# Overland

# Praise for *The Land as Viewed from the Sea*

"...Collins' prose has a simplicity that delivers a compelling read, dreamlike and lifelike at the same time. He has a flair for, almost a nonchalance with, structural surety, and this grave short novel, good on romantic tensions and on the hopeless repeating patterns of any romantic cycle, is threaded through with a subsconscious elegant homo-eroticism that insists nothing is ever quite as it seems."

Ali Smith – *The Guardian*

"...the two narratives weave in and out of each other with seamless precision, and the inevitably pullulating crossovers between reality and fiction are as untroubling as the tidal ebb and flow that is always in the background of this coastal tale."

Gerard Woodward – *The Telegraph*

"This is really a novel of images, the stormy lonely sea confronting the settled land of the past, a past only comforting insofar as it is set aside. The descriptions of life at sea and on land are rich and convincing."

Murrough O'Brien – *Independent on Sunday*

# Overland

## RICHARD COLLINS

seren

Seren is the book imprint of
Poetry Wales Press Ltd
57, Nolton Street, Bridgend, CF31 3AE, Wales
www.seren-books.com

ISBN 1-85411-420-4

A CIP record for this title is available from
the British Library

The publisher works with the financial assistance of the
Welsh Books Council.

Printed in Garamond by Bell & Bain Ltd, Glasgow

Cover photograph: Yiannis Bromirakis
                    www.bromirakis.com

To Flic, Kit and Peter

*When I was a young man*
*My mother said to me*
*There's only one girl in the world for you*
*She probably lives in Tahiti*

*I'd go the whole wide world*
*I'd go the whole wide world*
*Just to find her.*

Wreckless Eric, 1977

*My heart leaps up when I behold*
  *A rainbow in the sky:*
*So was it when my life began;*
*So it is now I am a man;*
*So be it when I shall grow old,*
  *Or let me die!*
*The Child is the Father of the Man:*
*And I could wish my days to be*
*Bound each to each in natural piety.*

William Wordsworth, 1802

# ONE

It rained continuously for two days but now it has stopped. This morning the sun has come out and it shines on the lake, making the water sparkle. All around the lake are large tree-covered hills but here, close to the town, is one small hill that is open and grassy. It's a tourist spot: well-maintained paths wind back and forth up the slopes to the viewpoint at the summit. I've been up there this morning to look down at the town and out along the lake. Now I sit on a bench at the foot of the hill with my ruck-sack beside me and wait for the next bus. I like this very much. Everything here is foreign. It's new and different and it's stimulating to me. And I like being about to move on to the next place.

Waiting for a bus makes me think of when I finished school. I travelled to and from school on the same bus for years. Every afternoon I walked out of the school gates and along some dull streets to the bus station. On the last day I walked out, just the same, but then found myself running fast and for no obvious reason. Except that I guess there was a reason: something to do with escape from everything that was commonplace and subur-ban and the same as it had always been. This was a couple of months ago. So it's good being here – different buildings and people and language. And I like the big hills that make it feel so different from the flat landscape I grew up in.

I sit on the bench watching swallows skimming low over the surface of the lake. Then I look back at the viewpoint hill and watch a woman with two young children coming down. She has one child in a back-pack and the other one is holding onto her hand and drags along behind. Both children have blonde hair, like their mother, and I think they are both boys but I can't be sure. The little back-pack child is asleep with his head lolling and the other one sucks the thumb of his free hand as he walks. They reach the bottom of the hill and she gets them into the red estate car that's parked there. She fixes them securely in their special seats and starts the engine but doesn't go anywhere. When she is sure that they are both fast asleep she turns the engine off and gets out again. She sits down on a bench almost opposite me. I look away towards the lake. A ferry boat crosses the water and moves in and out of cloud shadows.

When I next look across at the woman she is writing in a note-book. When she looks up I smile and she gives a hint of a smile back. She goes on writing but looks up the hill from time to time as if expecting someone. Then she's looking intently at me for a moment. But I'm used to this; punk is the big thing at the moment and I couldn't resist having my hair cut into a mohican, a spiky blue one, about five inches high, held up with glue. Here everyone looks but it's OK. I'm quite tall and broad-shouldered (but skinny) and now I have a mohican but no-one ever finds me aggressive looking. As soon as I speak or smile people are alright with me. I have been told that I have an open honest expression. Still, I'm surprised when she comes over to talk to me.

"Excuse me," she says, "But do you speak English?"

"I am English," I say.

She smiles, "I thought you were."

There's a pause and I'm thinking that she must have been really pretty when she was my age. Or she still is pretty. Or maybe handsome which is better in a way. Her hair is bobbed and she is smartly dressed but there's something a little bit creative or bohemian about her. Like she's not too straight.

"Can I ask you a small favour?" she says.

"Yes, of course."

"The children will wake up in a moment and I've got to get going. Will you give this note to my husband when he comes down the hill? He's got a foot in plaster and I'm afraid we've left him behind."

She passes me two or three pieces of paper tightly folded together; she must have torn them out of the note-book. There is a strange light in her eyes as she gives me them. She's smiling but I think that she might be angry.

"He'll be down soon. He's a big man with a beard. And because of his foot he's walking with a stick – you really can't mistake him."

"I'll be sure to give it to him," I say.

"Thank you," she says and gives me one of those really nice smiles that some women give to reward you for doing what they want you to. That's OK with me. And then she's across the road and into the car and gone and I'm left holding the note. My bus turns up very soon but I can't get on it because I have to wait for the husband. I really don't mind. I've been away from home for four weeks, travelling alone, enjoying being free and open to whatever comes along. It doesn't matter which bus I get.

I sit and wait. Part of me is right here noticing how steep the sun is climbing and how soon it gets hot. And how the lake is big enough to have waves that I can hear lapping against the shore. And noticing that the town further down the lake is lit by the sun and is pink, not grey like the towns at home. Another part of me is thinking about how good it feels to be me right now and how bad it felt a few weeks ago. I had left school feeling that I didn't want to go on to college this year and I should get a job for a while. But I couldn't find work so easily and I was bored and feeling strange. With nothing to do and no plans either I felt uncertain about my identity. It was scary. Just for a week or two things felt very dark. But I had some money from my aunt and I set off travelling and now things are good and I seem to have a sense of purpose.

Further down the lake a big cloud passes over and the pink town disappears in the rain. Here the sun still shines and the bells in a nearby clock tower chime twelve for midday. And a big man with a walking stick appears at the bottom of the path down from the viewpoint. He stands and looks around for the car, smiling but perplexed. He has a very round face and wears a beard. His hair is short and he has deep furrows on his forehead. But he looks likeable. There's something about his face that suggests that he spends a lot of time smiling. I put my rucksack on the bench where I can keep an eye on it and walk across.

"Your wife gave me a note to give you. She's been gone about half an hour."

He looks at the mohican and grins.

"Nice," he says and takes the note. "Thanks."

So I've done it. I'm free to go on. I go back to the bus-stop and try to decipher the timetable. Two hours to the next bus so I guess I'll walk to the main road and hitch. But I'm undecided and sit down on the bench again. The husband stands where I left him and reads the note several times over. Then he limps across the road towards me. He's a powerfully built man but it looks to me as if he has prematurely gone to seed. He is heavy from lack of exercise and he's sweating. Without speaking he sits down on the bench next to me. This is strange as there's a bench on the other side of the road where his wife had sat next to her parked car. He turns and speaks.

"You're English?"

"Yeah."

He holds out his hand for me to shake, "I'm Oliver. I used to live round here but now I've moved down south."

"I'm Daniel." I can't think of what else to say.

"I like your hair," he says. "But the punk thing's not going to catch on round here. They all like to look the same."

Then he's silent and reads the note again. He folds it and puts it in his pocket. He shakes his head, sighs, laughs. Thinks for a while.

"Daniel?"

"Yes."

"Can you drive a car?"

"Yes."

"Are you busy right now? I mean, well, excuse me for asking but what are you doing here? And are you in a hurry?"

"I'm on a trip but I don't know where to. I don't have any plans."

"But are you doing anything right now?"

"No. I walked up the hill and looked at the view. I was going to get on a bus. Your wife gave me a note to give to you."

"Look, I know I'm a complete stranger to you but I'm in a fix and you seem like a nice guy. Do you have a couple of hours? You see I've broken my foot and ..... And it's hard to explain. Just a couple of hours, I promise."

This man Oliver has an appealing manner. There's something likeable about him and he has a problem.

"What do you want me to do?" I ask.

"I just want to catch up with my family. They won't have got far. Will you drive for me? I would be really very thankful."

This is the point at which most people would think for a moment before making a decision. I never do that.

"I'm all yours," I say.

"Then we should hurry."

So we walk off into the town together, me carrying a rucksack, the man, Oliver, limping and using a walking stick. We hurry along slowly. Fortunately the sun has gone behind a cloud and it's not too hot. We arrive at a hotel and he goes in for a moment leaving me on the street. Then he limps out again and passes me a set of car keys.

"It's around the back."

As we walk around the block he explains, "This is where we stayed. This place has a lot of memories for me and Lizzie so it was the last place on the trip. Today we were turning back and heading for home. This hotel is good. I know it's not grand but they know us here. So they've let me take the car for a couple of hours. They're alright about it."

He seems in a serious hurry now. I unlock the car and put my rucksack on the back seat. Oliver bangs his foot as he gets into the passenger seat and he swears. Then we're away. Round the narrow streets of the town centre, Oliver navigating the one-ways. Then out past the bus-stop at the bottom of the hill and onto the main road along the lake shore. I like driving and I'm going fast even though I've never driven on this side of the road. Oliver says nothing but I feel a sense of urgency. The road winds up into the woods for a while and then it's back along the edge of the lake, passing through little fishing villages with cobbled streets. There are pantiled roofs, ornamental church spires, people on donkeys. Mostly the traffic is very light as we pass into the early part of the afternoon. We drive south into the sun. After a while we come into an area of gentler slopes and vineyards and then later we drive down onto a flat peninsula that juts out into the lake and which is all fields and dairy cows. Then we are in steeper wooded country again, the road is shaded and I don't have to squint against the brightness of the light.

Oliver is tense and looks ahead all the time. I'm hungry but I don't suggest stopping for food; I'm having a good time and I'm here in the moment. He said a couple of hours but they've gone by now. He doesn't explain anything – we're just trying to catch up with his wife and children. He's silent much of the time but when we see a red car ahead he lets out a joyful *yes*. Then it pulls into a lay-by, we pass it and I hear an unspoken *no*. Then he's laughing out loud.

"I'm so happy," he says, not to me especially but to the world, "I'm going home. I've really made up my mind."

I think there's something a little bit crazy about this man.

As it gets later the traffic is heavier and I'm getting tired. We will have to stop soon – I'm not used to driving here and I will have an accident if I go much further. There's a lot I don't understand but for some reason I like the man sitting beside me and I don't mind helping him. I don't mind that he has taken over my day. The road is straighter for a while and my mind goes back to when I was sitting on the bench waiting for him to come down off the hill. It was boring after a bit. I shouldn't have done it but it really was too tempting. There was no-one around. No sign of a man with his foot in plaster. I opened the note and read it.

*Oliver*

*I've driven off and left you. This is like some sort of test. Just get yourself home and come in through the door a quite different man from the man you were last night. First you have to get home. I imagine that you have some money on you. You won't starve. Then I have to hear that you've made a decision. So you've had these little flings over the years and I've thought I can cope because you love your family most of all. But last night was one time too many. I don't know what happened. All I know is that you were very drunk and chatting up some sexy young thing in tight clothes. And you were very late when you finally made it to bed and I felt humiliated. This was meant to be our family holiday.*

*You have to make a commitment and an effort and it has to start right now. If you are serious about us, about me and the children, you must make up your mind and I will see you at home. Or maybe you will catch up with us on the way...*

*love*

*Lizzie*

I can't ask Oliver for an explanation because I already know more than I should. And I understand that it's the last words of the note that dictate our actions now – *maybe you will catch up with us on the way...* OK that's fine. But how long is this going to take?

# TWO

I wake in the middle of the night, at home, in my own bed. The room is dark and shadowy but I can make out the shape of familiar things: the pattern of the window frame, the big ugly wardrobe, my desk and chair. I feel such a sense of disappointment. How did I get back here? I was travelling but now I'm home and trapped. All momentum is gone and it will be a long time before I can get away again. A sadness like inertia overcomes me and holds me down on the bed with its weight. I want to cry out. Perhaps I do. And I wake up into a strange room, a foreign early morning, the sounds outside of a cock crowing and a car engine starting up. I feel relieved.

The room I'm in is painted a garish lilac colour and has very little contents: just two small beds, a wardrobe and a wash basin. On the walls are pictures on religious themes: Jesus, Mary, some saints. It feels very old-fashioned here – not at all like 1978. I look at Oliver in the next bed, lying on his back, eyes open, staring at the ceiling. He turns his head towards me for a moment. I must have smiled.

"Fucking hell," he says, "That's all I need. Someone who's happy first thing in the morning."

He looks rough. His eyes are watery and his face is expressionless. He rolls onto his side and faces the wall. I want to get up and look around this new place. Seven o' clock. I'll have a wander and come back for breakfast later.

I get dressed, spend a moment in front of the mirror straightening my mohican (which always gets flattened in the night), and leave quietly. Our accommodation is in a house in a side street with just a little sign outside advertising rooms. Oliver offered to pay so he chose the place. It's a little walk down to the town square and I make my way through the early morning activities. Last night when we arrived here it was close to sunset so I haven't really seen anything of the town in daylight. I love this first-thing-in-the-morning-new-place-to-explore feeling. Maybe it's an ordinary town but it's special to me because it's new and it's foreign. I really haven't been abroad much before and certainly never on my own. When I was little my parents took me and my sister away sometimes but when we got older they didn't have the money. So ordinary foreign places are special to me. I understand that all the components of life here are the same as at home: people work in shops and offices or outdoors doing gardening and building work; there are postmen and delivery vans on the streets; there are schools, churches and bars. But what I like is the way that all the details are different. The buildings have wooden shutters, flaking painted plaster and huge front doors. There are old women dressed completely in black and smartly dressed businessmen incongruous on bicycles. I walk around and just look. I sit on a bench and watch the people going by. Then I go back for breakfast.

Oliver is at the breakfast table and he smiles at me when I come in.

"I'm sorry I was gruff earlier," he says, "I'm really no good at all until I've had my first cup of coffee – which I have had, you'll be pleased to hear."

I sit down to eat and look across at him. I think I can tell his mood by the way he holds himself. When he first came down that hill yesterday I saw a big man; big in physique and in personality too. My first impression was of someone who was outgoing and a little bit larger than life. And he had laughed out loud in the car when he felt that it was all going to go right for him. Now, at the breakfast table, his smile is fixed like it's something he's been doing for a long time but the original meaning has fallen away and just left a fading imprint. And his shoulders have dropped down as if in weariness. We eat and are silent. I don't know what to say – this is his thing that we're doing.

When we've finished our food he speaks: "I need to thank you a great deal, Daniel, for driving me here. What I think has happened is that we drove too far. We overtook them somewhere. Or maybe they went up into the mountains – that's possible too. But the thing is, you were good to help me and I can't expect to take up more of your time."

*Or can I?* is what I hear at the end of the sentence but I say nothing.

"Perhaps I should explain," Oliver says, "The note you gave me from my wife... Well, she's fed up with me, rightly as it happens, and I'm being tested. I was bad and she's upset. But sometimes when you and I were driving along yesterday I felt good. I felt that things are clearer for me than they've been before. More obvious. More certain. All I have to do is catch up with my family. They're the most important thing for me. Home, the people I love – I've been putting it all at risk. All I have to do now..."

His sentence peters out. He pours himself more coffee and is lost in his thoughts for a while.

"There was a chalet that we used to stay in, up in the mountains, very high. We wanted to take the kids there but a couple of weeks ago it seemed too early in the year – the road would still be blocked by snow. But it's been so hot. It's like summer now. You see Lizzie is altogether brilliant – she wouldn't just end the holiday completely because I'm not there. I think she has gone up to the mountains and is staying in the chalet. I think they're on the hill above the place right now playing about on toboggans."

Oliver's face takes on a far-seeing expression as if he has a picture of them all in his mind.

"Are the mountains near here?" I ask.

"No. We took the wrong road." He looks at me. "What about you helping me for another day? Will you drive for me again? Just for today, that's all."

"OK," I say. It will be fun.


We start off again, back the way we came at first and then off up into the hills. Oliver doesn't need to look at a map as he knows his way around this country. I'm more relaxed at the wheel than I was yesterday. I think about how it had been towards the end of the day when we reached the town and I tried to go the wrong way around a roundabout. Stressed out, I had stopped in the middle of the road and got out. Oliver sat in the car laughing as the traffic came to a standstill. I stood on the pavement and watched. The car was like a log across a stream with everything building up behind it. As the traffic stalled drivers put their hands firmly on their car horns and kept them there until a fabulous cacophony developed – people express themselves well around here. When I felt I could face it I got back in the car and sorted it out. Oliver was very amused even though he thought I was going to walk off and just leave him there. As we drove away he wound down the window and good-naturedly shouted and waved his fist at the other drivers.

But today I'm more confident. I've got the hang of this wrong side of the road thing now. And Oliver helps me out a bit. He watches the road carefully and says helpful things like: *you should have given way there, Dan, but it's alright, he could see you weren't going to stop,* or, *there's a lorry coming now, we need to be on our side of the road for a bit.* At one point I touched a curb a bit fastish. But it's really going OK.

The only thing is that I don't see much. It's travelling but not travel; all I get is a superficial glimpse of the landscape through the window like I'm watching it on television. I like benches best. I like sitting and watching people like I did in the town square this morning. Oliver doesn't see much of the country from the car either. Whenever I look at him he's watching the road. But we don't anticipate seeing the all-important red estate car here and he's not so obsessive. I can ask him questions.

"What did you do to your foot?" I say.

"Oh, I fell awkwardly. I was in a tree showing off to the kids. I missed landing on them when I fell but my foot got trapped and twisted on the way down. It was a week ago and it hurts less every day. The plaster is mostly precautionary. I'll have it off soon."

Maybe it's Oliver's foot that smells. It must get very hot. Or maybe he needs a change of clothes. I should have offered him one of my clean t-shirts this morning; I have my stuff with me but he has nothing.

We drive further and further into the hills, the road winds up and up, and something funny happens to my ears. Sometimes I can see the mountains ahead, except that they can't be mountains, they take up half the sky. They must be jagged clouds.

"See the snow, Daniel?" Oliver asks, pointing at what aren't clouds after all. "Gives you a special feeling doesn't it?"

He's right. There is something other-worldly about the massiveness of it all. But I have to keep my eyes on the road. And I begin to wonder about the man sitting beside me.

"What do you do at home?" I ask him.

"I'm a business man. I can't work for other people, there are always problems, so I've built things up myself. I have a small hotel and two tourist shops. It's not a noble calling, I know. But Lizzie and I work well together – she's the practical sensible number-crunching one and I'm practical too but I have crazy ideas that sometimes work out."

Then he's turning towards me and smiling, thinking of home.

"Dan, you must come and visit. It's a really special place. It's like an island where we live but it's connected to the mainland by an isthmus. The sea is green and very clear – it's wonderful for snorkelling. In the season we might be able to find some work for you though I can't promise anything. What do you think?"

I think this is how travelling should be. New opportunities. Unexpected things happening. This bend in the road, for instance, is unexpectedly tighter than I thought it would be and I'm skidding a little as I brake.

"Can we go a little slower?" Oliver says. "We're not in such a hurry as we were yesterday. If we go steady we'll arrive in the early afternoon."

I slow down more for the next bend but the wheels still screech.

"Teenagers are immortal, aren't they?" Oliver says.

I don't know what he means. "Yes," I say, "I suppose so."

He laughs.

As we go higher into the mountains we go backwards through the seasons. Some of the trees here are bare or only just coming into leaf. The air is cooler and I wind my window up. Very often we pass swollen streams coming down the mountainside and some-times there are quite impressive waterfalls. I want to stop and look but I carry on. I feel a little as if I'm Oliver's employee and I have to do what he says. I think it's because he paid for the food and lodgings last night. But it's a temporary job – I can quit whenever I want.

But by midday I am stressed out with driving on these bendy roads and I suggest that we stop. We pull up by a small isolated roadside café. Oliver gets me to park away from the road for some reason and we go in and have soup and bread. Afterwards I wander along the edge of the road to give myself a break before going on. We are in a steep-sided valley with a big mountain stream in the bottom and lots of smaller streams coming down the slopes to join it. I look down to the water; it's clear and icy blue like snow-melt. A small bird sits on a twig near me, opens its mouth and its whole body vibrates with singing. But the valley is full of the sound of rushing water and I can't hear it at all.

Then we drive for some more hours. Oliver wants to know more about me but there's not much to tell. I feel like my life proper has only just started. And it seems that travelling, just experiencing the world, is the thing for me to do now. I think of old school friends talking about saving up for their first mortgage and I know I want something different from them.

"What about your parents?" Oliver asks. "What do they do?"

"My dad doesn't work any more. He's had some bad health. He was a lorry driver and eventually transport manager for a small firm. But now he's at home all day. Mum works in an office. And I have a little sister but she's going through a weird spell."

"And do they call you Daniel at home or Dan?"

"Both. And they called me *Madness* at school."

"*Madness?*"

"Yeah, it's just a nickname. It doesn't mean anything."

I hit one of the patches of water that flood across this road. Oliver wants me to slow down but I like the splash and the momentary floating sensation.

"Why did they call you that?" Oliver asks.

"Just silly things happened. One time I found some tunnels around one of the old school buildings. They were connected to the cellar and stretched out a little way – I don't know why. There was a manhole and I came up pushing the lid off and emerging at the edge of the playground. It was just bad luck that I came out at the feet of the headmaster. And there was another time when I got onto the roof. They called me *Madness* because things happened to me. But it was unfair. It could have been anyone."

I speed up for the next patch of water.

"I think I understand," Oliver says.

We drive on through the early part of the afternoon, taking a small winding road that climbs steeply through conifers. As we get higher there are big dirty heaps of snow at the side of the road that must have been pushed up by a snow-plough.

"This is good," Oliver says. "This road would have been closed a few weeks ago."

Then we are out of the trees. The road climbs a little more and then levels. I want to stop and look around for a moment so I pull to the side and get out. We are in a wide open space surrounded by snow-covered peaks. The land here is hummocky grassland, stretching for some distance, dotted with patches of old snow that look like fallen clouds. At the foot of the steeper slopes the patches join together to form an unbroken mass of white that goes on up to the mountain tops. I've never seen anything like this before. Oliver is impatient for me to get back in the car so I can't look for as long as I would like to. We drive on but now I go rather slowly.

"I thought 'breathtaking' was just a daft expression," I say.

"It's good up here, I know," Oliver says. "But we're nearly there and I have a feeling we're going to find them."

Oliver is expectant and excited. He's lost his sometime slumped look and seems bigger again – like he's ready to burst out of the car. We carry on along the narrow winding road through the high pastures. And then there is a little cluster of wooden buildings by an icy lake.

"It's a seasonal village," Oliver explains, "where they stay when the cows graze up here in summer."

But there are no cows yet. No-one about at all. Only one red estate car parked between the houses.

"Yes!" Oliver shouts, making me jump. He bounces in his seat. He punches the air with his fist and hits it accidentally against the roof of the car.

"Yes!"

We stop in the village on a firm looking piece of ground and get out of the car. Oliver hops round to me and gives me a big bear hug and a kiss on both cheeks. I recoil a little, *we don't do this at home*, I think, but I'm smiling. He limps over to the red car and then to the chalet behind it. His body language is different again; he's a big, jubilant, extrovert force in the world. The chalet is locked and empty but there are muddy footprints, large and small, on the steps that lead up to it.

"Do you want to have a little look around for them?" Oliver asks. "I'll sit on the step here and wait."

I wander off through the village, which consists of about fifteen wooden houses next to the dark half-frozen lake. Then I get out into the open land. The grass here is flattened and the ground saturated with water as if the snow has only recently gone. Small purple and yellow flowers are pushing up out of the mud. I aim for high ground where I might be able to see Oliver's wife and children. With every step the view changes. I like being here and it's not only because I'm relieved to be out of the car. I walk along the higher ground around the lake until I can look down over a wide area. There's no sign of anyone. I go on, away from the lake and into the beginnings of a small valley that leads down to it. Along the bottom of the valley is a strip of snow that covers a stream. I can hear the muffled sound of water on rocks coming from below. I won't go that way; I think I would fall through the snow and into the stream bed. So I start to climb the steep snow-slope above the valley. The sun comes out from behind the clouds and I can't look at the snow without my eyes hurting. I go on up the slope with my eyes shut, turning round and opening them from time to time to look at the changing view. I can see the lake surrounded by high pastures, the top of the wooded slopes below, and a glimpse of the valley floor below that again. If I carry on up the view will get even better.

I get into a repetitive rhythm of a few breathless eyes-shut steps upwards, stop and turn, repeat. I go up and up, feeling like I'm a mountaineer. Then there is a pleasant sloughing sound and the world starts to move strangely or perhaps I do. The snow and

I take off down the hill and for a few moments I'm surfing a big white wave. Then it's too fast and I'm tumbling over and getting smothered. I curl into a ball and wait for it all to come to a stop. It does. The stillness is a wonderful sensation.

I'm covered by the snow but there's light above me so I'm not buried too deep. I wriggle and push to make more space but the snow below me gives way and I tumble down into water and rocks – the stream I had sensibly avoided earlier. I'm wet, bruised and tremendously exhilarated. The snow has collapsed into a shallow steep-sided crater with me in the bottom and blue sky above. I stand, brush myself off, and begin to climb the crater side. The snow gives way and I slide back down. I try again but can't get a grip. I dig my hands and feet in and climb carefully. No use. I pick a soft looking patch of snow and try a strange upward wriggle that's completely useless. I'm wet through but warm from my exertions. The depression I'm in is only perhaps fifteen foot deep and getting out of it seems such a small problem. I try again and again. But when I get tired out I have to rest, leaning back against the snow. It's then that I start to feel a little woozy. All this snow is doing something to my brain; a nice something but there could be a problem. I feel sleepy then I have a little adrenaline rush of fear. I stand and shout for help. The sound of my voice is small and softened by snow but I carry on shouting at intervals and then resting.

Soon there's a shout back, "Daniel are you there?"

"Yes," I say. "Oliver, help me get out of here, please."

"I don't want to come close to the edge. I'm going to throw in an ice-axe. Watch your head."

And then it's easy. I can climb using the point of the tool and pulling myself up. I'm soon out. Oliver has rescued me.

"We need to get back fast," he says. "It will be nearly dark by the time we get to the village."

We set off back across the avalanche snow and the muddy pastures, Oliver limping and slipping, me very tired. As the sun gets lower the snow slopes above take on a gaudy pink colour.

"Things just happen to me," I say.

"I know."

By the time we get to the village I'm cold, weak and shaky. The sun has gone down and it's getting dark. The red estate car has gone.

"Damn," Oliver says, "I wanted to see my kids."

He changes shape, his shoulders slump and he diminishes in size. He paces about awkwardly in front of the chalet.

"Too late to go after them now," he says, in a voice that is almost tearful.

He's standing in front of me and he seems to be shrinking. I realise that I'm the same height as him and I put my hand on his shoulder sympathetically. But I don't understand why he has to be so emotional – he saw his children yesterday morning.

"I'm sorry," I say, then I realise that it's my fault, "I'm really very sorry."

Oliver reaches under the steps of the chalet and brings out a key.

"Things just happen to you, don't they, Dan?" he says.

"Yeah. They just do."

We spend the night in the chalet; there's no question of me being able to drive on again until tomorrow. There's a stack of firewood against the wall and tinned food in the cupboard. I change into dry warm clothes and try to lend some to Oliver too but there's no way any of them will fit him. We eat and then sit next to the wood-burning stove, Oliver wrapped in a blanket. There's a cassette player in the room and I dig out a tape from the bottom of my rucksack and put it on. Most of it is speedy, angry punk rock and Oliver hates it. I wish I had some music that would cheer him up. He's very low and somehow I feel responsible for his well-being. I turn the tape over and just play the first track: Wreckless Eric's *I'd go the whole wide world just to find her.* OK, I know he's got a whiny voice but it's a good song and I identify with the words. Perhaps Oliver does too.

Then we sit in silence and I think about the events of the last two days. Travelling is so brilliant. New places, new people all the time. Life is so rich and full. Waking up this morning after dreaming of home, walking down to the town square and sitting on a bench to watch people – it seems months ago to me now.

And it occurs to me that maybe Oliver saved my life today in that snow. He's over-emotional, I know. But I screwed things up for him, he could have caught up with his family and yet now he doesn't say a word against me. He is a good-hearted, big-hearted man. I decide that I will carry on helping him for as long as it takes and I tell him so.

"Off again in the morning," he says. "We'll catch them up, I'm sure. I know exactly where they will go next."

# THREE

There are big differences between me and Oliver. He is excitable and outgoing but sad too. I'm just carefree. In the morning the differences are most apparent. He wakes up looking shell-shocked, his face grey-white above the stubbly beard. He is middle-aged – late thirties or something. He looks worried some-times. And he's irritable before breakfast.

So first thing this morning I slip out of the chalet and go down to the edge of the lake. There are big patches of last winter's ice floating about, rough textured like they've been marked by sun, snow and rain. But much of the water is unfrozen, dark and still, reflecting the mountains behind. I breathe deeply, taking it all in. I look up at the mountains; I've never seen so much snow. And there are little patches of snow along the lake shore too. I walk along until I find one big enough for me to make a piss pattern in. I try to write my name but I lose interest when the N goes wrong. I woke up very happy this morning. I am carefree. But now, as I look down into the steaming yellow lines in the snow, the dreams I had last night come into my mind.

I dreamt of snow, of course. But not of the avalanche, only of climbing an endless steep snow-slope and struggling to not lose my grip and slide down. And climbing up more, feeling that if I get high enough I will see something that I need to see or want to see. Something that will explain things. The dream had a disquieting taste, an atmosphere rather than a meaning. Then I dreamt that I was looking out of the bedroom window at home and watching my father walking down the street towards me. *My father walking*. But I've had this dream loads of times. Now I've finished pissing. I zip up my flies and look up at the mountains again.

Back at the chalet Oliver has washed and had coffee. He wants to get going. The cold morning air has made me hungry and I get some rice pudding from the cupboard and eat it straight out of the tin. I could eat more but we must go. We lock the chalet and set off. I drive slowly at first, not wanting to leave the mountains. I experiment with seeing how much of the view behind me I can see in the mirror and still keep to the road. There is no other traffic at all so it's fun. The road winds and winds and it's at a particular place on each bend that I get a momentary picture of snowy peaks and blue sky appearing in the wing mirror. But then we're in the trees again and soon we are back down in the valley and on the main road.

There is an unpleasant smell in the car and I think it's Oliver's plaster encased foot. He got it wet in the snow yesterday when he rescued me and afterwards spent part of the evening with it propped up by the wood-burner, steaming and drying out. He didn't complain. I think he's physically tough but mentally he's up and down. There's a body language thing with him and he doesn't have to say anything to let you know his state of mind. Now we get stuck behind a big lorry, it starts to rain, and I put on the wind-screen wipers. This goes on for some miles. Oliver fidgets in the seat beside me and I turn over in my mind all the different moods that I can see in him without him even speaking. It's like this:
1) Oliver first thing in the morning – tired but tense, irritable, crest-fallen;
2) Oliver later, in the car – upright, alert, expectant, willing us forward, occasionally expansive, huge smiles, large as life;
3) later again, still in the car – restless, deflated, shifting position continually like he's in the most uncomfortable seat in the world, or the most uncomfortable body, or, and I guess this is it, he's itchy with uncomfortable thoughts;
4) later again – more slumped, more deflated, motionless, a small sad man with even worse thoughts but I don't know what they are. I wonder if he remembers his dreams.

We turn off onto another road that runs down a wide valley of farmland. Less traffic here, no lorries, and a strange thing happens. The sky has cleared behind us but a heavy dark cloud hangs over the valley ahead. We are travelling directly away from the morning sun, towards the cloud, in and out of rain. And then there's a rainbow arching across the valley, bright colours against the dark. It moves as we move, going always away from us, leading us on. On each side of the valley a rainbow foot travels across the countryside, passing over the fields, right through herds of cows, touching the edge of a small wood, lighting up a farmstead. I slow down so I can watch the progress of the one on the left. It slows down too. Then I accelerate and start to drive fast towards what has now become a double arch. The rainbow speeds up as well. I go faster as if I can catch up, drive under it, and win some sort of race. Of course I can't. It merely moves on ahead, unobtainable, and as the rain ceases it fades away.

"I get a buzz out of stuff like that," I say. I can't express myself more clearly but I want to say more. "I always have done." I lift my foot off the accelerator and the car slows down again. "I think I always will."

It's only mid-morning, it's turning out to be another special day and I'm having a good time. Now I feel that Oliver is looking at me.

"The child is father of the man," he says.

What on earth? He smiles broadly and carries on staring at me as if I'm meant to say something back.

Later in the day we stop for petrol and also buy some fruit juice, bread and chocolate. Oliver doesn't want us to hang about here, we will stop and eat further along the way. Meanwhile we're on the road and he's restless again.

"Where are we going?" I ask, interrupting his uncomfortable thoughts.

"First to an old ruined watermill further down the valley. It's a quiet place to rest and eat a little. Then to a town with a big castle. I think Lizzie and the kids have gone there and they will stay more than one day. It's somewhere we've always wanted to take Otis and Daisy but it seemed too far out of the way on this trip. But they were at the chalet so now they will go to the castle."

"Otis and Daisy?"

"That's right. Otis is four, Daisy is two-and-a-half. Yeah, it will be good to introduce you to them."

"I had it in my mind that they were both boys," I say, "I saw them when your wife came down the hill with them and drove off."

"Of course, you've seen them," Oliver says and drifts off into smiling reverie.

"I would like to understand more," I say, "I've been hoping for a bit of explanation. I don't want to be nosy but it's the third day now. I don't know how long it will take to catch up with them and all I know is that she drove off because you did something wrong."

"Today or tomorrow we will catch up with them, I'm sure of it," Oliver says. "And as for an explanation. Well, the funny thing is that I didn't do anything wrong. I was drunk and flirting around. Then I went on to some guy's place because he had some cocaine. I stayed up most of the night. Lizzie thinks I slept with another woman but I didn't."

"So why didn't you explain in the morning?"

"I was building up to it. Look, the truth is that I have been unfaithful to Lizzie more than once. So it's not so strange that she doesn't trust me. It's my fault. But in the morning she was hard to speak to. I was building up to it. She stomped off up that fucking hill. Then she raced back down it again. So I never got a chance. But it will be OK."

"You sound doubtful."

"It's scary. She's strong and assertive. She gave me a warning once before but I didn't really take it in. She said *I do love you but I don't need you.* I think I understand what she was saying now. She was warning me. So now I've decided to be faithful and loving and everything else but that doesn't mean that she'll take me back. I mean – she could be getting on fine and thinking *do I need this man?* I don't know. I'm worried."

I've hitch-hiked a bit and I've noticed this thing with strangers where you talk very openly. It's happening now. I didn't expect Oliver to come out with all this stuff. I think it's the car. You sit side-by-side not looking at each other. Just the road ahead and a voice.

"Sometimes I feel very positive indeed," he says, "it's so clear what my priorities are. A brilliant happy family, like we are most of the time. I've just got to catch up with them. But sometimes I'm more worried. And I think *what if it's all over?*"

I feel I know these thoughts of his. At least I know how they look from the outside. Positive equals larger than life Oliver, expectant, excited. Worried is the uncomfortable in his seat stuff. Then there's the slumped and deflated *what if it's all over?* business. I really want it to be alright for him. I'll do what I can.

Oliver gets me to turn off into a little wooded valley. A couple of miles up it and we pull over into the trees by a ruined building.

"The watermill," he says, "Lizzie and I were going to buy the place and do it up. This was a long time ago, it wasn't so over-grown then."

We get out. I explore and eat at the same time, clambering over the ruin with half a loaf of bread in one hand and a bar of chocolate in the other. The roof of the mill has completely gone and I can walk along the top of the walls. I look down on Oliver. He leans against the side of the car, eating, staring straight ahead. I balance my way up and down one of the pointed gable-end walls. It's pretty solid, only one stone gives way and tumbles to the ground. From the back wall I can see Oliver through one of the windows. He's absorbed with what? He's certainly not here in the world I'm in. He said he had been here with Lizzie so maybe that's it – memories. Does he see himself and her as they were here years ago? Or he's remembering what they said to each other. He looks sad. This is another big difference between us: I'm living in the moment and it's good but he's always wrapped up in thoughts or memories. Nothing is fresh and new for him.

When I come over the other gable-end he catches sight of me and starts. I hold the remains of the bread between my teeth, climb down through the branches of a conveniently placed tree and join him by the car.

"You made me jump," he says, "I'd really prefer it if you didn't die by falling from a great height. I need you to drive."

"That wasn't a great height," I say.

He smiles and shakes his head.

It is mid-afternoon when we reach the town. Oliver is upright in his seat, expectant, smiling. The main road brings us in alongside a broad green river and then we wind up through narrow, seemingly ancient streets, to the castle. This is just a square edifice of featureless grey walls and turrets. Closed steel gates indicate that it's not open to visitors. But on one side there are flower gardens and a view over the town. We park in the shade of the castle walls and walk (limp in Oliver's case) through the gardens and into a children's play area. We make our way to a bench in the shade of a big tree and sit down. There's no-one else around.

"We wait," Oliver says, trying to make himself comfortable.

"No, I can't wait. We'll ask around."

So we get back into the car and drive to the hotel where his family are most likely to be. I wait outside and Oliver goes in and makes enquiries. Then he's out again, we drive a short way and repeat the whole thing.

"Well, that's the two hotels where we stayed before," Oliver says.

We drive around some more but there's no-one about in the heat of the afternoon. We check in at a small seedy hotel, shower, have something to eat. We sit in the little courtyard garden out the back. I look at the flowers but I can smell the dust-bins. Oliver is restless in a nervous way. It occurs to me that I would like this stuff to be over soon so that I can be free to do my own thing. Perhaps he reads my mind.

"I owe you one, Daniel," he says. "You've been very good."

"It's OK."

"If you want to come and stay at my place some time you will be very welcome," he says. "Whatever happens." He looks at his watch. "Let's go back to the castle for a while," he says.

So we drive up to the castle again. Oliver gets me to park in an out-of-the-way corner as he did before. I wish he could walk and we wouldn't have to drive all the time; I feel that I've seen too much of the inside of that car. We go to the children's park and sit down. It's very busy now with the noise of small children playing. Oliver smiles benignly at everyone, large and small, but there's no sign of his family. I'm bored. Oliver likes watching the children play and I follow his gaze, not smiling as he does and clearly not thinking the same thoughts. There's a couple with a very small toddler, first child perhaps, just learnt to walk. They watch his every move rapturously, faces lit up with silly expressions. It makes me cringe. Then there's an awful little girl who's pirouetting around saying the same words over and over. I don't understand the language but I think it's *look at me mummy, look at me daddy*. The child's parents watch with brainless intensity and gormless expressions. I want to puke. A baby cries inconsolably close by. The mother is making sympathetic noises. *Poor baby* her expression seems to say. *Poor me* I think – what a racket.

I wander over to the flower gardens and to where the slope drops away and there's a view over the town. It's late in the afternoon now but still too hot. I liked it in the mountains but I don't like small towns. Right now I wouldn't mind being in a big dirty grey city with a soft rain falling. *What? Did I just think that?* Yes, I did and alongside the thought is a weird yearning sensation. This is new to me and I don't want to believe it – I think I've just had the first twinges of home sickness. I look back towards the park where I can see Oliver, now in slumped mode with his chin resting on his hand. A father and small daughter walk towards me through the flower gardens. She reaches up, stretching her arm, to grasp one of his fingers. *That's nice* I think, in a suddenly sentimental frame of mind, *I would like that one day*. And it's *did I think that?* again. That's another completely new one for me.

I go back to Oliver and we agree that I should explore the town, keeping my eyes open, and he will stay in the park, the most likely place to find them. I turn and look back on my way out. Laughing happy families for the most part. And one man on a bench, hunched up, grim-faced, alone.

It's better to be on my own for a while; Oliver is hard work twenty four hours a day. And the sun is lower now, it's getting cooler and things begin to look good in the evening light. I think I'm still enjoying travelling but some time soon I would like to stay put somewhere. Oliver's place? I'm not so sure about that but maybe. I walk down through the town. People are dark here, black hair, brown eyes, olive-coloured skin. The young women are gorgeous. Bicycles are the big thing at the bottom end of town where it is flat. I notice the great range of different ways a rider will carry other people on the bike. Children are on little seats attached to the handle bars or on the back. An old man, a grandfather, has a little boy standing on his crossbar with one arm around his neck. Girlfriends sit on the crossbar or sideways on the back rack. Best of all there's a young man riding past with his girlfriend standing on the rack behind him with her hands on his shoulders. Her long hair is blown back in the wind, her dress clings to her body and she has a sensual smile on her face. I think I need to get a bicycle.

I walk along the pavement between the main road and the river, the rush of traffic with its noise and fumes on one side and the dirty riverbank and green water on the other. Across the water, on the opposite bank, there are old buildings, fine trees and lots of people milling about. I can see a blonde-haired woman buying ice-creams for her two small children. They stand out very clearly as foreigners, as I suppose I do. And they must be Oliver's family.

I shout and wave my arms but they can't hear and don't see me. Maybe I'll be more visible from the riverbank. I vault over the barrier that separates the pavement from the river and drop down onto the mud. There's a great stinking squelch as my feet come down and I sink up to my knees. I have to pull myself out with my arms and I'm covered in mud when I clamber back onto the pavement. A passing couple laugh at me. But I have to hurry. I run towards the nearest bridge, wet muddy shoes slapping on the pavement, everybody I pass turning to look. I cross the bridge, dodging pedestrians by going onto the road and getting hooted at by cars. I run down to the other side of the river to where I saw the woman and children. Of course they're not there now. I climb onto the pedestal of a statue to look around and I get some disap-proving glances from passers-by. I realise that I'm clinging on with one muddy hand on the statue's ample left breast. I can't see any sign of a blonde-haired woman or a red estate car. I climb down and frantically run up and down looking into courtyards and side streets, a very obviously deeply crazy man, stared at suspiciously by increasing numbers of people.

I rush back to the bridge and confidently walk into the road to stop the red car that's coming towards me. I raise both muddy arms and the car comes to a halt. A terrified old couple stare at me through the windscreen. I go round to the driver's side and speak to the man behind the wheel, "I'm sorry, I'm looking for a woman," I say; *I am a crazed foreigner about to murder you* is what they hear and the car pulls away fast. It is at this point that I realise how ludicrous this has all become. I laugh out loud. An old man who was crossing the bridge towards me quietly turns and goes back the way he came.

When I arrive back at the children's park by the castle Oliver takes a look at the state I'm in and starts to laugh. I have to go over my story several times for him before we go anywhere. He struggles to keep a straight face. He doesn't say much but for the remainder of the day he looks at me from time to time with a smile like he's going to start laughing again. At night we share a room in the dingy hotel. We lie on our single beds, side by side as we were for much of the day in the car. A little stray light comes into the room from other buildings. Exotic smells drift up from the dustbins in the yard below. I'm not completely sure that the woman and children I was running after were Oliver's family; I never got a close look at them. But he's certain, he knows we will catch up with them tomorrow, and he's happy.

"I like you, Dan," he says.

"Why's that then?"

"Things just happen to you, don't they?"

I can still hear him laughing quietly to himself as I drift off to sleep.

# FOUR

Here's the story of my fourth day with Oliver:
1) we go to the children's park by the castle and wait for his family to turn up – they don't;
2) we sit at the edge of the main road out of town and wait for a red estate car to come along and stop – it doesn't;
3) I take Oliver to the hospital because his foot smells very bad and he needs the plaster removed – we wait for hours but get it sorted;
4) we go to the shops (open in the evening here) and Oliver buys new clothes;
5) while he's in the changing room I look in the mirror, realise my mohican is leaning over at a ridiculous angle again, and before the evening's over I have it cut off, it's gone for ever;
6) I ask Oliver *don't we ever have to take that car back?* and he says *it's OK.*

Day five. We're in the car again. Oliver is dressed neatly and smells sweetly. His foot is bandaged, not in plaster, and he wears two different sized baseball boots on his feet, the other non-pair sit on the back seat next to my rucksack. All morning he has been smiling a very competent smile, the one I've noticed before, the mask. For a while his feelings are hidden and that's a relief – he can be hard work. *One more day, perhaps two* he said this morning, *if you fancy it.* I think he's coming round to the idea that we won't catch up with his family but that he'll see them at home soon and sort things out there. I don't understand about the car. Oliver still can't drive because it hurts his foot when he presses the brake pedal. He won't be taking the car back and I have no intention of doing it (I want my journey to go forwards not backwards). So what's going to happen?

We are driving across country, on minor roads, in order to get to a place where his family might be. The road goes right through the centre of little villages which is a bore. People milling about.

Donkeys again. Lorries being unloaded. Cobblestones. A herd of goats across the road, supervised only by a child and an old man. Strange vehicles that are really three-wheeled mopeds with a tiny cab and a flat-bed behind for goods and they go very slow and are impossible to overtake. And too much driving. I come into one village a little bit too fast but it's OK. People have a good chance to get out of the way. But there's an old woman with a walking stick and a young woman with a baby who maybe I was a bit close to. We hit the open road again and are travelling through an area of scattered woodlands, all the trees bright green with spring foliage. I can feel that Oliver is tense. Then he crashes his hand down very hard on the dashboard and roars *stop the car*. I panic, skid a little, and pull to the side of the road. Oliver gets out, slams the door of the car, and walks off down the road back the way we came.

I like Oliver very much but now I'm scared of him. He is so angry and he's a powerfully built man – flabby but strong underneath. The plastic dashboard has cracked where he hit it. I wait, concerned, a bit angry myself now, wanting an explanation. Oliver disappears round a bend in the road. Ten minutes later he returns and sits down on a grassy bank next to the car.

"Sorry," he says, "I'm upset. It's not just you that I'm angry with."

He seems much calmer now. That's good.

"But I *am* angry with you, Daniel."

I wonder what I've done.

"Things *just* happen to you, don't they? Do you really believe that?"

"Yes," I say, but I'm made to think about it. "I'm accident prone I suppose. Perhaps it's me that makes things happen. But I'm unlucky too."

"When you walked on the walls of that water-mill, you remember? That was actually dangerous. It's not quite normal to do that."

"I see."

"But it's just you being you. If you fall maybe that's alright. Take a chance. Live life. I was a bit like that when I was young."

He pauses. I feel that I'm being lectured to.

"Your driving is dangerous. I think to myself, *OK, Daniel will have a minor smash up one day, he'll survive with luck, he'll learn a lesson. Then he will slow down.*" Oliver looks me in the eye. "But it's not OK. Do you understand why I'm upset?"

"No."

"Because you nearly hit two pedestrians back there. You will kill someone if you carry on like that. It will probably be a child." He turns away, angry again, exasperated, and then turns back to me, "Do you understand?"

"Yes." And I do actually. I think he's probably right. I'm pissed off but at myself, I guess. "I'm sorry," I say.

"I'll buy you lunch," Oliver says.

We get back in the car and drive to the nearest town. I go very slowly where there are people and houses. We stop, eat lots of greasy food and drink beer. Oliver announces that he will drive this afternoon; he'll try it and if his foot hurts too much I'll have to take over.

"I can't believe you passed your test," he says.

"I haven't taken it yet."

"But you said... You said you could drive. Well, I suppose you can, after a fashion."

"And when we first set off you said that we would be back in two hours at the most. I thought it would be alright for a couple of hours. But that was quite a few days ago."

I like the idea of being a passenger for a while; watching the land go past while Oliver drives. But the food and beer has an effect on me and I fall asleep. Later I wake up into a dreamy state behind closed eyes, turning thoughts around in my head, barely aware that I'm in the car. I think about Oliver's anger with me over my driving. I didn't like it but it's a learning experience. I've always been spontaneous, even reckless sometimes. I like heights very much, the little buzz of fear. And that bravado stuff makes me feel good – like I'm special. But he's right about the driving. I just wasn't thinking about other people. And I don't feel quite so good about myself now, I'm at a low point. My eyes are still closed, bad feelings and apathy keeping me in this state close to sleep and the comfort of dreams. But eventually I open my eyes and come back into the world.

The world is hilly, green, sometimes wooded and sometimes agricultural, viewed through the window of a car. Soon, I promise myself, I will have some car-free, staying-in-one-place days.

"Do you remember your dreams, Oliver?" I say. It's the first thing to come into my head.

"Oh, you're back with us. Dreams. Let me think." He changes down a gear for a bend. "Yes, I remember my dreams."

"That's good," I say, not sure of whether or not I should ask more.

"I dreamt, last night, that I was in a car driving very happily along, fast, with Lizzie in the seat next to me. And she wasn't very happy because I kept driving too close to the edge of a cliff. *It will be alright* I thought, *what's the problem?*"

"I'm sorry, that's my fault," I say.

"No. I don't think that's it. It's definitely me and Lizzie. I'm driving. I think it's to do with taking chances with our relationship – that's the cliff edge."

"Do your dreams work like that?"

"Oh yes. I know there are lots of pointless dreams but there are some where you're being told something that you need to know. Something that you know deep down but don't want to think about consciously. I get dreams like that."

We are driving along one of the few flat straight pieces of road around here, regularly spaced trees on either side, a sort of avenue. There's a very strong wind blowing, tearing at the leaves, bending the branches, but it's happening outside, we are distant from it in the car.

"I get parental anxiety dreams," Oliver says. "In one dream my son, Otis, has climbed high into a tree, too high, and out onto a dead branch. The branch breaks, he falls, and I wake up feeling really terrible. A nightmare. And it tells me that I worry about the children more than I admit to myself. It tells me about how much I love them. I get lots of dreams like that at the moment. And I remember them in the morning. Do you get big time serious dreams, Dan?"

I dream of my father walking. I'm hundreds of miles from home and I still have that dream sometimes.

"No," I say. "No, I don't have serious dreams." Then I think again. "Actually I did have one where I was back home and it was grim because I wanted to be still travelling."

"Being at home was grim?" Oliver says.

"Yes. Or at least boring."

"I'm looking forward to getting home very much," he says, quietly. "I guess we're very different in that."

Later in the day I'm driving and we're stuck behind a lorry. The high sun shines in through the windscreen, burning hot on my legs, and the air coming in through the car window is full of diesel fumes and heat off the tarmac.

"Why try to catch up with them?" I ask Oliver. "Why not just go home and if you're there first you can wait?"

"Lizzie's got my passport," Oliver says. "I don't think she knows she has it but it's in my suitcase in the back of the car. I've got cash and a credit card but there's one border to cross to get home. I can get across maybe but I don't want to get into trouble with the police – they could be funny with me. Some years ago they were unpleasant but they have been alright with me since I became a model citizen. Still, I ought to be careful."

"Were you not a model citizen in the past?"

"They thought I was a drug courier."

"But you weren't? Or were you?"

"I needed money to set up a business. It was a short term career move."

"And you never got caught?"

"No, I was careful and I was lucky."

I try to think of Oliver smuggling drugs. I can't imagine him being self-possessed enough to carry it off – he shows his feelings too readily. Then I think of the not-showing-his-feelings times, the fixed smile that he can do. And he can be charming too.

"Did you mix with heavy people?" I ask.

"Not at first, but in time, yes."

"You shouldn't tell me this," I say.

"I don't generally talk about it. It's not dinner party conversation. But you're a friend, Daniel. I trust you."

The lorry turns off, I accelerate and we get a cooler breeze coming in. I'm not a timid person, sometimes I like something with a hint of danger, but I would never do that stuff. I admire Oliver for this; I guess he has a toughness in him and a cool nerve. But I wonder if he's someone I should really trust. He's been open and honest with me about everything except maybe this car we're driving. I'm aware that we always have to park in out-of-the-way places and I feel an inhibition about asking why, like it's not something to be discussed. Now Oliver gets me to turn onto a minor road and a few miles later we come into the grounds of a grand house that is open to the public. I'm not surprised when he asks me to park away from the entrance.

Oliver pays for us to go into the grounds and we wander around. Everything is very ornamented, symmetrical and tame. Little gravel paths lead around rose gardens, lawns, statues and fountains. We pass through a tunnel made of the interlaced branches of small trees that are covered in hanging yellow flowers – it leads to the back of the house where the garden is terraced up the slope towards beech woods. We go up the steps and across each terrace to the top of the garden where we are close to the trees.

The garden here is made up of rocky places and grottoes, luxuriant vegetation, narrow paths winding between deep pools. I find a place where I can sit and look over the roof of the house and out to the landscape beyond, rows of hills stretching in the haze and distance. Oliver is focused on closer things; he walks each path between the rocks, looking at the small detail of his surroundings, preoccupied, saying nothing. He disappears into a grotto. I like it here but I'm very hot. I find myself looking into the water of a small deep fish pond. This is the most secluded part of the garden and there's no-one around. I take off all my clothes and lower myself into the water. It's very deep and I can sink right down below the surface. I pull myself up and out onto the flag-stones, realise that I've not cooled off enough and go back in. Then I get out and put my clothes back on. I sit on a bench, dripping and steaming in the sunshine, feeling good. The cold water has sharpened my senses and the colours of the garden seem more intense. I find myself feeling very alive, very here and now, lost in the experience of my surroundings. Oliver appears and comes to sit on the bench next to me.

"You went in the pond, didn't you?"

"Of course I did. It's very hot here. I recommend it."

He shakes his head.

"We were here two weeks ago," he says, "so that's what I see now, Otis running down every little path, climbing the rocks. Me with Daisy on my shoulders." He sighs. "There are things that they do – the *look at me* stuff, sharing their happiness with you, drawing you into their world. And the hiding behind things and coming out all smiles, excited to see you again. And then they look right into your eyes, smiling so much. And of course sometimes they're crying and won't stop – there's that too. But the kids really loved it here. I just thought they might come back."

The man sitting beside me is shrinking. He goes into himself and his memories. I suppose the place is very different to him without his family here. He sees their absence. But to me this place is shiny and new and I'm here in the moment, awake not dreaming, very much alive. I feel that Oliver and I are in the same place but at the same time in different places from each other, like we're in parallel universes. Is it always like this, people only seeming to be on the same planet as each other? I look at Oliver, hunched up, lost in thought. I'm sympathetic but also I'm fed up with him. I feel I want to spend some time with someone who shares my universe. I want it very much.

On the way down through the garden we take a different path, a shady track under the trees. Half-way down Oliver stops suddenly to pick something up off the ground.

"Well, how about that?" he says, holding out his hand to show me a small green felt dinosaur. "It belongs to Daisy," he says. "Come on, we need to hurry."

At the gate he speaks to the woman who sold us our entry tickets. I can't understand what they are saying but he's very excited. We get in the car, Oliver in the driving seat, and set off again. He drives very fast, keeping the engine revs high, accelerating around the bends like a rally driver.

"They were there in the garden today," he says. "They left an hour ago."

Oliver concentrates on the road, slowing down only at places where Lizzie might stop: roadside cafés, petrol stations, lay-bys. I'm the disconnected one now, only half watching the road and the landscape, half thinking about how I get to meet someone who's on the same planet as me. Someone female.

A couple of hours pass and we cover a distance on fast roads. We are moving away from the hills and into a flatter landscape, more like home to me and therefore less attractive. We speed by large fields of what I guess is young wheat or barley. From time to time there's a huge tractor spraying some obnoxious chemical onto the land. Sometimes the road crosses a large river. Villages sit on low hills above the arable land and we turn off to visit the nearer ones to see if Oliver's family have stopped there. When we stop for petrol Oliver asks if I will drive; his foot hurts badly and it's spoiling his concentration. I drive better than before, fast but concentrating, trying to be safe.

We are on a boring four-lane road with heavy traffic. I get stuck in the inside lane behind a big car driven by a little grey-haired old man. A long queue of cars are overtaking steadily and I can't get out into the fast lane. Now a red estate car is passing, driven by a woman with bobbed blonde hair, with two children fixed safely in their special seats. Oliver bounces up and down and starts shouting.

"For God's sake – Lizzie, it's me – Daniel press the horn, sound the horn will you?"

The horn isn't in the centre of the steering wheel. I fiddle with the switches and manage to turn the headlights on, spray the windscreen with water, and start the wipers going. Oliver is waving his arms wildly as the car passes. Then the overtaking traffic slows and we are drawing level. Oliver shouts so loud it hurts my ears. He waves frantically and the little child in the back seat smiles and waves back. Then they pull away again and we continue to be trapped in the slow lane. When I do find a space to pull out the red car is maybe twenty or thirty cars ahead, hidden from us in the mass of traffic.

"OK Dan, just keep steady in this lane. Find out where the horn is. We can't go wrong now."

"Your little girl will tell Lizzie she saw you, won't she?"

"She's two-and-a-half years old – she might do, she might not. If she does, Lizzie won't believe her." Oliver starts laughing, a big mad laughter of joy and excitement and frustration.

The road rises ahead over a low ridge. At the top of the slope is a roundabout; one of those where the main road continues in a cutting and the roundabout traffic passes overhead on two bridges.

"Straight on?" I ask.

"I think so."

We drive past the slip road and then as we approach the first bridge we are both looking up at the traffic overhead. The red estate car with Oliver's family inside passes over as we approach.

"Yes," Oliver shouts, seeing them so close, "No," he shouts, as he realises that we can't get to them. "Do something, Daniel."

I change lanes and pull over by the slip road for traffic coming down off the roundabout. I start reversing as fast as I can up towards the roundabout, against the flow of traffic. I only have to go maybe two hundred yards backwards then we are after them again. But it's difficult to keep the car in a straight line and the cars coming down have to swerve to avoid me. I have the engine roaring at full revs and cars coming down the hill are hooting at me and flashing their lights. Oliver is shouting for me to go faster or slower or something, I don't know what. I feel very good that I'm keeping my head and managing to concentrate. I'm at the top. I reverse carefully onto the roundabout itself and then hit forward gear.

"Yes, yes, yes," Oliver roars.

I accelerate into the traffic.

"Which turn off? How can I tell which way they went?" I ask.

"This one. It *will* be this one I know it."

And I turn the way Oliver says, onto a wide road with little traffic on it. I overtake one slow car. Then when I pull out to overtake the next one we can both see Lizzie's red car not far ahead.

"Daniel, I'm going to kiss you," Oliver says. "You are the best driver in the entire..."

But he's interrupted by the sound of a police siren behind us. I look in my mirror and see a blue flashing light. I'm going to have to pull over.

Oliver looks over his shoulder as I slow down.

"I just do not believe this," he says.

## FIVE

Oliver has been spirited away somewhere and I'm in what I suppose might be called an interview room. There's no window to the outside world and the air is stale. There's no colour: the walls and ceiling are white, the floor is covered with hard grey tiles, and the plastic chairs and formica topped table are grey too. A policeman in an elaborate shiny uniform sits expressionless on the chair next to the door. The clock above the table shows the minutes passing painfully slowly. And the hours.

All I did was drive backwards up a slip road and now I'm locked away in the back of a police station where the cells are. It seems a bit over the top. It's awful because I don't speak a word of the language and they don't speak English; perhaps they are waiting for a translator and then things can be cleared up. Meanwhile I have no idea what's going on. It's awful because I've never been on this side of things before; no-one I know and no-one in my family have ever been in trouble with the police. What happens is this: in the front of the police station people come and go freely, making enquiries, talking politely, smiling helpfully at each other; then there's a door which is locked and behind which there's no contact with the outside world and you feel that you're a prisoner and it feels like you're underground – which is strange because you don't go down any stairs. I think of Oliver and his shady past – what if he had drugs in the car and they think I'm his accomplice? No, it's not that, but then again the police might have something on him and see me as being involved.

It's early evening and the policeman by the door is replaced by a colleague. Then a plain-clothes man comes in and speaks to him. They look across at me from time to time and then the plain-clothes man goes out. The policeman by the door catches my eye, gives me a kind smile, and says something I don't understand, maybe *don't worry*. I do worry but I try to find some mental game that will while away the hours. Perhaps they won't get hold of anyone who speaks English until tomorrow. Now the plain-clothes man comes in again, this time carrying an ice-cream. I look away but he says something recognisably like my name *Mr Brownlow* and passes me the ice-cream with a smile. Very good ice-cream. Kind man. And this is surreal.

An hour later I'm moved to a cell. It looks like I'm going to be staying the night but there's a few hours to pass before I go to sleep. In here it's worse than the interview room. There's the same grey and white colour scheme of course and there's also a heavy iron door with a barred window through which I can be watched. There's a bed, a plastic bucket to piss in, and a table with a pitcher of water and a cup. Stale air again. I take my shoes off and lie on the bed.

I know that I can make myself be somewhere else in my mind. I think of a clear blue-green sea and a sandy beach. That's where I'm headed when I get out of here, south to the sun, sea and that other thing but this is not the time to think of that. I could go to Oliver's place but I feel uncertain about my friendship with him now. I wonder if he's in here in another cell. Somehow I don't think so. I concentrate my mind on the beach and the sea, somewhere I've never been but I've seen in holiday brochures. But my mind goes to the wrong place, to a greyer dirtier cooler sea. The sound of gulls. Deckchairs and sandcastles. Candyfloss. Crazy golf. I'm remembering childhood holidays, the feeling and smells of those times. I remember being on high wooded slopes above a deep gully in something like a big park in a seaside town. Looking down on the holiday-makers walking along the narrow path below me. Hiding. Climbing the stunted pines. Running and jumping with a child's energy. Feeling like a hero in a landscape of adventure and excitement. Exultant, above the world.

And I remember my father as he was in those days, the man who would pick me up and put me on his shoulders. Who could make the dog do tricks and who told silly jokes at breakfast time. My mind moves on now to my childhood home, not the place we've lived in recent years but to where we lived before in the leafy suburbs. Mostly I remember the big conker tree on the edge of the garden. Me and my friends climbing and swinging, building aerial dens of old pallet wood among the leaves, out-daring each other in the topmost branches. Or at night time on my own, high up in the dark, hidden from and looking down on the lights of the grown-up world. That was a long time ago, before the bad stuff.

Along with the pictures, sounds and smells of those times, along with the feeling of being a small hero, come the words Oliver said after we saw the rainbow, *the child is father of the man*. What's that all about? I try to make the words fit in somehow with my day-dreams of home but I don't think they mean anything. It's just a sentence with the word *child* and the word *father* in it. Oliver's been going on about his kids and I'm locked up and lonely and far from home and it's all getting mixed up in my mind.

In the morning my rucksack and passport are returned to me and I'm released without explanation. Outside the police station I am met by Oliver. He looks concerned and apologetic and he carries a plastic bag in one hand.

"I've bought you breakfast," he says, "and I owe you an explanation."

We walk to the town square and sit on a bench under the trees. Traffic circulates around us, a man in overalls waters the plants, an old woman walks her dog. It's great to be out in the world again. Oliver pulls out of the bag a carton of orange juice, a loaf of freshly baked white bread, some peaches and a bar of chocolate. Another morning, another breakfast and a new place. Part of me feels good.

"It's about the car," Oliver says, "we stole it. I didn't have permission from the hotel to take it, I just went in and took the keys off the hook and walked out. That's why you got arrested – for stealing the car. I'm very sorry. I had a sense of urgency and I acted fast. Now that I come to think of it it's amazing that we got so far."

I'm smiling but I don't think it's a nice smile. I guess I'm annoyed.

"How come they let me out?" I ask.

"I've been busy. I've been on the phone to the hotel to get

them not to press charges. I explained that you didn't know, you're young, foreign, and it was my fault. They've known me for years so with a bit of persuading they let it go. They told me they didn't want to see me there again – that's not surprising."

I carry on eating bread and chocolate and I say nothing. I need a moment to think.

"Why didn't you tell me that the car was stolen?" I ask. "Then I would have had a choice. I wouldn't have got locked up."

"I'm sorry," Oliver says, "but I got you out."

*You got me in*, I think, but I don't say anything.

It's very hot in the middle of town. I think I will carry on south now and down to the sea where I can swim and cool down. Maybe just a couple of days hitching and I'll be somewhere really good. I finish the orange juice, stand and pick up my rucksack.

"It's been nice meeting you," I say, but it comes out sounding bitter and sarcastic. "Good luck in catching up with your family." I look around and try to decide which way to set off. "And thanks for the breakfast."

I don't know the name of the town and I only have a vague large-scale map. Where to go? I wander through the streets aimlessly but hoping to reach a major road and the edge of town. I remember that I have a compass in the top pocket of my rucksack. I take it out, let the needle swivel and come to rest, make a mental note of the direction south, set off. I am myself again. My haphazard, almost mapless, certainly planless way of travelling is at least *my* thing. I delight in it. At the edge of town I set off along a small badly-maintained road running along the side of a low hill and above a river. The day has become cloudy and a breeze sounds in the leaves of the big poplar trees. I like being here, going my own way, not inside a car. I walk past small-holdings with vegetable gardens, fruit trees and chickens. Then it's dry open land with yellow grasses grazed by goats. Why *not* take this small road through the countryside? It feels right. It's a shame there's almost no traffic for hitching – just the occasional lorry.

I walk. Sometimes the sun comes through a gap in the clouds and shines on the river below me. Sometimes the wind picks up and rattles the leaves above. Lizards scurry across the road or sit on rocks close by; one of them has no tail. I run my hand through the feathery leaves of roadside plants that smell of aniseed. Then a lorry is coming and I turn to hitch. The driver doesn't stop but makes a sign with one hand, a circular motion that means he's turning soon. But everything is pleasantly stimulating to me, good because I'm alone and not tied to Oliver and especially good because I'm not locked up in a police cell.

Further along the road I look up at a truck coming towards me and recognise the driver as the one I tried to hitch with earlier. He's going back to town already. He doesn't look at me as he passes. Now there's a very faint smell in the air; it's sweet, maybe putrid. I don't recognise it at all but it affects my stomach. And the smell makes the landscape *look* different. It's becoming unwelcoming to me, somewhere I don't want to be. The change in my mood has come quickly. I take off my rucksack, put it down and sit on a rock. I want to know why the place has changed for me so fast. I look at the components of the scene: river below, small hills, poplars, wild fig trees, lizards. The things that looked pleasant before now look sinister. I think back to a couple of days ago when I was in a garden with Oliver, him painfully aware of the absence of those people who were there before, me seeing just a bright new world, senses awakened by cold water on a hot day. How much we project our own stuff onto what we see.

But the wind changes and it isn't my stuff out there, it's that smell again and it's stronger. I have to move on a little. I walk on around the next bend where the road ends abruptly with a turning place beside an old quarry. There's an open gate in a barbed wire fence. I go through and on to the edge of the broken tarmac where there's a sheer drop. The abandoned quarry is the town rubbish dump. Below are old fridges and cars, torn rubbish bags. I can see the legs of a dead cow that has come to rest exactly upside down. On the dusty slope to one side are three dead sheep, two of them blackened over with swarms of flies, one being pecked at by a crow. I guess there are other corpses, ones that I can't see because they are covered over with rubbish. The smell is bad enough now to make me want to throw up. I think I took the wrong road.

Later in the day I'm on the edge of town again, standing at the side of a slightly larger road that leads due south. The sky has clouded and darkened and it begins to rain, big heavy drops wetting the tarmac and releasing the smell that comes with rain after sunshine, the smell of summer at home. A small car containing a big family pulls up and the driver offers me a lift. *No good* he says, pointing up at the sky. I cram myself into a back seat, rucksack on my lap, children heaped against me, heavy rain outside and the wipers going full belt. The mother has an outsize baby on her lap. Its big round cuckoo face creases up into a grimace and tears run down its cheeks. After a while it begins to howl for no reason at all. The children in the back are fidgeting against each other. The boy pokes his sister on the sly and she yells in a high foreign voice. I'm not enjoying this but the parents are unperturbed. I think of Oliver for a moment, his longing for his kids. I'm puzzled.

We pull in by an unpleasant small modern house and the man makes a sympathetic face to me. *You eat?* he says and invites me in. Inside the house the woman cooks while the man sings to the baby and tosses it into the air to stop it being bored and crying again. We eat a big lunch, the rain stops, the children argue, the man smokes and I thank them and set off carrying a mental snapshot of their busy crowded life.

There's little traffic now and I feel that I'm a person here and not the anonymous figure that I have been by the side of busier roads. I'm actually more likely to get a lift. Sure enough a three-wheeler half-truck-half-motorbike stops for me and an unsmiling old man directs me into the back. We travel maybe ten miles in half an hour, not much faster than on a bicycle, the man in his tiny cab waving to people on the road, me in the open behind him, watching the world go by at a leisurely pace. I like this; I don't have the chore of trying to make conversation with someone who doesn't speak my language and I can see the land passing by without being separated from it by window glass. We pass vineyards and dairy farms and go through small villages of pantiled houses surrounded by flowers. In time we get to the edge of a town and stop by a supermarket. The man points out the way for me and says good-bye.

On the opposite side of town I'm standing by the road again. A young man in a smart car stops and gives me a lift. He looks educated to me and I try to start a conversation in English with him. With a great deal of effort and some humour we succeed in communicating almost nothing. He drives slowly and keeps turning to smile at me. I feel a certain warmth coming from him even without words, like he's on my wavelength. On a straight stretch of road he slows the car and puts his hand on my thigh. I jump and say the word *no* a few times. He laughs and moves his hand away. Half a mile later he drops me off at a lay-by, smiles, says something that might be *sorry*, and turns to drive back towards the town. He raises his hand to me as he goes off. He looks sad.

Now I have a long wait but eventually get a lift in a big truck. The inside of the driver's cab is festooned with photographs of what I imagine are his family and friends, as if he's not the silent truck driver sort at all but would rather be surrounded by people. He wants to talk but it's hopeless; we have little common language, the truck is noisy and he needs to watch the road. I look at the photographs. Everyone is looking at the camera and smiling. They are better company for him than I am so I allow myself to fall asleep. When I wake he has stopped at a junction and he motions for me to get out. He tries to explain something with his hands – I think he isn't allowed hitch-hikers and has to drop me off here. I get out and he turns off onto a smaller road, sounding his horn to say good-bye.

It's early evening now and the road is very quiet. The junction is in the middle of a forest of tall trees, beech I think, and in their shade, under a cloudy sky, and with evening coming on, I fade to invisibility. The few vehicles that come along pass me by. I decide to walk. I plod on through the forest, stepping out of the road when there are headlights coming, pushing myself a little in the hope of reaching somewhere to stay before nightfall. As it gets darker there's little to stimulate the senses and the smell of the dead animals in the rubbish dump keeps coming back to me. I don't feel that good. Around midnight I'm still in the forest and I'm exhausted. I climb the bank above the road, settle down on a pile of leaves and pull myself into my sleeping bag. I have travelled across the surface of a few people's lives today and passed by some places. I fall asleep with a procession of images running through my mind.

I wake up late in the morning after a bad night's sleep. I tumble down the bank to the roadside, clothes in disarray, shoelaces untied, eyes adjusting to the morning light. My sleeping bag hangs half out of my rucksack and I'm pushing it clumsily back in when a car stops. There are two men with hippy-length hair looking out at me through the dirty windscreen. The one in the passenger seat winds the window down and speaks to me in English,

"Do you want a lift?"

I get into the back seat of the car and we drive off. The passenger-seat guy turns and smiles at me. "You look very much like you wouldn't refuse a good breakfast," he says. "You can come up to our place if you want. You might even decide to stay a while."

He has a strange eager expression on his face. I don't know what to think.

## SIX

Some good things about this place:

1)   The old buildings around the courtyard, some of them half-restored. I think they were built for usefulness but by someone who had a good eye for shapes and proportions. In semi-dereliction they look great. Perhaps the guys are right and the place was originally some sort of religious settlement. There is certainly a special stillness here. It makes you feel calm.

2)   One building in particular, not so different from the others, from the outside it looks similar to an old barn or store room. I go in but the others don't like it. There's something like a psychic force in here; I don't know what I mean by that, I don't mean haunted. Perhaps the accumulation of all the special feelings over the years has left a residue. I get a serious erection in here, very nice, well actually uncomfortable. And it seems inappropriate; not what you'd expect to happen to you in a chapel.

3)   The gorge. Push your way through the tangled scrub-turning-into-woods vegetation behind the buildings, go maybe three or four hundred yards and you come to the edge of the gorge. The cliffs are sheer on each side, quite close together in places, and made of a fawn-coloured hard rock – I think it's limestone. The water at the bottom is clear pale blue; it runs shallow over pebbles, then over a waterfall into a pool, then between pot-holed rocks and out of sight. I *will* find a way down there.

4)   The guys. Jay is the walking bass one. He sits down, pushes his long hair behind his ears, rests his guitar gently on his lap and plays. Ragtime, blues, folk tunes, sometimes a little Bach. And always with a regular walking bass, rhythmic, certain, not too fast, sure to get there. Jay is tall and he walks like that, talks the same, even chews his food to the same regular rhythm – well, it seems to me that he does. I like him, his pock-marked face, that very subtle smile. The other man, Rob, is small, wiry, energetic, has

long blonde hair. He plays guitar with a pick and gets a very bright tone. He tells me that he was once lead guitarist in a rock band. His blue eyes open very wide when he speaks – like headlights.

5)   Emma. I don't know. She's very quiet. She seems kind. She watches me a lot – maybe mistrustfully? No, I don't think so. Like the guys she is three or four years older than me. She has long mouse-brown hair, usually tied back in a pony-tail. Is she pretty? I'm not sure.

Some not so good things about this place:

1)   The big poster in the kitchen. It says *The peace of God, which transcends all understanding, will guard your hearts and your minds in Christ Jesus.*

2)   The small poster in the bathroom that says *The truth will make you free.*

3)   The one at the top of the stairs that says *I have come into the world as a light, so that no-one who believes in me should stay in darkness (John 3:14).*

These people believe in this stuff.

But I like it here very much. They speak English, they are kind and lots of fun, the guys are good musicians. And the place is very quiet, far from anywhere, beautiful in its way. Also it's a mess and there's lots to do. They have asked me if I want to stay for a few days and help out in return for food and a bed. Yes, I do want to stay here.

It is early evening. It has been cloudy, breezy and cool all day but now the clouds break up and there are patches of sunshine on the tree tops. We have eaten supper and we are sitting outside in the courtyard. Jay has just finished finger-picking (with walking bass) *Jesu, joy of man's desiring* by J S Bach – that's what he said it was, I didn't know it but it sounded familiar.

"Devotional music is the best," he says, "and anyway, Bach aids the digestion."

Overhead swifts are wheeling around and making that screeching noise. They nest in the buildings and now and then one will plunge down and in through a broken door or window.

"Thank you for asking me to stay," I say.

"It's OK." Jay says. "You sound like you need to be in one place for a while." He looks at me carefully. "Can I ask you a question?" he says.

"Yes."

"Why are you travelling?"

"I just wanted to get away from home because it's too normal. I wanted a change."

"You don't think you are looking for something?"

"No," I say, "Just exploring."

"Not going anywhere in particular?"

"No. I like the idea of not knowing where I'm going. Just seeing what will turn up."

"That's good," Rob says. "That's how we found this place. Well, it wasn't us that found it, it was Peter and Christie. They'll be back in a couple of days and you'll meet them. They were just travelling around seeing what would happen – leaving God a little space to do his work. Everyone should do that sometimes."

"Maybe," I say.

"Can I ask you something else?" Rob says. He's smiling a lot. I don't feel that I'm being interrogated.

"Yes," I say.

"When we picked you up you had slept rough under the trees but you said that it wasn't as bad as the night before."

"That's right."

"Well, what happened the night before?"

"I was in a police cell."

And I have to tell them how I got there. It's a good story. When I've finished Rob speaks again, "That man betrayed your trust. Lying to you like that."

Betrayal is a heavy-weight concept. I hadn't thought of it like that.

"Oliver is not a bad guy," I say, "I like him. I think of him as a friend. He was in a difficult time."

"If he was your friend then why did you just go off and leave him?" Rob says.

"OK. Maybe I was angry. It's true that I trusted him and he let me down. And we didn't have a car anymore."

I think to myself that I do make pretty fast decisions. I wonder how Oliver is getting along. I hope he's alright. I wonder if I'll ever see him again.

Jay gets up. "We have our prayer meeting now," he says. "We don't use the chapel, we've got a clearing in the trees. You're welcome to come along, Daniel."

"Not tonight, thanks."

"We won't press you. Come in your own time." He goes indoors to put his guitar away.

Rob is smiling at me. "You know we'll get you in the end," he says, in a teasing voice. Then he looks more serious, he does his eyes-very-wide-open-like-headlights thing, "Seek and you will find, knock and the door will be opened to you," he says. I guess it's a quote. Then Jay comes out of the building with Emma and the three of them walk off quietly into the woods.

I am working with Jay and Rob on the roof of an old cattle shed on one side of the courtyard. It's raining but too warm for water-proofs so we wear just shorts (actually swimming trunks in my case) and trainers; our bodies glisten with a coating of mixed rain and sweat. Both the men have their hair tied back in pony-tails and as Rob's blonde hair is dark with the rain they don't look so different from each other as they usually do – they could be brothers. We are taking all the tiles off and storing the best ones for use in repairing the roof of the main building. I'm at the top passing tiles down to Rob who passes them on to Jay at the bottom – he's afraid of heights. The roof is slippery but we have ladders made out of poles they cut out of the woods. Jay and Rob are cracking jokes and talking about football, remembering particular goals scored in matches played years ago. I never liked team games so I can't really join in. But I like these guys; they certainly don't fit with my preconceptions of serious believers.

"How did you get to be Christians?" I ask.

"I was brought up like that," Rob says. "Then I rejected it in my teens and did the whole sex and drugs and rock and roll thing, playing in a band. But I wasn't happy. I was always coming down. Down off drugs or the high of performing. I had a lot of casual sex which made me feel bad – it seems unlikely I know." He laughs. "But it made me feel bad inside. There were girls who just saw a man on a stage with a guitar. They didn't want to know who I really was. And sometimes I didn't give a shit, I really didn't. And deep down I knew I had a moral standard that was being destroyed. I felt ashamed of myself, so that meant I used more dope."

We've stopped passing tiles. Jay watches from his ladder at the edge of the roof, listening carefully, though I guess he must have heard all this before.

"Then I packed it up. I left the band and the lifestyle that went with it," Rob says. "I bet you can't believe a healthy young man would give all that up."

"I can believe it," I say. "I like drugs, acid best of all. But drugs aren't that important. And I've had sex that felt bad afterwards. Like I wanted something different."

I've never said this to anyone else and I certainly didn't think I would say it to another man.

"What was the something different that you wanted?" Rob asks.

"Oh, I don't know."

I go quiet because I do know. I dream of a big-time soul-to-soul relationship; the someone-on-the-same-planet-as-me stuff. But my planet is so out on the edge of things. I don't know if it will ever happen.

"How old are you, Daniel?" Rob asks.

"Nineteen."

"I think you'll make a good Christian someday."

"Oh my God," I say, in horror.

Rob laughs. "Did you hear what you just said? You're half way there."

We move some more tiles but I realise that I haven't heard the whole story.

"So you gave up rock and roll. How did you become a Christian again?" I ask.

Rob looks down at Jay. "Do you want to tell him or shall I?" he asks.

"Go on," Jay says. "It's your gig."

"I went out of my way to help an old school friend, a very lovely bloke who was trying to get off heroin. He succeeded with God's help. It changed us both." He looks down at Jay as he says this.

"Are you the lovely bloke?" I ask Jay.

"It's my middle name," he says.

It scares me that they are such brilliant guys. I want to be like them but more than that I desperately want not to be.

Rob does that headlight thing with his eyes again, "We know that we have passed from death to life because we love our brothers. John: three, fourteen."

It's OK, I feel safe. The bible stuff really turns me off. And there's a weird vacancy about them when they speak that way. It's like they lose something of themselves, their healthy scepticism or something more than that, I don't know what. I do know that whatever it is, it's something I don't want to lose.

Every evening after supper Jay, Rob and Emma go off for their prayer meeting. I don't join them but I set off in the opposite direction. I walk through the scrub along what is becoming more like a path each time I go this way. I clamber over old dry stone walls that are covered with creepers and brambles; I guess this was farm land once and it's been abandoned in recent years. Nature is taking over fast. As I get nearer to the edge of the gorge I can hear the water below. It draws me on.

There are places at the side of the gorge where I can stretch out flat on the rocks and look over the edge. It's hot here, still and humid under the clouds, and the water below looks inviting. My eyes rest on the pool below the waterfall. It's deep enough to bathe in, maybe swim a few strokes. I've already tried a couple of ways down and didn't get very far. It's a sheer drop and my heart goes pretty fast when I first lower myself over the edge. But the rock is hard, perfect for climbing, safe. And if I get stuck I know that I can get back up again; it's always easier than going down.

Today I try for new routes. I push through the vegetation in a number of places and look down. Where it is less steep there are creepers, bushes and even small trees holding onto the rocks. I realise that the most nearly vertical sections are the safest; just clean hard rock, space, and the river below. Getting started is the hardest thing but if I clear away some soil and vegetation from the top of the cliff I can lower myself from good hand-holds. I find a possible route that will bring me down to the river above the waterfall. I set off very slowly, trying to move only one hand or foot at a time so that I've always got three safe holds on the rock. The adrenaline buzz makes me clear headed and logical. I wish the people who say that I'm impetuous could see me now.

I soon come to some easier rock with big hand-holds and I move a little faster but still with care. Then it changes again, the rock below me is smooth, like the inside of a cave that was once hollowed out by water. I can't go down here but must move sideways until I find a way past or across this surface. In time I find a place where there are two cracks running down diagonally. I use the cracks to descend, hands in the top crack, feet in the bottom one, and, because I'm going diagonally, I can see ahead of me all the time and move with a steady rhythm. But the cracks get shallower and soon I'm holding onto the rock with not much more than toes and finger tips. There is a safe ledge below me, not too far, and I keep going. The trouble is that I'm tiring and my fingers hurt. I'm sweating very much and I smell bad – not the usual smell of physical exertion in the heat but something more. I recognise it and I don't like it; it's the smell of my own fear. So now, stupidly, my legs start shaking and holding on becomes even more difficult. And it gets worse.

Two things are happening: the top crack is getting bigger and the holds easier; the bottom crack is fading out to nothing, there's nowhere for my feet to go. But the ledge is quite close and anyway I'm too weak to go back up. I shift myself down using only my arms and with my feet hanging useless against the rock; I mustn't waste my energy scrabbling for foot-holds that aren't there. I can't do this for long but I don't have to. Quite soon I let go and drop onto the ledge.

I can rest easily here; my feet are on a firm surface and I can lean back against the rock and relax. The shakes come on, first in my legs and then for a moment my whole body is trembling. Then I get calmer, my breathing slows and I stop hearing my heart beat and start hearing the sound of the water below. I scramble down the last part of the cliff, take off my clothes and paddle along the shallows to the waterfall. The water descends maybe ten or twelve feet into the pool. Not far. I guess where the deepest part of the pool is, jump, and hit the water feet first. I touch bottom before coming up again. I duck-dive, swim, float on my back, dive again, swim to the edge and get out. I sit on a boulder and rest.

I think about the worst part of the climb. I've always had these I-wish-I-hadn't-done-that moments. I know that whatever I try to tell myself I will have scares like this again. I don't want to but I will. It's usually something to do with climbing. The time I got up on the school roof it caused more trouble than I could have imagined. And I climbed a crane once but it was in the dark and no-one knew. I can't help it. I like the buzz.

When I get back to my Christian friends I don't tell them what I've been doing. I'm pleased with myself that I made it to the river and I have a great appetite for supper. All they have done is have a prayer meeting but they look high too. Rob is non-stop headlights, Jay's soft smile hangs around his face all evening and Emma is elated though she looks like she's been crying. I don't normally ask them about their meetings. The general assumption is that I'll go to one eventually. Maybe I will. But after supper Emma and I are doing the washing up together and I can't think of what to talk about.

"Good prayer meeting?" I ask.

"It's always good," she says.

Then she's wiping down the cooker and I'm about to go outside to listen to the guys playing guitar.

"Daniel," she says.

I stop at the door and turn.

"I prayed for you."

She looks into my eyes with such an open frank expression. She holds my gaze and I find that I'm smiling. I don't know why.

# SEVEN

We've just had breakfast and the guys are making music already. Jay finger-picks chords and Rob is sitting with his guitar on his lap, not playing but singing. They are doing something that sounds like an old folk tune, not my sort of thing. But when you're travelling you don't hear much music and the things you do hear get stuck in your head. This one has grown on me. The words are meant to be Jesus saying *just believe, do what I tell you, everything will be alright.* Rob sings it gently so that this Jesus sounds like your best friend, favourite uncle and brother all in one. After he has sung two verses and choruses he plays the tune and some variations on his guitar, a single line of clear melody above Jay's chords. Then they put their instruments away and we get ready for work. It's a nice start to the day.

We begin work in what was, isn't now, but will be again, the meadow above the courtyard. The grassland has half-disappeared under a new growth of brambles and thorns and our job is to cut them back and open it up again. The plan is to have animals grazing here some time in the future. Jay and Emma are cutting the grass at the edge with sickles. Rob and I are using slashers, sharp hooks on long handles, to cut down the heavier vegetation closer to the trees. Rob is a hard working vigorous little guy and I try hard to keep up with him. We manage to keep a conversation going as we work.

"You said there are two others who are coming back some time," I say.

"Peter and Christie. They started us off here. Peter's sort of our leader here though nobody says it. It's true though. Peter was brought up very strongly in the faith and he has a deep understanding. He doesn't preach but he leads our meetings."

"Are they a couple?"

"Yeah, they've been married three years. She's from a Christian background too. They are our inspiration. I'm looking forward to you meeting them."

"Will they approve of me being here?" I ask.

"Oh yes. It's our aim to get more people here. Like a community."

The sun has come out from behind the clouds and it's very hot work. I've got my shirt off but I don't have shorts like the others.

"Have you got any scissors here?" I ask.

"Yes." Rob stops and looks at me questioningly. "If you need them they are in the kitchen drawer."

I disappear for a while and come back with my jeans cut down to shorts. Rob takes a look and laughs.

"Praise the Lord," he says.

"What does that mean?"

"It means you've got very white legs."

I look down. It's true, they do glow in a luminous white sort of way.

"Praise the Lord," I say, half-heartedly.

"I think we're getting to you," Rob says, smiling, teasing me. "But can you work a little further away from me, Daniel? I'm worried that you're going to take my ear off with that thing."

I move away a little and get into some serious hacking of brambles. It's cooler in shorts but I'm not as skilful as Rob and I'm getting scratches on my legs.

"When are you coming to a prayer meeting?" Rob asks.

This subject keeps coming up. I like these people and I want to stay here. I think I'm earning my keep by working alongside them. But I know they want something more.

"Maybe you'll come when Peter and Christie get back and it's five of us," he says. "Then we can help you."

"What do you mean *help me?*"

"You know, to find Jesus. But move further away with that thing. It's very sharp you know."

"I'm not sure that I want to find Jesus," I say. I feel sad that I might be offending him.

"Give it a try," Rob says. "Open yourself up, Daniel."

I swing my slasher round to the other side at the same time as

Rob swings his and they crash against each other with a metallic crunching sound. He looks at me with a patient expression.

"You're dangerous," he says.

Now it's early afternoon and Rob has asked me to swap places with Jay and work with Emma. He said that working alongside me was too stressful for him. Emma and I are using sickles to cut the long grass on the edge of the meadow close to the courtyard. Actually it's not just grass; the meadow is half other plants, some of them have scented flowers and some are herbs which give off rich smells when the leaves are cut or crushed. When we need a change we stop and rake it up into a heap. The work is rhythmic and the air is full of the fragrance of cut vegetation drying in the sun.

I don't know what to say to Emma. I feel bad because I've been here quite a few days and have made friends with the guys but ignored her. It seems rude. But she's reserved and has said very little to me; maybe it's not my fault that I'm awkward with her. Emma generally wears one of a number of loose men's shirts that must be comfortable and cool in this climate. This morning when the sun came out she took off her shirt and now works close to me in a little thin cotton vest. She has a beautiful body. I try not to look but I don't entirely succeed. Maybe the shirts are a deliberate covering up – guys around, hot weather, she doesn't want to give anyone the wrong idea. I do have the wrong idea; I can't help it. I find it hard not to look at her breasts, her nipples showing through the thin cotton. I try to concentrate on the work but my mind wanders then my eyes wander too. I need to talk to her and make her a person and not just a sexual presence.

"Have you always been a Christian?" I ask.

She stops her work for a moment and looks at me. She has this way of looking right into your eyes.

"No," she says, "But I had a special experience. A life changing moment."

Somehow I don't want to ask about this. "What did you do before?" I say.

"Not a great deal. I went to university and smoked a lot of dope. I wasn't a great success."

"Are any of us?" I say.

"Well yes, actually. My family are. They are all clever. My older sisters are both doctors like my father. My brother is a classical musician."

So maybe I understand a little about her straight away. That posh accent that comes through even when she tries to disguise it. And being ordinary is a problem for her because her family are clever. And dope. Then Jesus. But perhaps I'm making it too simple.

"What did you study?" I ask.

"Art. But I didn't finish."

"Why not?"

"I didn't feel good enough. I thought my work was worthless. And that was me being sorry for myself but it was true in a way. Without Jesus in our lives we are nothing."

She looks so sad. Her body language is *it's only me, I'm nobody much.*

"I don't believe that you're anything other than pretty special," I say.

I only mean to be kind but the words come out of me with a lot of conviction. She looks into my eyes again and smiles. I notice that her eyes are brown but with flecks of green. Her smile is like a physical touch; it's intimate and it makes me feel good. Now she lowers her head and turns away. She is still for a moment before going back to work. I move away so that I can swing my sickle properly and I turn my back on her. I try to focus on the work, on all the smells of the herbs and all the shapes and colours of the flowers I'm cutting down. But with the heat of the sun on my back I'm feeling very sensual. And though I try to think of other things I can still see that smile of hers – it felt like she had put her hand down the front of my trousers. Now she calls me and out of politeness I have to stop what I'm doing and turn towards her.

"Daniel."

"Yes."

She has one hand on the small of her back as she straightens. She stretches and I'm looking at her body even though I don't mean to.

"I think you will become one of us here."

She's smiling in the same way again. I feel like I'm being flirted with and manipulated. I have to remember that she's a Christian, she only wants me to find Jesus and all the sexy stuff is in my head. It's just me being a randy teenager. I guess it will be different when I get older. Easier, I imagine.

It has been a physical day and I'm too tired to climb down into the gorge this evening. I sit in the kitchen because it's the coolest place to be. But I'm not terribly comfortable here, my legs sting with sunburn and scratches and, worse than that, I keep looking up and seeing the poster, *the peace of God, which transcends all understanding, will guard your hearts* and so on. I turn my chair to face the door but the words are stuck in my mind. *Transcends all understanding* sounds about right. Restless, I wander out and into the chapel at the side of the courtyard. It's cool in here too and there's a special stillness. I wonder why they won't use this place for their prayers. I remember that I once went into a big cathedral and marvelled at how it was built to have a particular effect on people. The light coming through stained glass windows, sounds echoing in the vast space between stone walls, ridiculously high ceilings to make you feel small as if in the presence of some higher power. This place has none of that. I look carefully but there's really nothing in the construction of this building that is different from the others here. The only cross is outside on the roof. So why does it have this effect on me? I feel moved in some way. I have an erection – that happens every time I come in here. I pace up and down in the cool empty space, wondering what has happened to the pews and all the religious paraphernalia that must have once been here. I have a strange urge which I act on immediately, as I always do.

I go across to the meadow and use a pitch fork to lift the half-dried grass and herbs that we left in a pile there. I carry as much as I can over and into the chapel, making three or four journeys. Then I spread it to cover the whole of the stone-flagged floor. A warm fragrance fills the air. I stand right in the middle with my eyes closed, just breathing it in, feeling a little dizzy. My friends want me to become a Christian like them. It's not going to happen. I wonder what you have to do to become a pagan.

We are sitting around the table about to have a light lunch of bread, cheese, tomatoes and olives. The air is heavy with moisture, thunder sounds in the distance and the door is shut to keep out the great variety of insects that are about today. We bow our heads and Jay begins to say grace, *Lord Jesus who was sent from God to save us from...* but he's interrupted by the sound of a vehicle coming up the track from the village. Rob gets up and opens the door.

"It's Peter and Christie," he says. "Praise the Lord."

We all go out into the courtyard to greet them. A landrover pulls up and a short round-faced man with a Christian sort of beard gets out. His face beams with religious fervour or maybe just the pleasure of coming back to his friends; I'm not sure which. Then a woman gets slowly out of the passenger seat. She's small, wears thick glasses and is heavily pregnant. Jay, Rob and Emma bustle around them, smiling, giving warm hugs to each of them in turn. I'm introduced.

"Daniel, I'm very pleased to meet you," Peter says, looking me up and down, opening his arms for a hug from me too. I'm not used to this sort of thing and I'm awkward. I hug Christie and bump against her bulge.

"I'm very sorry," I say, embarrassed. "They didn't tell me that there were three of you."

Peter is smiling at me. "It might be four of us. We think it could be twins," he says and everybody is laughing.

Peter sits at the head of the table, says grace and we eat our lunch. I'm quietly watching them all, sensing the change in atmosphere. There's still plenty of humour but Peter makes it feel different; he's much older than the rest of us, maybe thirty, and he has a patriarchal manner. Rob and Jay are respectful towards him and not quite so relaxed. Emma makes herself invisible. When lunch is over and Christie has gone upstairs for a rest, Jay tells Peter about all the work we've done since they've been away. He's kind enough to say that I've been a good help.

"And have you been to our prayer meetings, Daniel?" Peter asks. "I'm building up to it," I say.

He looks at me silently. He's only little but he sits very upright at the end of the table and I feel I'm being looked down on with disapproval. I think that tonight I've got to get myself to prayers. First time and last time, I reckon.

I think the wind must have changed direction. The sky has cleared, the air is cool and all the afternoon's humidity has been swept away. We stand outside in the courtyard waiting for Peter and Christie. Rob and Jay are talking about football and making jokes. Emma watches me out of the corner of her eyes. I feel nervous, like I wish I hadn't agreed to go to this evening's prayer meeting. At last Peter comes out of the house.

"Christie is very tired," he says, looking disappointed. "We'll go down without her this time."

I wait for the others to set off and follow after, last in the single file passing along the narrow path through the trees. We come to a clearing that is pleasantly unspooky. We spread ourselves into a little solemn circle and stand with heads bowed. There's silence for a while. Then Peter speaks:

"*I am the resurrection and the life. He who believes in me will live, even though he dies; and whoever believes in me will never die.*"

Silence again.

My head is down and I'm looking at the ground, at the five pairs of sandalled and trainered feet and a line of black ants going about their business. I can sense that Jay, who is on my left, is swaying gently from side to side. Rob is on my other side and he begins to mutter a phrase over and over. I listen carefully as his voice rises and I can make out the words *I have been crucified with Christ and I no longer live, I have been crucified with Christ and I no longer live.* His voice has changed – it's not the Rob that I know and like. Peter is now chanting but I can't make out a single word. It doesn't sound like English. I keep my head down and wonder how long I have to stay. Then there's a loud sob and an out-pouring of incoherent biblical sounding nonsense from Emma. I look up and see that she's swaying and turning her head from side to side. She gradually becomes silent but her lips are still moving and tears are running down her face. This is appalling. It's madness. As quietly as I can I slip away.

I go back and sit outside in the courtyard. Swifts are whirling around in the air above me, screaming, plunging down and into the buildings where their nests are. The sun is low and the red-tinged light touches the underside of their wings as they fly. I'm happy to watch this for a while, it makes me feel sane but nicely alive. Then I start to think of alcohol. I would love to have a few beers and feel even more nicely alive. Yes, this would be just the right time to walk down to the village bar and meet the locals.

I'm not used to long periods of clean living and I like a little wildness: sometimes I smoke enough cannabis to make the room spin around me in an interesting way; I've had scary and not so scary acid trips; I've stayed up all night on speed. Easier than any of that is alcohol in large amounts. You can buy it anywhere and it makes you feel a great warmth for your fellow human beings. And if you drink enough there comes the need for inspired craziness with or without the companionship of others equally inspired and crazy. I like drugs and alcohol. I like the release of energy, the uninhibited nonsense, the altered state of consciousness. And long periods without that release make me feel constrained.

But the bar in the village is drab. I try to talk but there's no-one who speaks enough English to attempt conversation with me. I sit in the corner with a bottle of rough red wine and a tumbler on the table in front of me and watch people. They all look so old. And I don't want to be watching, I want to be acting up in some wild way. The people here are drinking not for craziness but for mild sedation; they are quiet and restrained, good-natured and dull. This is the wrong place for me but I stick it out, drink my bottle of wine, smile at people, start on another bottle, scowl at people, leave.

Then I start walking back up the hill to Christianville. I plod unsteadily along, tripping over ruts, loosing the edge of the track from time to time in the darkness. Above are stars, no moon, just too many thousands of bright stars. I think my father would like to be out here with his telescope tonight. But I don't want to think of him now and the night sky is an irritation. I start to run, weaving from side to side deliberately, taking the chance that I might go off the track and tumble into the bushes. And soon I trip on a tree root and crash onto the ground. But it's nothing, only a little pain in my arm and shoulder. I want more than this. I want to climb, that's what I usually do when I feel like this. At home it's out of the pub and secretly up onto the tower of the ruined church. In town I once climbed a crane. Here the only possible place is the gorge and that's a climb down rather than up. It will do. Just thinking about it gives me an adrenaline buzz and my head begins to clear.

# EIGHT

The path to the side of the gorge is well trodden down now and easy to follow even on such a dark night. In the absence of light and colour I hear the sound of the water much earlier than I usually do. I'm excited, focused, and aware of all the different gurgling, splashing and rushing noises coming up from the river, the different rhythms beating against each other. I believe I can smell the water from here; I can certainly smell the pale night flowers that I pass by. My feet know their way along the path and I can look up and see bats, their black shapes making jagged movements across the stars. When I reach the edge of the gorge the water sounds louder, my heart is beating fast, but my mind is still. I find the familiar hand-holds and lower myself over the edge.

The climb is a journey of easy and hard parts. The first section is straight forward and I've done it quite a few times before. My hands and feet move easily into the right places and my hold on the rock is skilful and certain. I can see very little and my sense of touch, of finger-tips against stone, is sharpened. Then comes the section I really like – the bit where the two diagonal cracks cross the smooth rock face. Here I try to keep the rhythm that I have in daylight but I'm slower; feeling for small hand-holds takes longer than seeing them. And now the best bit: the foot holds run out and for a few yards I'm holding on with my hands only, shifting along and down until I can drop to the ledge below. But how far do I go before I make that drop? Even the starlight is limited here in the gorge and I can't see the ledge at all. I know my movements are slower in the dark so I go a little further than seems right before letting go. I hit the ledge awkwardly and fall sideways against a smooth surface where my hands can't get a grip. I have a slow-motion sense of the rock pushing me away into space and darkness.

Of course it's not far to the bottom from here and it's not a sheer drop. I descend in a series of small hard bounces and land on my side in the shallow water that runs over pebbles. I get to my feet quickly and wade down to the big rock above the water-fall. I stand here for a while breathing fast and shaking all over. When I've calmed down I move my arms and legs carefully, one by one, to see they are in working order. Only bruises and some blood on one forearm. I feel exultant. I take my clothes off and stand in my usual place on the rock. I look up at the narrow ribbon of stars that is all I can see of the night sky from down here. Then I step forward, drop to the pool, and plunge down through the cold water.

My way up out of the gorge is by a slightly different route. Up is always easier than down but there is one bit of serious climbing a little way up from the floor of the gorge. When I've done that section everything else will be straight forward. I've shivered myself dry, I'm dressed and I start to climb. I come to the diffi-cult stretch. It's smooth rock with small hand-holds but it's not dangerously high and it doesn't normally take long. But this time I'm in difficulty. There's a place where I have to hold my weight with my left arm while shuffling my feet to new holds. When I try it now there's a great pain in my shoulder and I'm forced back. What do I do? I can't find an easier route up in the dark so I must try again and I must overcome the pain. But it hurts too much and I can't concentrate on finding the right place for my feet. I try three more times but it hurts more each time. I can't make myself do it. I descend to the bottom of the gorge.

It must be something like midnight now. I'm shivering, sweat-ing, hurting and very wide awake. And I'm going to have to stay down here until daylight when I can find an easier way up. I don't think sleep will be a possibility. I feel my way to a gentle depres-sion in the rock face and sit, leaning back, eyes open onto the dark, waiting for dawn. I will feel very cold later but that's OK. I don't need to worry, just pass the time. I try to think of a song to sing and come up with Rob's *Jesus makes everything alright* number. I sing it over and over and begin to believe in the words. I can see Rob's face in front of me, his blonde stubble and long hair. After a while Rob is Jesus in my mind and it's all become silly nonsense. I laugh out loud. I try to think of other songs and go through my record collection back home, album by album, song by song, trying to remember one that really means something to me. It's like I've moved on from them, not one song tells me how it really is. I spend some time before dawn in something like sleep, still going through the albums, still searching. I don't know what it is that I'm looking for.

I spend two days and nights in bed, shivering, sweating, sometimes delirious, sometimes lucid. The bruises are painful but it's the satisfying pain of a body injured and repairing itself. In my head I feel good; I needed some sort of release and I found it. People come in to see how I am. Rob is great, full of excitement after hearing about my little adventure, wanting to climb down into the gorge himself now that he knows it's possible, irritated by the others telling him that it's out of the question. And he relates to my craziness. It reminds him of his younger self and it makes him believe that I will find Jesus like he did. I won't but I don't want to tell him. Jay comes in from time to time with his guitar and finger-picks blues and jazzed-up hymns. He doesn't say much but it feels kind – I like him for that very much. Christie I don't see; I think she's having a difficult pregnancy. Peter comes in and asks politely if I need a doctor. He doesn't say it but I think he wants me to leave when I've recovered.

And Emma. Well, it's her room, they put me here because they thought I should have a comfortable room of my own for a couple of days. Maybe she offered. The room is nice. There are dresses hanging against the wall but I've never seen her wearing one. There's a cross above my bed but I can't see it most of the time so it's alright. There's a mirror; the only one in the whole place I think. Emma is very kind and brings me soup. If she thinks I'm asleep she stands by the side of the bed and prays for me; I can hear her muttering and I keep my eyes closed. One time she comes in and I feign sleep because I don't feel like talking. I can hear her pulling out drawers and I open my eyes a little to watch her changing her clothes. I shut them again when she turns but I think she knows.

On the second day I'm standing naked in the middle of the room, holding her little mirror in front of me and trying to look at my bruises. She comes in.

"I've brought you some food," she says, showing no embarrassment.

I get back into bed, pulling the sheet over me.

"Are you OK?" she asks.

"My head's spinning and bits of me hurt but I'm alright. Thanks."

She puts the bread and tomatoes on the bedside table and waits quietly beside me until I've finished.

"Why did you climb down there?" she asks.

"For the buzz."

"What does that mean?"

"You know. Excitement. Feeling very much alive."

She watches me very intently while I speak. There's kindness in her look and something more. I like it.

"That's what I was like for years," she says, "wanting to feel more alive. But nothing could do it. I smoked lots of dope. Had far too much sex. I was a very desperate person. I always felt very empty inside. Hollow. Is it the same for you?"

*No, it's not like that at all,* I think. My life is full and I don't feel hollow inside. I suppose I'm girlfriendless – that doesn't feel so good. My mind isn't completely clear and I start thinking about her having *far too much sex.* Why did she have to tell me that?

"It's the same for me," I say, not at all sure what I mean.

Emma gives me one of those caressing smiles. "I think the prayer meeting frightened you," she says.

"Oh, I don't know." But I do know. I just can't explain.

"I want you to stay here with us," she says.

"Alright," I say, not meaning *alright I'll stay* but only *I heard what you said.*

She turns her back to me and starts to get clean clothes out of her drawers. Then she stands very straight, arching her back like she's stretching, using a completely different body language from the Emma I see when the others are around.

"I'd better not get changed in here, had I?" she asks.

"No."

She takes some clothes and goes to leave. But she stops at the door, turns, looks at me and gives me a very warm conspiring smile. When someone does that you smile back in exactly the same way. You can't help it. You just do.

It's the third morning after my night out in the gorge. I don't think that anything extraordinary will happen today. I'm well enough to feel restless so I get up, get dressed and go outside. I know that Jay and Rob have gone off into town to do the food shopping. I don't know where the others are; maybe Christie is resting in her room. I walk to the edge of the gorge and look down at the water. I go to the clearing where my friends hold their meetings. I go to the chapel but only look in through the open door. I want to be outside. There's a strong fresh breeze blowing and it's a good day to be not indoors and not in bed. My shoulder hurts but it's OK. And the bruises are only bruises. But I have been poorly; I got a serious chill from my night out and I still feel weak. I sit in a patch of sunshine by the kitchen door but my head is spinning and it's no good. I have to go in and lie down.

A little later I'm woken up by the sound of the car coming back up the track. I lie in that comfortable state where your body is still resting but your mind is functioning well. I can hear the car stop and I can hear footsteps and voices. There's a voice that doesn't belong here but it's very familiar. Perhaps I'm not as much awake as I think I am. Something strange has happened like time is all messed up and someone from another time, it seems long ago now, has been transplanted here into this out of the way place. I climb out of bed, my head spinning, and put my home-made shorts on. I go down the stairs still feeling weak and spaced out from my tiny bit of morning exercise. It doesn't seem possible but I'm right about the voice. There in the kitchen talking to Jay and gazing around amiably is my old car-stealing friend.

"Oliver," I say.

"The very same. You didn't think you'd see me again, did you?"

Oliver and I sit at the very edge of the gorge, our feet swinging out into space. I have to tell him the story of my little adventure here even though he's heard it from Jay and Rob. I never told them that I was pissed that night but I can tell Oliver. He is my friend even though he let me down. Seeing him here has given me more energy again and I have ignored Emma's out-of-character assertive pressure on me to go back to bed and rest.

"Things still happening to you then, Daniel?" he says.

"Yes, you could say that. But you still haven't told me your story."

I last saw Oliver less than two weeks ago and in that short time he's changed. He's pleased to see me but he looks subdued, worried and his face is drawn as if he's lost a little weight. And he's curiously symmetrical in his manner, not walking with a limp, even wearing two of the same size baseball boots on his feet.

"Mostly I've been hungry," he says, "and I've been frustrated, worried and tired. But things will be alright again, it's just taking longer than I thought. And your friends Rob and.... what's the taller one called?"

"Jay."

"Rob and Jay gave me lots to eat in town before they brought me back here. So that's good."

"You were hitching and they picked you up?"

"I was hitching. I'm not a very pickupable person. I've been dejected. I try to smile but after an hour at the side of the road I lose it and I'm this sulky unlikable sort of figure and the chance of someone stopping becomes rather slim."

"But I don't understand," I say. "Why are you hitching and how come you've only got this far and you haven't got home yet?"

Oliver lets out a sigh. I shouldn't have used the word home.

"It's simple really," he says. "I took the car back. I had agreed to do that so I did. Then I went to the bank to get money out but they refused me and kept my card because I've been blacklisted. Well, I was surprised but not totally surprised as we've been over-drawn for a while. I phoned Lizzie but I couldn't get through. The phone to our place is notorious, it's always going off – that's not strange either. But I was left in a difficult situation. I had to hitch. And I'm not very pickupable as I've said."

"But Rob and Jay picked you up."

"Yes, and when I told them about myself they recognised me from your description and brought me here."

"And what now?"

"About fifty miles from here lives an old friend who's offered me work for a week or two. She'll pay me and I can get home. Easy."

But the last word was said unconvincingly. I hope Oliver isn't getting into something dodgy.

"What's the work?" I ask.

"Landscaping. I can do that. I've done plenty of it before."

"So it will be alright?"

Oliver shrugs and smiles weakly. I don't know if that's a *yes* or a *no*.

We sit in silence for a while. I remember how much he misses his family and understand that the last week or so has been bad for him. I'm willing to help him again if I can. Only I'm slightly mistrustful – I can't help that.

"Rob and Jay are brilliant guys aren't they?" I say, not knowing what else to talk about.

"Very nice young men. They were kind to me straight away. I'm not so sure about the girl though."

"Emma, she's called."

"Yeah, Emma. She didn't like me as soon as I walked in the door. I think she's got the hots for you, Daniel, and she thinks I'm going to take you away."

"Perhaps you should," I say, "I've probably outstayed my welcome here."

Oliver goes silent. He's turning something over in his mind. I shuffle back away from the edge of the gorge and lie down; I'm beginning to feel shaky again.

"I know I wasn't honest with you, Dan," he says, after a while. "I also know that I shouldn't ask for your help again." He pauses. "But if I tell you exactly what's on my mind you can decide. I won't be offended if you say no."

"OK. What's it all about?"

"This friend. I phoned her up. She said she wouldn't lend me money but I could do some work for her."

"And?"

"And she's an old lover. She's a clever woman. She's made a lot of money by working very hard. But she's more than that, I don't know how to say it.... She's admirable. She's strong. And she's very sensitive too. I can't explain but I don't want to be there on my own. I want you to come and help me. And some of the work will involve heavy lifting so two people will be better than one. Think it over. Maybe if you feel better in a couple of days..."

There are seven of us sitting round the kitchen table about to eat supper. Peter is sitting at one end, very upright, saying a lengthy grace like a sermon. My eyes are lowered respectfully as usual but I raise them a little before he finishes. The Jesus people all have their hands clasped together and their eyes firmly shut like devout children. But Oliver sits normally, his hands on the table, looking at them with interest. He catches my eye and winks. At last Peter has finished and they say *Amen*. Oliver raises his glass and makes a toast. *Good health* he says with a cheerful grin. I see Peter wince. It makes me smile and I have to look down at my food.

"Chelsea had another good season then," Oliver says, looking across at Rob. I think he's deliberately trying to undermine any attempt at solemnity. He's an awkward subversive presence here. I like him for this very much.

Rob's eyes light up, half-way towards the headlight thing, then he glances at Peter at the head of the table.

"Oh, I don't follow football so much these days," he says.

"That's not what you said in town," Oliver says. "You and Jay couldn't stop talking about the cup final. And the locals all liked you talking about English football. I think you're making good friends with the kids here."

"We are getting to know people. They're good fun. And we're picking up more of the language all the time," Rob says.

I look around at everybody. Rob and Jay are smiling uncertainly. Emma is in her invisible mode. Christie, behind her thick glasses, is on another planet – planet new-baby-on-the-way I think. I look at Peter and the words *righteous indignation* spring to mind. He looks like he's having difficulty swallowing his food.

"Our commitment here," he says, "our commitment is to the word of God. It doesn't leave us much time for other things."

"I understand," Oliver says, with just the smallest touch of irony: "And what exactly is your project up here?" He smiles pleasantly.

"We do God's will," Peter says. "We are setting up a community and a retreat. A place where people can come for spiritual refreshment."

"God's will, eh? You're a lucky man, Pete. You and God seem to have similar ideas about things." Oliver speaks with a completely innocent expression on his face.

"You are very welcome to spend the night here," Peter says, looking at Oliver and attempting a patriarchal manner. I think he means *don't think of staying longer than that.*

We all get stuck into our food, Oliver eating with particular enthusiasm. Then Jay turns to Peter. "Oliver has offered to go to the builder's merchants with us," he says. "He's lived round here, he knows the people and the way they do things. If we can persuade them that we're going to be around for some time..."

"We are," Peter says.

"Yes, but if we can convince them of that we can get a good trade account. We should get thirty percent off."

Peter is thinking hard. Then he offers Oliver some more pasta. "That would be very good," he says. "We have a great deal of renovation work to do here. Thank you Oliver. Praise the Lord."

"Who works in a mysterious way," Oliver says.


I'm not so ill now and I thought I should give Emma her bedroom back. Oliver and I are sharing a room tonight, a little empty attic space with just two mattresses on bare floor-boards. We lie on our backs looking through the skylight at a handful of stars.

"Just like old times, Dan," he says. "I'm glad that I came to rescue you from these people. They're completely bonkers." He doesn't make any attempt to keep his voice down.

"I think I'm safe," I say. "I went to one of their prayer meetings and I got out in one piece. And if they're crazy they're still kind. I like them."

"The girl is the worst," Oliver says. "There's something sinister about that one."

"She's been very kind to me."

"But the others don't like her. She's only tolerated and I think I know why." Oliver has lowered his voice.

"Why?" I ask.

"Well, I'll tell you what I saw. I was in the kitchen after supper. I got into that big armchair in the corner and I was half-asleep. Emma came downstairs at the same time as Peter came in through the front door. She had a letter in her hand. *I got another cheque from my father* she said, and handed it to him. He looked at it and made some very appreciative noises. Big dosh I think."

"I see."

"And there's something else. She put her arms around him and gave him a very warm hug."

"They do that here all the time," I say.

"Yeah, sure," Oliver says.

I don't know what he's getting at.

I think everybody has gone into town in Peter's landrover, mostly to sort things out at the builder's merchants but in Christie's case to look for baby clothes. It's raining outside, a continuous fine drizzle, and I'm hanging around in the kitchen. I pick up the big book that's lying on the table. It's the only thing here to read and I'm bored. I like the first bit, the Garden of Eden, because it's about growing up and loss of innocence and the onset of sexuality. Then I open the book at random a little further in and read a passage about the treatment of mildew – apparently you should cut out the offending piece of cloth, burn it, then get help from a priest. I really needed to know that. Then Emma, who obviously hasn't gone into town, comes in and I put the book down guiltily.

"I knew you would begin to read the Bible," she says.

Of course she knew. There's nothing else in the house, not even a newspaper.

"I can't find the juicy bits," I say. "Perhaps you can help me out."

"Read the New Testament," she says. "Read about Jesus."

"OK."

She stands and looks at me but I don't want to read with her watching.

"Or try the Song of Solomon," she says, and goes up to her room.

I check out the Song of Solomon. It's a love poem, quite raunchy in places. I wonder how Peter would explain that. I put the book down but it's still raining and I'm bored. I wander over to the chapel.

All the herbage I spread out a week ago has dried and filled the place with good smells. I bend and turn some of it over with my hands and release more scents into the air. Then I separate out different flowers and herbs so that I can smell them individually. There's an old table against the wall and I go over and begin to make a collection of individual plants, spreading them out on its surface. I get more and more immersed in my task, wandering about the chapel and turning over the vegetation; picking out new specimens and taking them over to the table to compare them with others; adding them to the collection. Back and forth I go – absorbed like a child at play. It's an innocent sensual Garden of Eden kind of activity. I even think of taking off all my clothes but I decide against it.

The rain makes a continuous noise on the roof and I haven't noticed that Emma has come in. She is watching me – it feels like she's always watching me.

"Come and see," I say, and she comes over and looks at my collection.

"Guess which one gives off the best scent."

She chooses a squashed poppy and sniffs.

"Try again."

She picks up a gaudy, daisy-like flower; one that has barely any smell at all.

"Keep trying."

I leave her to choose and walk to the other side of the chapel. I sit with my back against the wall and daydream. I've never seen any of my Christian friends in here before and I have a vague feeling that I know why. This place always has an atmosphere that doesn't seem connected with their religion. I wonder if Emma feels it too. Sensual images from the Song of Solomon drift into my mind, *let him kiss me with the kisses of his mouth because thy love is better than wine*, something like that. And lots about vineyards and ointments and pomegranates and lying all night betwixt breasts. Now I'm confused. This stuff is in their book too. And it was Emma who suggested that I read it. I get up and wander back to her. She turns to me and her face looks pale, her eyes are open very wide, the pupils dilated in the dull light. She has chosen one plant, a nondescript grass.

"It smells of summer," she says, "childhood summer."

I'm not sure if either of us can really distinguish one scent from another now. My turning over of the vegetation, and perhaps the walking backwards and forwards on it too, has released a great mass of gorgeous smells into the air. I feel dizzy; perhaps I'm not quite well yet. Perhaps I am. Emma begins to braid some of the faded flowers into her hair. They don't look very good but I smile anyway. I'm aware that she has a dress on, one of the ones that normally hangs on the wall in her room. I've not seen her in anything but faded jeans or work trousers before. I have a little thought and as she's standing quite close I act on it straight away – that's what I always do. She kisses me back.

# NINE

Yesterday's rain has gone, the sun is out, and the world is new. Oliver and I are walking down the track from Jesusville to the village. I've got my rucksack on my back and Oliver has a few belongings in a cheap little suitcase. We're off again.

Half-way down he interrupts my thoughts with a question.

"Did you take any precautions?" he asks. "I'm sure she can't have been on the pill."

I didn't tell him and I really can't imagine how he knows.

"Safe time of the month," I say.

He doesn't ask any more. That's good, I really don't want to talk about this. I guess it just happened because it was going to happen. That's OK. But actually I know I want something more. I have this soul-mate fantasy, this notion that one day I'll meet someone who sees the world in the way I do. I want a real connection with someone; a connection that's better than any I've made so far. I have friends I suppose. Except that I didn't say good-bye to Rob and Jay and I realise now that I don't have the address of the place – I'm unlikely to ever contact them again. And as for Oliver: well, I seem to have this link with him that started when his wife gave me that note. He's a special man and he's a friend. But he's on a different planet from me – planet family-man. What I want is someone who's on my planet, someone my own age, female, rather beautiful.

I realise that I've never *slept* with a woman. Had sex, made love, whatever you want to call it, yes, but never woken up in the same bed in the morning. That would be nice. I like being on my own much of the time but I have this uncomfortable feeling right now. It's like Oliver missing his family. I think we're in the same boat. I look sideways at him and I can see that he's in good spirits, excited and optimistic. And it is a beautiful day. But I wonder if he feels the same thing as I do. A little twinge of loneliness.

Later on we're on a bus together and heading towards the nearest big town. The bus has been turning off into every village to pick people up and we haven't got very far. Now there's a stretch of flattish unpopulated country and a fast road. We're really moving.

"I'm going home, Daniel," Oliver says, turning to me and grinning in a self-satisfied way. "I'm going home."

There are huge arable fields on either side of the straight road and there's not much to look at. The people, mostly old people, on the bus have settled down into mumbled foreign conversations. It's a good time for quietly turning over the things that are on my mind but Oliver wants to talk.

"I thought she was a very sexy young woman," he says.

"Yes."

"Well done, Dan."

I thought we might keep off this subject. I don't know what to say but there's a question that's been on my mind for some time and it just comes out.

"What made you sleep with other women?" I ask.

"Ouch," Oliver says, and hesitates. "That's a question and a half." He pauses again and is thoughtful. "Because I wanted to and because I could. It was for sex and for ego – it fed my self-esteem."

"Self-esteem?"

"No, not that really. Ego, I guess. Yeah it was something to do with ego. And women are so beautiful and it's difficult to be good. Look Daniel, it didn't happen very often. I love Lizzie very, very much. I'm just stupid. And casual sex happens. Like you and that Emma. It happens, doesn't it?"

I wish he wouldn't keep bringing this up.

"Yeah, it happens," I say and I think about how good it was and I smile to myself. But there are other feelings too.

"It happens but I want something more," I say.

"Yes, I know," Oliver says, like he really understands.

And I think he does understand and what started out as a conversation about sex has changed to something else. And there's another question I want to ask him. A question I've been wanting to ask someone for a long time.

"How do you know when you're in love?"

"It hurts," he says without any hesitation.

"Always?"

"Every time."

"That's something to look forward to then," I say. I'm not sure that I believe him.

"You know Dan, we *are* travelling in the same direction," he says.

We're sitting next to each other on a bus, the world is rushing past at sixty or seventy miles per hour. What does he mean? Of course we're travelling in the same direction.

When we reach the town I have to change travellers cheques. Oliver has no money and I don't think we can hitch together so I'm buying the bus and train tickets. It's OK, he can pay me back sometime. We go to the train station, get our tickets for the next part of the day's journey and board the train. There's a few minutes to go before the train leaves and I pull some money out of my wallet, leave it on the seat and rush off to buy ice-creams. It's an averagely impetuous thing to do. I leave the door of the carriage open so that the train can't go off without me. I buy two ice-creams off the man on the platform and turn to see a railway worker slam my door shut, raise a flag and blow on his whistle. At that second the train begins to move. Carefully, so as not to drop the ice-creams, I run towards the train. I'm running alongside one of the doors when the guy starts blowing his whistle frantically. Just for a moment I think he's stopping the train for me and I slow down. The train accelerates away and that's it. I'm left behind.

This is not a nice moment. I look at the timetable on the wall to find out when the next train will be. Tomorrow. An image of the departing train replays in my mind as I come to a realisation – my rucksack and all of my belongings, my wallet, my passport, travellers cheques and money are on that train. And my ticket. All this rather useful stuff is sitting on the seat next to Oliver and travelling away from me at speed. I eat the ice-creams. When they are gone I have nothing – just the clothes that I stand up in. The world is suddenly different. It's divided into two different types of people: those with money in their pockets, homes to go to, friends or family around them; and the others, people who have none of these things, people on the outside. I feel that I'm moving into the second category. But I like a new experience. A challenge.

Now I have to decide what to do. I can wait here for Oliver to come back and get me or I can hitch to the town the train's going to and catch him up. If I go and he comes back that's difficult. If I stay and he waits for me there I'm stuck. What would he expect me to do? Hitch I guess. I walk into the town and find a shop with maps. I take a good look at the route to the place the train's going and memorise road numbers. I'm tempted to steal the map but I remember how it felt the last time that I was on the wrong side of the law. I walk to the edge of town and start hitching. It's cloudy now and I hope I get a lift before it starts raining. There's lots of traffic but no-one wants to stop. I feel invisible and anonymous. It starts to rain and I have no coat – OK, invisible, anonymous and wet. The rain increases and I can't allow myself to get soaked to the skin so I run back into town a little way and shelter under a shop awning. *I like a challenge* I think. *I like new experiences.* I have to keep thinking these things for an hour because that's how long the rain lasts.

Then it's back to the edge of town and hitching. I need a good lift, a lift of some distance or I won't make it before nightfall. And it happens; most of the journey in one lift in a smart fast car and then two shorter hitches as the afternoon turns to evening. Now I'm on the outskirts of the town where Oliver will be waiting for me. I feel very hungry but I'm on a high. I like this roller-coaster ride feeling of things going bad and then good again. I only feel a little uncomfortable when I see the big sign at the roadside. But I've seen this thing before where there are two different spellings for the same place name. It wouldn't happen at home but things are different here.

I need to get to the train station. I can't see any signs but I know the word for station and I ask an old man on a street corner. He shakes his head. I ask someone younger and when they don't understand I try English. The guy looks bemused and just says *no station, no station.* I walk into the centre of town. There's no way I won't find the station or at least a sign for it. It's evening now and people are out as couples or in families and I begin to feel uncomfortably alone. Also it's not so warm in just a t-shirt. And I'm hungry. Things take on a dreamlike quality as time passes. After a while I feel that I've explored the small town pretty thoroughly. I approach a large middle-aged woman and try to ask for directions but she looks at me nervously and hurries away. Now I'm self-conscious too. I realise that I have ice-cream stains all down the front of my t-shirt and that I look stressed out. *I like a challenge*, I say to myself, *I like a challenge*. But I have a picture in my mind of my friend Oliver and all my possessions speeding away from me on that train. And here I am at the train's destination. In a town that has no station. I go into a book shop and look at a map. I notice how similar to each other two of the place names are and then it all suddenly becomes very clear and very simple. I'm in the wrong town.

I sit down on some steps and think. Inside my head I say those words again a few times – *I like new experiences, I like a challenge*. They seem like the most empty pointless meaningless words ever. I don't like this and that's the truth. My next thought is to find some English speaking tourists and ask for help. I go to an attractive square that I passed through earlier and wander around. The smell of food from the cafés is a real problem – my stomach starts churning like it's eating itself. But there is a middle-aged couple walking towards me and I can tell that they're English – they look a bit like my mum and dad.

"Excuse me. Are you English?" I say.

"Yes." They look at me uncomfortably.

"I'm in a bit of trouble and I haven't got anywhere to stay the night. I wonder if you could lend me some money?"

The woman looks scared but the man laughs.

"Yeah, sure," he says and I feel a tiny moment's relief before I realise that he's being sarcastic. I can't think of anything else to say as they turn and walk away. Now all the uncomfortable stuff hits me at the same time: hunger, tiredness, cold, fear, and loneliness. And more. I've got a feeling that I'm on the outside of things, there's a barrier between me and other people. I don't want to be on this side of the barrier. I'm going a bit crazy and it feels difficult to approach anybody else. I wander around the square hoping to find some dropped money or a wallet. Some chance. Perhaps I should steal.

I leave the square and walk the streets of the small town. What do I hope to find? Only food, warmer clothes, money, somewhere to stay the night, someone to talk to. Or a way of magicking myself to where Oliver is waiting. But that won't happen; I have to stay the night here somehow and hitch in the morning. I come to a well-lit park where people are sitting around talking. Children play. Old women watch them and chat to their friends. I follow a small path into the trees hoping to find a pile of leaves that I can curl up in later when I'm really tired. Of course the place is immaculately tidy and inhospitable. I leave the park and walk the streets again. Maybe I'll find some thrown out cardboard boxes to keep warm in. Nothing doing. Hard cobbled streets, hard pavements, parked cars, foreign people walking past talking a language that I don't understand. More unbearably good smells from restaurants. And then I see a policeman standing on the street corner ahead of me, very smartly dressed and intimidating like they all are round here. I turn off down a side street before I get to him and hurry away guiltily. That's strange as I haven't done anything wrong. In only a few hours I've moved to the edge of things. What would I be behaving like after a few days of this? Or weeks or months? It's so easy to fall out away from straight comfortable society. I can see that it might not be so easy to get back in.

The street I've taken brings me back into the big square again. There are two people of about my age walking towards me. They look about as English as it is possible to look. The guy wears torn jeans held together with large safety pins and a t-shirt that says *fuck art lets dance.* His hair is formed into a glorious multi-coloured mohican. His girlfriend has matted green hair and a nose-ring and wears a leather jacket. Everybody stares at them but they take no notice. They are outsiders. They look so beautiful. They remind me of home.

Later on I am sitting in the back of a camper van with my new friends Spunk and Angie. They have given me something to eat and we have very quickly polished off a couple of bottles of cheap red wine and are now well into the third. I have told them about Oliver and my bad luck at missing the train and being separated from all my belongings. In the back of my head I can hear Oliver's voice saying *things just happen to you, don't they, Daniel?* I talk on about the Jesus freaks, the stolen car, my night in a police cell, the chase after Oliver's wife Lizzie.

"If you hadn't of met that bloke your life would have been a lot easier," Spunk says.

"Yeah but dull," Angie says, "and he sounds like he's alright. I like him even though I haven't met him yet."

They slump against each other affectionately on the back seat of the van. Then Angie sits up and rolls a cigarette.

"You're good value, you are, Daniel," Spunk says. "You can tell a story or two. But what are you really up to? Is there somewhere you're going to? A destination?"

"No, honestly. I just want to see what happens. And see new places and new people. And it's been brilliant. I think I'm a travelling sort of person."

"That's not what you were saying a couple of hours ago when you came running up to us in that square," Angie says.

"OK. That was a low point and I didn't know what to do. I felt alienated like I was outside of society. And I was desperate." I look across at my multicoloured, pierced and tattooed friends. "Don't you ever feel like that sometimes. That there's a barrier between you and everybody else?"

"No, it's not like that any more," Angie says. "It was a bit a couple of years ago but now everybody wants to talk to us. People stop us here to take our photographs. It's OK. And the thing is, my mum and dad are from round here so I can speak the language. We're different but we're not outsiders. But you don't speak the language, do you? That's what puts you on the outside of everything. You should be able to speak to people otherwise you're just travelling over the surface of things. You're just seeing the scenery, aren't you?" She looks at me critically.

"When I set off I didn't know what countries I was going to so I didn't think about languages. It was more of a spontaneous thing. And it doesn't feel to me the way you describe it. It feels to me like I'm on a very special journey. Not travelling over the surface of things."

But what Angie said makes me think. What I like is the continuous change of moving on even if I don't get to know the people I meet or the places I go to very well. I feel like I'm a traveller – that's who I am. And surely experience is the substance of life, not staying at home and saving up for a mortgage like some of my friends.

We are all quiet for a while. Spunk has drunk more of the wine than Angie and I have and he's falling asleep. His head lolls back and his mohican brushes against the window of the van.

"Spunker," Angie pokes him in the ribs, "Spunk, you're falling asleep and we've got a guest."

He opens his eyes and smiles drunkenly. "I know she loves me when she uses my full name," he says, slurring his words. "Spunk is just an abbrevie-whatsit. How do you say it?"

"It's an abbreviation, sweetheart. Spunker is your full name, the name I gave you. But we won't be telling Daniel all the details of that story." She leans forward to whisper to me. "His real name's Nigel. Don't let him know I told you."

She laughs and leans back against him, kissing him on the cheek. He smiles as he falls asleep.

Spunk and Angie pull up in front of the station and let me out of the van. It's mid-morning but I'm still badly hung over and my neck hurts from sleeping awkwardly on the front seat.

"Go and look for your friend and we'll wait here to see you're OK," Spunk says, checking his hair in the rear-view mirror.

I find Oliver sitting on the platform with my rucksack on one side of him and his little suitcase on the other. He's staring into space, half asleep. When he sees me he stands up, smiles, opens his arms out to hug me and begins to laugh.

"I was worried about you," he says, "But I thought the best thing would be to wait for you here."

Spunk and Angie come walking down the platform. I introduce them to Oliver, "These people saved me from oblivion," I say, "And then got me pissed on cheap red wine."

Oliver shakes their hands warmly and then gives them big hugs that they don't expect. Then we all stand looking at each other, awkward but smiling, unable to think of anything to say for a moment. Angie starts to roll a cigarette. Spunk looks at the floor.

"I went to the wrong town," I say.

"Yes, I wondered," Oliver says and then turns to my punk friends, "I don't know how to thank you enough. I thought I'd lost him."

"It's alright," Angie says, "Any time."

"Least we could do," Spunk says. "Yeah, we'd better be off. Take care of yourself Dan. Don't do anything I wouldn't do." He winks and they both turn and walk away.

As they leave the station I shout "Thanks," and they look back. Angie waves and Spunk smiles and holds up his hand in a V sign.

To get to the house of Oliver's friend we have to get a bus up into the hills and there's a three hour wait. We leave our luggage at the train station (which is fairly close to the bus station) and can wander around town.

"Where do we go?" I ask. "You've been here before. What are the sights?"

"There's a botanical garden and arboretum. It might be worth looking at."

"You've not visited it before?"

But Oliver just gives out a fatalistic sigh that might mean something but I can't guess what. We buy bread, fruit and chocolate as usual. I know that this is the standard picnic that Oliver always had with his family and it's like a nostalgic habit with him. We walk through the town and into what is to me just a normal park except that everything is labelled. "Let's eat up here," I say and we walk up onto a little grassy hillock and sit down.

Oliver goes quiet and eats very little. He stares intently at the very ordinary view of grass and trees and his shoulders slump into the thinking-about-the-kids position. I'm a bit bored with this by now but I suppose I have to be sympathetic.

"You've been here before?" I say.

"Yeah, that's right. It's what I call a memory place."

"Isn't everywhere a memory place for you? All the places we've been you've already visited with Lizzie and the kids."

Oliver jumps as if I've said the wrong thing.

"No, not this time. Well you're sort of right – I've travelled and hung around and worked all over this part of the world and I can't seem to go anywhere without seeing people and times from before."

"Your family?"

"Other people too. This is big love affair country. I split up with a girlfriend right here in this garden many years ago. I came back once and I got to the gate and looked at this hill and then turned around and went. I didn't want to come in."

This is strange for me. It's such an ordinary unspecial park in an ordinary unspecial town. And I don't understand this man. He has mixed with dangerous druggy people and stayed cool. He has a strong physical presence and the one time I saw him angry it was scary. He's not young, he's been around, lived in different countries, set up his own business. But he really is a big softy on the inside. He's travelling like I am through the same sometimes interesting and sometimes commonplace world and it's not such an awful place to be. Why does it have to be such a big time emotional trip for him? I suppose he feels insecure. Maybe all that family stuff makes a man like him into something softer in time. I don't know whether that's a good thing or not. And I've not thought of it like this before. I always thought you would get tougher and stronger as the years pass.

"Yes, it was here that I got dropped from a great height by someone I was very fond of," Oliver says. "I don't like coming back."

"What do you see here?" I ask, thinking that the ghost of his old girlfriend is walking around the garden in front of him.

"Well, I came back that one time and looked through the gate and saw this hill. It seemed much bigger than it does today. It made my stomach turn over and I thought of Hollywood."

"Hollywood?"

"Yes. You know that big sign on the hillside? Have you seen pictures of it? Right here on this hill something was spelt out in huge letters in the same way."

"But not Hollywood?"

"No, the word was emptiness or loneliness or something like that. I'm not sure exactly. But it felt like that – like it was written up there for everyone to see. Except that people didn't see. They went walking on by as if everything was normal."

This stuff gets irritating after a while. I'm used to being with people who aren't so sad all the time. Or at least if they are they don't keep talking about it.

"I think you live a past-tense life," I say. "You didn't seem like that sort of person when I first met you but you are."

"I'm going home, Daniel. When I get there the clock will start going forward again and there'll be no more of this nonsense. I just have to get home."

"And we have to see this old friend of yours first?"

"I need the money."

"You haven't even told me her name."

"Caroline. She's sort of English and she lives out here and she's called Caroline."

He says her name with something like weariness or resignation. I can think of another question to ask him but I don't.

# TEN

There's a time travel feeling about the journey up to Oliver's old girlfriend's place and it starts even before we leave the bus station. I get the impression that all the most rustic and weathered members of the local population are gathering at this place. There are old ladies dressed in black, old men with walking sticks and some slightly younger people (there's no one here my age) wearing out-dated clothes. Once inside the bus all this peasant-stock rural conservatism is concentrated into a small space – an essence of times past. Oliver and I are out of place, the only late twentieth century people in an otherwise nineteen-fifties setting.

We set off and do some time travelling through the landscape too. We leave the outskirts of the town and pass through some large-scale modern farming country with enormous sprinklers watering the fields. Then we start into the hills and it turns to small-holdings with a big variety of crops and animals and, as we get higher, more and more fine trees. I recognise oak and ash but there are also big-leaved trees with yellow splashes of things like straight catkins. Oliver tells me that they are sweet chestnut trees and that the chestnuts are a crop here, harvested and sold in the autumn. The road winds and climbs, crosses a ridge, drops again, and continues up and down through the intricate landscape. In the higher places the big chestnut trees grow spaced apart over sheep-grazed pastures. Sometimes there are old buildings of stone and timber, farm houses and barns built of local materials, home-grown, part of the land itself.

Oliver is in low spirits this afternoon and I make a feeble joke; "We're still travelling in the same direction then."

"Yeah, yeah." He stops looking so worried and smiles weakly.

"Can you tell me more about the work we'll be doing for this woman?" I ask.

"I've not seen Caroline's new place but she says it's nice. Simple but special. She wants us to build a bridge and lay paths and do some building work. We will probably only do the bridge. Then we will both be richer and we can go."

We get off the bus in a village small enough for people to notice us as strangers and turn to look. Oliver consults a scrap of paper that has some directions on it and we set off on foot along a road through pastureland. After a while we turn off down a track through some woods and out into the open again. Then we come to Caroline's house set among some trees on a change of slope. It looks like an old farmhouse for a once prosperous family. It's large, is built of stone and weather-boarding, has a pantiled roof. Vines and fig trees grow against the walls. Oliver pushes open an ornamental iron gate, a dog barks and a woman appears through an archway at the side of the house.

"Oliver, it's nice to see you again."

"Caroline. You look good."

There's a long silence and I'm lucky to have the dog to make a fuss of. They look at each other and then look away awkwardly. Oliver puts an interested expression on his face and inspects the garden. Then he becomes aware of my presence.

"Caroline, this is Daniel. He's my friend and he's come to help with the work here."

She gives me a thin smile and a cool looking over. "Daniel. I'm pleased to meet you. You are very welcome here." Each word is carefully pronounced so that I know they are only words, a formality; I mustn't think they have a literal meaning. Or perhaps she's being ironic and means the precise opposite of what she says. Oliver picks up on this and is very firm.

"Daniel is my good friend. I want him to work with me."

"OK. Come in both of you. Come and have tea or a glass of wine."

The house is more modern inside and open plan but tasteful with exposed woodwork, a stone fireplace, framed pictures on the walls. Oliver looks around at the structure of the building and the furnishings. Either he's very interested in interior design or it's a displacement activity and it means he can avoid looking at Caroline. She watches him carefully, waiting for comments. I look at her, listen to the silence, and wonder what I've got myself into. This goes on for a long time and it's difficult and ludicrous too. I don't want to be here but at least it's interesting, very *what's going on with these two?* And I like looking at this woman. She has shortish black hair and blue eyes, very pale almost translucent skin, high cheek bones. She's dressed in loose clothes so I shouldn't be able to tell but I'm sure she has a perfectly beautiful body. And she looks tough and vulnerable at the same time. Sensual and nervous. Intelligent. Maybe scary. But all of this is a first impression and I know it's likely to be wrong. I'm thinking all this nonsense about Oliver's old girlfriend and she will, no doubt, seem very different to me in the days that follow.

The awkwardness continues. Oliver has insisted on cooking supper and is in the kitchen. Caroline and I are in the living room and she plays the piano while I sit and turn the pages of an expensive art book. The piano is a cold instrument to me – not my favourite sound. I'm against it in principle but it gradually gets through to me that Caroline plays well and that she's expressing something. She sits very upright and her fingers move lightly on the keys. It's classical music and I don't recognise it but it sounds like it's about emotion being controlled.

After a while Oliver calls us both to the table and serves up something made of pasta, fish and strange vegetables. They won't talk to each other and Caroline politely asks me about myself. She feigns interest but seems disdainful. She asks about my parents, what subjects I did in school, what my plans are.

When we've finished eating we sit in the living room on the three big sofas – one each. Caroline asks Oliver about his present life and he talks about his business, not a word about Lizzie or his kids. He asks her about herself and she describes how she came to find and buy this house and the land around, how long it takes her to drive to work and why it's worth it to be able to live here. When the conversation peters out they try not to look at each other.

I know that when I'm bored or irritated I wind people up by asking questions. I did it a lot at school and it didn't go down well. But I can't help it.

"How long ago was it since you two last met?" I ask.

Oliver jumps. "Seven years?" he says, looking across at Caroline, "A long time ago."

"Eight years," she says. "Eight years this summer. Not such a long time really."

I have a picture in my mind of a grassy hill in a botanical garden. It's probably the wrong picture. There's another long pause before anyone speaks.

"You've given up smoking then?" Oliver asks.

"Yes, of course."

"Me too."

"I noticed."

And so it goes on haltingly. I do the washing up and make plenty of noise so that they can talk without feeling that I'm listening in. When I come back into the room they are silent and looking away from each other. I think they need to talk and I need to not be here.

"I'm tired," I say. "Is there anywhere to sleep?"

"Yes, it's getting late," Oliver says. It isn't, it's barely dark. "I need to turn in too."

Caroline laughs out loud as the daftness of the situation hits her. "I suppose you need your beauty sleep," she says. "I'll show you to your rooms and tomorrow I'll put you both to work. I intend to get my money's worth, you know."

She has an upper middle class accent. I get on with all sorts of people – I really do. But what with the patronising tone and the indifferent manner too, well, I can't help it. I have a feeling I'm not going to like this woman.


Caroline has taken a few days off from her job to supervise and look after us and after breakfast she takes us out to show us the work she wants doing. We are accompanied by her dog, a big mottled thing with floppy ears. First we walk through her garden and look at the herbaceous borders and roses and fruit trees. She obviously cares about it very much and has worked hard to make it so beautiful. Oliver knows the names of flowers, can ask intelligent questions, and makes the appropriate noises of what sounds like genuine admiration. He compliments Caroline without having to say anything personal. This morning they can both talk of the place and not of themselves. It's easy.

At the end of the garden we pass through a gate into some woods. We walk some distance to a gully that carries a small stream. We scramble down, cross the stream, and climb up the other side onto the new piece of land that Caroline has bought. A short distance further and we are out of the trees and there's a view of a wide valley. A small ruined building stands alone at the top of the slope.

"All I need is a good path," she says. "And a bridge across the gully. And this building restored to something like a refuge or a studio or a summer house. I've asked around here but the one or two people I trust to do it tastefully want to charge too much. They think I'm terribly rich."

"You are," Oliver says.

"I'm certainly not. Not as rich as they think. And I work too hard to want to throw it away."

Oliver inspects the ruin and looks out across the valley. "It's a fine spot," he says.

"Yes, it's an extraordinary view," Caroline says. "Not so much now but in the autumn when the air is clear. Or in the early spring. I have come here often over the years, trespassing of course. When the owner discovered that I liked the place he stopped me and threatened to build a fence. I asked if I could buy it. I had to offer a great deal of money for a tiny piece of land."

"Which is what he was planning on," Oliver says.

"That's right. If I was poor he would have said nothing and I could have had the view for free."

"So there is some justice in the world."

"If you say so."

Oliver walks around the building and looks in through the open doorway. Caroline watches him expectantly.

"I need thinking time," he says. "I need to be alone until lunch time and then I'll tell you what I'm willing to do." He looks at me. "Are you up for it, Dan? A little creative manual labour in attractive surroundings."

"Yes, I think so."

"Then you need to both leave me alone to scratch my head for a while. We'll talk some more this afternoon."

Caroline and I walk back to the house together. The path through the woods is too narrow to walk side by side so I follow on behind. She walks very lightly, gracefully, like a girl. I think of the contrast it makes with her grown up business-like way of talking. When we arrive at the garden gate I see that she is quietly smiling to herself. She calls the dog and he comes ambling along, wagging his tail.

"He's a good dog," I say.

"He is very good but I'm afraid he's very keen on the wood-land smells and always gets left behind."

The dog comes to each of us in turn to be stroked.

"He likes you," she says. "You should feel honoured. He doesn't take to everyone."

Caroline looks at her garden as if she's seeing it for the first time. She admires the flowers and then starts pulling up tiny weeds. She's pleasantly preoccupied and I am invisible to her.

"I'll go for a walk," I say, interrupting her thoughts. "Shall I take the dog with me?"

I think he knows the word *walk*. He runs to the front gate and back again excitedly. I guess he'll come too.

I call the dog and set off up the track towards the road. He looks at me from time to time for instructions but I don't have anything to say to him. The track takes us through grazing land and woods and then we're at the road that Oliver and I came along yesterday on our way from the village. I go the opposite way now, just walking without destination, for the hell of it, calling the dog to me when a car comes. It's a level road along the ridge top, a dreaming and thinking road like the one I take out of the village at home when I've got nothing else to do. I haven't thought of home for a while but I do now. I'm not thinking about my parents or the house we live in but about the land around the village and the road over Victoria Hill. That's a doubly misnamed place – no Victoria and no hill. The Vic was a pub but it was shut years ago. And the hill exists only in the minds of locals; the land there is flat, or so it looked to us when we first moved in. But there is a gentle slope up and a gentle slope down and in such a landscape it's enough to be named a hill.

But why am I thinking about this? I guess it's because when I left school and was at a loose end for a while I often walked that road. And I was longing to get away and walk a different, foreign road. I had one last walk over the 'hill' before I set off on this trip. I felt good. I carried in my mind a picture I had seen in a book of an African tribesman, a young warrior walking along with his head tilted back in a way that looked maybe arrogant or maybe merely confident and happy, full of himself. And that's the way I was walking that day. I tried to explain all this to my dad when I got back indoors. He's always pleased to see me and he always smiles. But he does look old sometimes. And as I talked to him his smile faded away slowly like it does. I was going on and on about walking and not thinking about what I was saying. And now I'm all this way from home and I remember this. Him smiling and the smile fading away.

After lunch Oliver takes Caroline's car and goes off on his own to find out about equipment and materials. I climb to the top of a large tree on the edge of Caroline's land. I know that she sees me when I'm making a grab for the first branches but I forget about her as I struggle to find a way up. It's nearly summer and the tree is in full leaf so I have to climb right into the skinny topmost branches to get any sort of a view. Now I can look down on the house and garden and some of the land around. And I can see over the top of the woods to the tower of the village church. Down by the house Caroline is sitting on the edge of a low wall and looking up at me. She raises her hand and smiles. I like being up here and I'm glad that she's seen me. I don't have a good enough grip with my feet but I can't resist letting go with one hand and waving back. I try to look relaxed and carry on check-ing out the view. But I can't see that much and I make my way down. When I drop to the ground from the lowest branch Caroline is still watching me. I walk towards the house and she applauds and calls out *bravo*. The dog comes running up wagging its tail.

"If you can climb you might do a job for me," Caroline says. "Would you mind terribly?"

"I came here to do some work," I say.

She takes me to look at a tree at the bottom of the garden. It stretches away from the woods and into the light and some of its lower branches are shading her flowers.

"I just want someone to cut those branches off without damaging my plants," she says. "Can you do that?"

"I can if you're willing to help."

We get a saw and some rope from an outhouse and I climb up onto the first branch. It's sturdy and heavy and I begin to have my doubts. I hope Caroline is stronger than she looks. I slide out along the branch, attach the rope to the right place, and drop to the ground. I give Caroline the other end of the rope.

"I'll make some saw cuts," I say. "I've done this before so I know how to do it. Then when I give the word you pull hard on the rope and walk backwards. Like you're in a tug of war. It should pull clear of the flowers as it goes down."

"You say *should*."

"It's up to you. We can wait for Oliver to get back if you want."

"No let's have a go. But I should be sad if we damaged the flowers."

I climb up again and do some sawing on one side of the branch and then on the other. When there's very little holding it I shout for Caroline to pull and I make the final cut. There's a wonderful cracking noise, I drop the saw (as planned), and grab onto the tree-trunk. Caroline leans against the rope, walks backwards and pulls the branch clear as it falls. OK, so she is much stronger than she looks. Or maybe she was standing too close. Or perhaps I attached the rope in the wrong place. The branch swings so far and so fast that it catches her and pushes her to the ground. I jump down and run across. I don't think she can be hurt but I do think she might be angry with me.

Caroline has more or less disappeared under the branch; only her legs are visible. I push the side branches away and find her lying comfortably on the ground. She gives me a wry smile.

"I'm fine thank you, Daniel," she says. "It's kind of you to ask."

I haven't said a word and I don't know what to say now. I try to look serious and concerned but I can't quite manage it. I try not to laugh and just about succeed.

"I'll get the saw," I say. "I think the easiest way to get you out is to cut off the end of the branch."

I go to the foot of the tree and pick up the saw. The blade has come loose and the pin that should hold it has disappeared. I search the long grass but I don't think I'm going to find it. I guess Caroline will be OK where she is for a moment. I go to the outhouse and find an old nail that will hold the blade in place. There's a bench and a vice here so the best thing is to fix it now. It doesn't fit very well and it takes a little time. Then I make my way back to the fallen branch. "I'm back," I say, but there's no answer. I push the leaves apart and look down on Caroline. Her face is still and expressionless; only her eyes move to look at me.

"Are you alright?" I say.

She smiles. "Very much so. You should have left me for longer. I've been looking at the sky through the leaves."

There's not much you can say to that. She certainly seems at peace.

Caroline and I spend the rest of the afternoon working together. We take down some more branches, cut them up and carry them away into the woods. She doesn't say much. There's a stillness about her manner even though she's working quite hard. When we've finished and made everything look tidy we stand and admire our work. This end of the garden certainly looks lighter now.

"Thank you very much, Daniel," she says.

"Sorry about that first branch."

"Yes," she says, and smiles a little dreamy vacant smile. "Yes. That wasn't quite me lying there looking at the sky from under a piece of tree."

"I don't understand."

"I'm normally so in control of everything. High powered job, beautiful garden, carefully planned dinner parties and so forth."

Do I understand now? I'm not sure. But Caroline is not so bad. I like the way she smiles.

## ELEVEN

There are three jobs Caroline wants us to do – the path, the bridge and the ruined building. We are going to re-route and fix up the path and build a rustic bridge. Oliver will draw up plans for the restoration of the building on the viewpoint and arrange for the work to be done by locals. He is very capable at this sort of thing and he's knowledgeable and imaginative. He also has a way with people and has begged, borrowed and rented various tools and pieces of equipment. Our first job is to collect some stone from a collapsed redundant wall on a local farm. Oliver has offered a small amount of money for the stone and persuaded the farmer to lend us a tractor and trailer to transport it. We can't get the tractor into the field so here we are, filling up wheelbarrows, running the stone down the gentle slope to the road, and loading it onto the trailer.

It's hot but there's a breeze and sometimes a cloud will hang about in front of the sun for a while. The work is nicely physical and rhythmic and it's easy to talk or not talk to each other. Most of the morning we don't talk. Oliver works hard, filling his barrow and getting down the slope to the road without losing control and spilling everything like I do. He's absorbed in the work and his thoughts and that's OK with me. Only when it gets near lunch time and we've slowed down does he speak.

"I'm not a past-tense person," he says.

"What?"

"You know, what you said to me in the botanical gardens. That I lead a past-tense life."

We are standing either side of the tumbled down wall with a wheelbarrow each, lifting stones up from the ground, the mirror image of each other in our movements at least.

"OK," I say. "I wasn't putting you down. It's just that all the places we've been to seem haunted for you."

"Maybe that's true. But this is just a tiny part of my life, these few weeks travelling towards home. When I get back I'll be busy with family stuff and no-one could be more present-tense."

"How's that?"

Oliver stops working and wipes sweat off his forehead with his t-shirt. "It's the stuff with the kids. They live in a very exciting brand new world every day. All sorts of little things are exciting to them. Something like the postman coming and bringing letters, things as commonplace as that. Otis will be jumping up and down and wanting to carry the letters up to my office. He'll say the word *Daddy* about twenty times in a row. And then when it's not the tourist season we can all go places together. There's an old castle we go to and Otis gets out of the car with his legs already going and he hits the ground running. Explores every corner. Climbs and jumps over everything."

"So he's very present-tense."

"Yeah, and Daisy is too. And when you're with them you're seeing things through their eyes. Happy when they're happy. It's what's called vicarious pleasure. And they're changing all the time – first steps, first words, first everything."

"But aren't they awful a lot of the time too?"

"Yes, Dan, there is that. Lizzie and I haven't had a night of unbroken sleep for three and half years."

"Sounds like torture."

"No, it's OK. It's what you go through. It's part of the deal."

I don't entirely understand. This could be my life some years ahead (but not for a very long time). Would I want this? Oliver is sentimental but it's real for him too. He smiles so much when he's talking this stuff – that is before he goes all sad again. Now he fills his barrow and is off down the slope before me. I follow behind, we pass each other as he comes up, then I catch up and we're working side by side again.

"I like travelling," I say. "I don't think I want to ever be tied down with kids."

"Bringing up children is a journey too."

"Yeah, sure." But I really can't imagine how getting woken up every night by crying babies takes you anywhere.

When we've got a good load of stone Oliver wants to drive back in Caroline's car leaving me to take the tractor and trailer. I can't believe the number of times that he tells me to go very slowly down the hill. He explains the gears but I've driven a tractor before and I know how to do it.

The way back to Caroline's place goes along a ridge, down into a small valley, and then up onto the village road. The tractor is an old one with no cab so I'm in the open air enjoying a cool breeze. Working here, driving the tractor, I'm more *in* the landscape than I have been in the last few weeks. I'm part of this foreign country-side. Every time I pass another vehicle the driver raises a hand in greeting and I wave back. I'm having a good time and I feel care-free. When I get close to the top of the hill I use the gears and the brake to slow the tractor down. I can feel the weight of the trailer pushing me along from behind. I know that I can't step on the brake too hard or the wheels will lock and I'll skid. I decide to use the low gearbox to bring my speed right down before I go over the brow of the hill. This is the sensible thing to do.

The problem is that I'm in neutral for a moment before I get into the low gearbox. It's a long moment and the top of the steep slope down is getting closer more quickly than it should. The tractor isn't slowing at all and I'm still struggling to get the lever into low gear. In fact I can't do it, I have to settle for high and step on the brakes hard. The back wheels of the little tractor lock and skid along the tarmac. The loaded trailer behind me pushes me firmly towards and then over the brow of the hill. Now the trailer, with all that weight in it, wants to overtake and it begins to swing the tractor round sideways. I lift my foot off the brake, speed up, and straighten it out. Then I have to brake again and the trailer is twisting me around in the same way again. I speed up, straighten out, brake, twist sideways, and so it goes on. It's not a wide road but it's straight and I can see all the way down to the bottom of the hill. I'm making a slewing, skidding, zig-zag way down but it will be alright. I can't stop but I'm in some sort of control.

A car comes around the bend at the bottom of the hill and starts driving up towards me. This is bad news. But the driver notices my crazy descent, stops and begins to reverse out of my way. OK, except that another car comes around the bend. Both cars stop and both drivers press their horns enthusiastically as I careen down towards them. Then the second car has seen me and starts to reverse. Car number one follow smartly and they disappear round the bend and out of sight. The slope levels out just before the bend but I'm still going fast. Round I go, not knowing what I will meet next. But the road is empty and flat and I bring the tractor under control. A hundred yards along the way I see both cars parked in a field entrance. The drivers raise their hands in somewhat expressive gestures as I pass.

After lunch Oliver tips the stone at the side of Caroline's track and takes the tractor and trailer back. He really doesn't want to hang around. Caroline and I sit in the shade at the back of her house and listen to the bees buzzing around her flowers.

"It's kind of you to help Oliver here," she says.

"It's OK. I think I'm going to enjoy it. And it's nice here. And he's my friend, I like working with him. But I didn't know he was so practical, he told me he was a businessman."

"Oliver is a very talented person," Caroline says. "He has what is called a creative intelligence." There is something like admiration in her voice. "I'm lucky to get him to do some work for me. He'll draw up a tasteful plan for the old building. And it will be more than tasteful, actually – it will be something imaginative, something that no-one else would have thought of. He won't even tell me how he's going to make the bridge."

Even sitting quite still Caroline is in some way graceful. Her skin is quite pale – maybe I notice it because Oliver and I have become so tanned over the last few weeks. And she has shadows under her eyes like she's been ill. But there's a posh gorgeous sensuality about her. She's attractive. Scary but I don't know why. And I can't imagine seeing her anywhere other than in this garden surrounded by her flowers.

"It's a beautiful garden," I say. "I like sitting here."

"Thank you," she says, but she looks at me with impatience as if she would prefer me to be somewhere else. Then she smiles. "I think Oliver brought you here as a chaperone. Is that right?"

"I don't know."

"Did he tell you that we used to be lovers?"

"Yes." And now I'm feeling uncomfortable.

"Sorry," Caroline says. "Sorry if I'm embarrassing you. And I'm sorry if I seemed unwelcoming when you arrived. Oliver didn't say you were coming. I suppose it was meant to be a *fait accompli*." She stares out across the garden but I don't think she sees anything. I can't guess what she's thinking; all sorts of happiness and sadness seem to be mixed up in her expression.

"How did you meet Oliver?" she asks.

I'm not sure what to say. "I just did. He came up and asked me to drive for him."

"To try to catch up with his family. He told me that."

"Well, that's right. That's how it started. Or actually before that when Lizzie gave me the note."

"You met his wife?" Caroline sounds shocked.

"Yes."

"He didn't say that."

"Lizzie gave me a note to give to him and then she went off with the two kids."

Caroline takes a deep breath and looks away like she's trying to remain calm. Then she turns and speaks in a cool voice that she thinks hides her emotions.

"What do the children look like? I expect that they are very beautiful."

"Just kids. Pretty I suppose. Long blonde hair."

"Blonde," Caroline says, as if this is deeply significant.

"Otis and Daisy. He talks about them all the time."

"Not to me, he doesn't," she says sharply. And she gets up suddenly to go away. She takes a few steps towards the door of the house and then turns and comes back.

"I'm sorry, Daniel," she says. "It's all a bit awkward, isn't it?" She smiles sadly. "But I'm glad you're his friend. I think your being here is probably the right thing."

She turns again and walks into the house.

In the days that follow Oliver and I get stuck into the work. We spend most of a day making a better path through the woods – digging out, cutting steps, shoring up the earth with pieces of timber. We spend some time wheelbarrowing stone to the edge of the gully and piling it up. Then we are digging and messing about on the slopes above the stream, getting cement and making some concrete footings where the ground is too soft. The next thing is to make two small stone piers for the ends of the bridge. Oliver teaches me how to build with dry stone and we work on either side of the stream. He comes over from time to time to help or correct my work. This stone-work takes two days to complete.

Caroline comes to see us several times a day bringing lemonade – not factory stuff but the real thing, freshly made in her kitchen. She's always excited about our work. She compliments me on what I'm doing but is deliberately cool with Oliver. She says very little but finds it difficult to leave. The evenings are awkward. There's no television in the house and after dark we must sit around holding books and pretending to read. Oliver is very controlled and polite – not himself at all. Caroline puts on a good show but I think she's nervous. I feel like stirring things up but I don't. For some reason I'm more thoughtful than usual and I even consciously go easy on the red wine.

One evening Oliver disappears soon after supper. I don't know if Caroline wants me around and I decide to go outside into the last of the evening light. Caroline comes out and sits by the French windows with a glass of wine. She watches me as I wander off down the garden and I feel guilty when the dog comes running to join me and leaves her sitting alone. I take the new path into the woods, the dog running ahead, sniffing the ground, wagging his tail. It's not much fun in the semi-darkness under the trees but I'm making for the old ruin and the view over the valley. I cross the stream and continue to the edge of the woods. When I step out into the open I see Oliver sitting at the top of the slope with his chin resting on his hand. The dog runs over and licks him on the face.

"Sorry," I say. "I didn't mean to disturb you."

"It's OK, Dan. Come and sit down for a minute."

I sit next to him and look out at the view. The sun has been down for a while but the sky is still light and glows softly. There are no clouds and no stars yet either. In the valley below us patches of mist form and drift together. A car travels along a distant road, its headlights showing the way, the sound of its engine carrying through the silence.

"You alright?" I ask.

"No."

We sit for a while. The valley gets darker and a scattering of house lights becomes visible. In the sky the first stars appear, faint to begin with, then stronger and more numerous, gradually outnumbering the few lights on the land below.

"You asked me about love once," Oliver says. "About how you know when it's happening." I can't see his face. He's just a shape in the dark and a voice. "And I answered that it hurts."

I can't think of what to say so I just sit and wait for more.

"And it does," Oliver says. He breathes in and out rather heavily. He laughs a little.

I'm getting cold now but I remember that this place is uncomfortably hot in the day with the sun shining down. That's because the slope faces south. Oliver sits facing south now, facing his home. Maybe it's just chance – a guy has to sit somewhere. But it seems obvious to me that he's thinking about his family.

"I'd better go now," I say. "Caroline is all on her own. I brought her dog with me unintentionally."

I can just make out Oliver's face turning towards me. "Yes, of course," he says. "But I think I'll stay here for a while."

It could be difficult finding my way through the woods in the dark but the dog goes ahead, sniffing his way confidently, and I can follow the sounds he makes. I cross the gully and the stream just above our half-built bridge. I can't hear the dog now because of the sound of the water and I stand still for a moment in the dark, wondering if I'm on the path or not. I have a picture in my mind of Oliver sitting alone above the valley. Then a picture of Caroline sitting alone outside her house. I don't know what to think about all this.

We've finished the supporting stonework and Oliver takes me off into the woods to show me the bridge itself. I'm not impressed. It's just a big old dead tree lying on the ground. He sets to work with a chainsaw and takes off all the branches so that only a length of tree-trunk remains. Then we carry a big hand winch and various ropes and cables into the woods and set about the seemingly impossible task of getting the piece of tree to the place where it's needed. We rope it up and set up the winch so that we can pull it down and across the slope. I work the lever of the winch back and forth and the trunk moves slowly towards me. Oliver guides it with old fence posts that he knocks into the ground and holds onto. Each pull of the winch lever moves the tree-trunk only half an inch and it's hard work. But sometimes it moves easily and I can work the lever back and forth quite fast. From time to time Oliver takes over and gives me a break but he prefers to be in control at the other end.

"Sometimes I think you don't trust me very much," I say.

"Too right," Oliver says. "Things happen to you – don't you remember?"

"But not so much recently. I'm getting more careful."

"Yeah. Well, the guy who lent me the winch this morning told me an interesting story. Things go round pretty fast in rural areas you know. He said something about an out of control tractor and trailer on a steep hill and two cars desperately trying to get out of the way."

"I forgot to tell you about that."

"I bet you did." He laughs.

When the tree-trunk is closer to the gully Oliver cuts a big lengthways slice out of it with the chainsaw so that it has one flat side. This will be the top of the bridge – the bit you walk on. There's a lot of noise and it takes some time. Then we attach the winch to a tree the other side of the stream and start moving it again. One end of the trunk is lifted off the ground and pulling this weight is slow hard work; Oliver has to take turns with me. The high end of the trunk is gradually lifted over one of our stone piers and then out across the gully. When the bottom end of the trunk is in place we reverse the action of the winch and let the high end down onto the other pier. Oliver twists and levers it so that the flat side is uppermost. And there it is – once a tree, now a bridge. Oliver does a little more work with the chainsaw while I make steps at each end with some stone we saved for that purpose.

"Not much more to do now," he says. "We've got to make some rustic-looking hand rails and that's it. We'll be finished some time tomorrow."

"I've got to get Caroline," I say.

I run off down the track to the garden where I find her cutting flowers for the house and looking rather cooler than I do.

"We've made the bridge," I say. "It's not quite finished but you must come and see. It's really good. You'll like it."

I guess I'm really proud of our work. Oliver is proud too – he's standing on the far bank of the gully waiting for me and Caroline to arrive.

"Is it safe?" she says.

"As houses."

Caroline smiles very beautifully and steps up onto the tree-trunk bridge.

"It will have hand rails on by this time tomorrow and it will look better and be safer," Oliver says. "You'll have to imagine it like that for now."

I watch Caroline make her way across. I can see the expression on Oliver's face as she walks towards him; he is smiling so much and so happily. It's like the way he looks when he's talking about his kids but more so. Of course he's very proud of our work. And I guess it's special because it's for someone he was once very fond of. When Caroline reaches his side she holds out her hand and Oliver is obliged to take it and help her down. She turns and waves to me, still holding onto his hand. She stretches up and kisses him on the cheek. They look like something out of a romantic film.

"Thank you, thank you, thank you. Both of you," she calls out. She looks radiant.

Oliver moves away and starts fiddling with the perfectly good steps I've built on that side. Then he walks up the bank a little further to look down on our work.

"So that's nearly it," he says. "We'll fit the hand rails tomorrow if we can find plenty of nice old timber. I've got to think a bit more about your ruined building, see a couple of guys and get another quote. Then we can be off. Daniel to more adventures. And I will be going home."

"Yes, of course," Caroline says.

She steps up onto the bridge and walks slowly back. She holds onto a very plausible smile. I turn away and start to collect up the ropes and cables. I can't bear to look.

# TWELVE

The bridge is just a log on two stone piers. The hand rails will make it safer but they've got to make it look good too. The word that Oliver uses a lot is *rustic*. When the rails are in place the bridge will be a handsome thing, a man-made artefact but one that harmonises with its surroundings. We explore the woods thoroughly, looking for dead hardwood branches on the ground or in the trees. The timber should be all of the same sort, preferably oak. Oliver is the man with the eye for what is needed and I follow him around ready to carry any pieces that he thinks are suitable. We've done the seriously heavy work and this will be an easy day. Oliver is in good humour. He seems relieved. I think in his mind he is nearly home. By lunchtime we have enough timbers but not enough of the big coach-screws that will fix them to the bridge. Oliver asks Caroline to go into town and buy some more and suggests that I should go too and leave him alone to scratch his head and think more about the renovation of the old building.

Caroline has a smart new car and we drive off along the up-and-down round-and-round road that Oliver and I travelled by bus a few days ago. She talks to me about the land here and the farming practices. She tells me the local gossip, explains that all the younger people are moving into the cities and leaving her in a community of deeply conservative older people. She describes her lifestyle – very organised and thought out and with all the trappings of wealth and success. She speaks brightly but sounds lonely. She can't really disguise it.

In town Caroline shops for food and I go to the builders' merchants and buy coach-screws. We meet up again and go out of town by a different route that takes us past the botanical gardens. I open my mouth to say something but change my mind. Then we're off into the hills again. Caroline drives fast and skilfully. She doesn't speak for a while but eventually lets out a random thought.

"I had a very happy childhood," she says, speaking to herself as much as to me.

"In England or out here?" I ask.

"Both. And other places too. My father was a minor diplomat and we had to travel. But we were lucky. A big happy slightly crazy family – except that I wasn't one of the crazy ones. We lived mostly in beautiful places. All of us grew up multi-lingual which is a great advantage."

"What does being slightly crazy involve?" I ask. "And how come they were and you weren't?"

"I mean they were creative. My siblings were creative and talented in a way that I never was."

"But you play the piano."

"I play other people's compositions – I don't make anything myself. My brothers could paint and draw and write. I'm afraid I was the sensible one. It's the same with Oliver. He's talented in all sorts of ways. You won't believe this but he used to write poetry. I don't think he has time for that now."

We lapse into silence. I think about Oliver the poet – that's a new one. Caroline overtakes an old car that's going too slowly for her liking but then she slows right down herself. My guess is that she's thinking about Oliver too. After a while she speeds up and restarts the conversation.

"What about you, Daniel? Did you have a good upbringing?"

"Good and bad. And different from yours. My dad was a small-time managerial type. He sort of retired early and we moved to the countryside. I think I liked it better in town."

"Have you got brothers and sisters?"

"One sister but she's weird."

"Your father was lucky to retire young."

"Well, sort of."

"Meaning?"

"He had an accident and bad health. But it's been OK. Really."

The road is narrow and bendy here. Caroline has to concentrate and doesn't say anything else. I think about her saying she had a happy childhood. She sounded wistful – like she's not so happy now.

"What do you want that you haven't got?" I ask.

It's like she hasn't heard. She just drives on, slowing for bends, accelerating on the straighter bits, always changing into the right gear. Then we reach a hilltop and she slows and pulls to the side of the road. I look around thinking there's something she wants me to see.

"You will understand more about women, Daniel, as you get older," she says.

I think I know a few things but OK I've got a lot more to learn – she doesn't have to say it quite like that. She hasn't turned the engine off so I guess we will start moving again pretty soon.

"What else do I want? What is there I don't have already?" she says. "Well, I'm thirty-five years old – I'll be thirty-six by the end of the year." She looks straight ahead as she speaks. "I'm thirty-five years old and I want to have a child before it's too late. That's all."

She puts the car into gear and pulls away again.

Sometimes when people are unhappy you don't want to be around them. It's different with Caroline. When she's happy of course you just want to be on the receiving end of that smile. But when she's unhappy – OK it makes you feel sad too. And yes, I don't understand women, I really don't. At least not that stuff – not the I-want-a-baby-now stuff. But the thing about Caroline is that when she's sad she's so beautiful. Profoundly beautiful, if such a thing is possible. I've not thought that about anyone else.

Caroline and I walk down the path through the woods, looking for Oliver, wondering how he's getting on. We find him on the bridge, right in the middle above the water, so absorbed in what he's doing that he doesn't hear us coming. We stop and watch him for a while from the bank above. He's doing something with a hammer and chisel, working very carefully like a craftsman. Perhaps that's what he really is – all that businessman stuff is just something he has to do to make money. He looks different from the man with his foot in plaster that I met by the lake a little time ago; much leaner, fitter and sun-tanned because he's been leading a healthier lifestyle. And he's modestly at home in the work he's doing and in his surroundings. Beside me Caroline is watching

Oliver with the same seriousness and concentration that he's giving to his work. I think she's taking in this image of him as completely as she can. A mental imprint. Made to last.

Oliver finishes what he's doing and catches sight of us. "Perfectly timed," he says. "I need both of you right now."

But he doesn't, he only really needs one person at first to hold the uprights while he screws them into place. I slip away and go to the viewpoint and leave Caroline to help him. I do it on purpose but I don't exactly know why. I do know that during the course of these few days they haven't once been alone together. I hang around by the ruin and eventually come back to find Caroline holding the last upright in place while Oliver winds in the coach-screws with a big spanner. Now he needs us to hold up the hand rails, bendy old heartwood lengths, while he fixes them. He has to recut some of the joints as we go so it takes some time. And he's always walking off onto the bank to check that it looks as aesthetically pleasing as possible. Caroline and I hold the wood this way and that according to Oliver's commands. He walks a few steps down the path and approaches again to look afresh. Goes to look from the other side. Narrows his eyes. Opens them wide again.

"He's a true artist," I say.

"An artist, yes," Caroline says, holding onto the wood patiently, standing quite still, as in a dream.

The three of us carry on for some time, linked together by the work, until the light begins to fade and we must go in. We can finish it tomorrow. We walk back through the trees, Caroline's dog in front wagging its tail limply. Another day nearly over.

Oliver is out for the evening; he has to see two brothers who will maybe do the renovation work on the ruined building and who have invited him to supper. Caroline is a great cook but this evening she's not interested and we have something reconstructed from leftovers. It's OK. I wash up, play with the dog and look through Caroline's art books some more. I get very taken with a particular picture and carry the book closer to the light.

"What is it?" Caroline says.

I show her the reproduction of an old landscape painting. "It's very much like where I live at home," I say. "See the church on the hill there? Well, our house would be here, below it, on the edge of the village."

I take the book away and sit down again.

"Do you get homesick?" she asks.

"No way."

"Do you miss your parents?"

"No, I don't. Perhaps I will some time."

"I'm sure they miss you."

I hadn't really thought of this but I guess it might be true.

"Do you write to them much, Daniel?" she asks.

"I've forgotten to for a bit. I sent them a postcard a few weeks ago."

"I think they must worry about you. I'm sure they'd like to know that you're OK."

I shrug. She's probably right. Now Caroline is thinking and frowning. She normally smiles (real smiles and fake ones too) or looks impassive or sad. Her frown is a funny thing – I'm not used to it. I guess it takes a while to get to know all the different faces someone will make.

"I'd like you to phone them," she says. "I feel responsible as you're staying here. Will you do it? I don't mind the cost and you can use the phone upstairs in my office."

I can't refuse but I feel awkward. She shows me where the phone is, tells me the international dialling codes and leaves me to it. My mum answers and it's strange, so far away like a journey back in time and of course I don't know what to say. Then I speak to my father. I tell him some stuff and he sounds quite excited to speak to me. He hasn't any news because he's not in a position to have news really. His hobby is astronomy and he starts on about that but stops pretty soon, realising that I'm running up someone else's phone bill. The whole thing makes me feel weird. When I get back into Caroline's living room I'm feeling sad.

Caroline is hurriedly closing a big book when I come in and neither of us speak. The wine is there on the table and I pour myself a big glass-full. Caroline comes up and refills her glass too. We sit down again, both of us quiet and reflective. There are some incredibly noisy insects making a racket outside the window – a much more foreign seeming sound than it was before I made that phone call. The dog is chasing rabbits in his sleep and barks with his mouth shut. Otherwise it's quiet like it has been here every other night. But it's a companionable silence, not awkward like it is when Oliver is here. I have more wine and I fill Caroline's glass too.

"What's the book you were looking at?" I ask.

She passes it to me without speaking and I turn the pages. It's a photograph album. All the pictures are of round here but in a different season, dull like winter. There are two people in the pictures but they are rarely in the same shot so it seems that they've been passing the camera back and forth between them. But in a few pictures the couple stand side by side with their arms around each other, their bodies pushed up close as if for warmth. They look very happy.

"Oliver looks funny without a beard," I say.

"It was a long time ago. We both look very different. Much younger."

"He looks younger but you look just the same."

"Oh, thank you. You certainly know how to say the right thing, Daniel."

I hadn't thought of saying the right thing. I rarely do. And I don't know what to say now even though I feel like this evening she and I are in similar states of mind – me time-travelling down the phone and Caroline time-travelling through old photos, both a little sad. I find myself just looking at her. I think she's beautiful in the photos and beautiful right now. I watch her expression change from a smile at my unintentional compliment to a look of unhappiness. She takes the album from me and puts it away and when she turns again big tears are running down her cheeks. I'm shocked. But I'm a bit drunk and uninhibited and I find myself wrapping my arms around her and giving her a warm hug. She cries and her body shakes with it and her breathing is strange. Her tears make a wet patch on the shoulder of my t-shirt. When she has quieted I let go of her and we sit down on separate sofas.

"Sorry," she says.

"It's OK."

"Thank you."

Then she goes to the kitchen, comes back with another bottle of wine and refills both our glasses.

"If I hear Oliver coming in I shall just slip away to bed," she says. "I can't let him see me like this. So don't think I'm being rude if I suddenly disappear."

"Alright. I understand."

"You're fond of him too, aren't you? He's a very special man. Very talented in all sorts of ways."

"Yes, I like Oliver very much. He's my friend. And I liked making that bridge. I might go and stay at his place some time. Maybe after we've finished here."

Caroline does the frowning thing again and it makes me smile. She notices and some of the smile transfers itself over to her but it doesn't last long.

"It might be good if you travel back with him," she says. "And make sure that he's alright."

"I can't imagine that Oliver needs looking after."

"But I worry about him. Will you go back with him? And let me know that he's got home safely?"

"If you want me to that's what I'll do. As long as it's OK with him too."

Caroline drifts away into her own thoughts for while. Then she has more to ask me: "You met Lizzie didn't you? What did she seem like to you?"

"Strong. Sensible."

"Yes, I thought as much. Oliver never went in for girly sorts – except for sex of course. And is she terribly attractive?"

"She's not as beautiful as you are," I say.

"Thank you, Daniel. You're very kind."

We sit in silence for a little time and Caroline finishes off her wine. Then she gets up to go to bed. She comes over and gives my hand a little squeeze and says good night. I sit for a bit longer but I realise that I don't feel like being around when Oliver comes in. I go up to my room and get into bed even though I think I won't fall asleep. I think of the photographs. They reminded me of somewhere round here but in another season. The trees in the background were all leafless so it looked different. I didn't really recognise anything but I reckon it was one of Oliver's memory places – the botanical garden.

It feels like this is our last day. There's a little more work to do on the bridge, fixing the remaining pieces of handrail, smoothing off rough edges and so forth. Caroline was late out of bed this morning so Oliver and I fiddle about until she comes. Then it's the three of us and the tasteful arrangement of bits of wood thing again; Oliver getting Caroline and me to hold the timbers this way and that until he's satisfied with the effect. He and she don't really speak to each other, that's nothing new. Caroline looks pale and has those dark lines under her eyes that I noticed when I first met her. But it goes well and we are all pleased with the thing in the end. We don't have a bottle of champagne to crack against it and we don't have a ribbon to cut – never mind. Caroline is pleased. Oliver is more than pleased and looks at the finished bridge from every possible angle.

"Well done buying this piece of woodland," he says to Caroline. "And the ruin too. It makes your place that bit more special." He's excited this morning. Maybe with the work finished he's not so focused on here but more focused on home. He stands on the bridge and looks down into the little stream. "This would be a brilliant place to bring up kids," he says.

What a thing to come out with. I thought I was meant to be the one who speaks first and thinks later and who doesn't understand women. I know I should turn away now, throw a stick for the dog or something. But I can't help watching to see how Caroline will be affected by this. She takes a couple of steps towards Oliver and speaks in a clear voice, loud enough for me to hear.

"Then give me a child."

And now it really is time for me to not be around. I call the dog and walk away towards the house. I don't know if either or both of them are following me or if they're both still standing there looking shell-shocked.

The rest of the day Oliver hangs around by the ruined building, still making different designs for how it might look. I want to go now. I like the feeling of being a person with limited connections, free to move on. But it's not so simple as that – I do have connections with these two people. I pretty much promised to Caroline that I would see Oliver home and so I will. And we start travelling tomorrow morning; two days to Oliver's place; then free. I can cope with that. I wander off and look around the village, spending the rest of the afternoon away from the claustrophobia and high emotion of Caroline's place. I come back in the early evening and grab something to eat from her kitchen. I go into the garden and find her there, tying up some plants that have grown too big.

"Daniel, I thought I'd frightened you away for good," she says.

"Not yet."

She seems pleased to see me. And I'm surprised to find that I'm pleased to see her too. She looks different to me now. Softer. Almost loveable.

"But it is a bit much, this place," I say.

"You mean the people in it."

"Yes, the people. Or the circumstances or something."

"I understand. It must be tiresome for you. You'll have to think of it all as an experience." She fiddles with the piece of string in her hand. "When I couldn't see you anywhere I looked up into the tree. I wondered if you'd hidden yourself up there."

"I'm not the hiding sort," I say. "I just like climbing. I do it for the adrenaline buzz sometimes when I'm bored or if I need shaking up."

"Perhaps that should be my new hobby. What do you climb?"

"Trees and rock faces. Buildings and cranes when I'm drunk."

"I thought you were a bit drunk last night. You didn't go off and climb something after I went to bed did you?"

"No," I say.

"I wish I didn't know that about you. I shall worry now. Please don't fall from a height and kill yourself."

"I won't fall. But I think I'll go out for a drink tonight. I fancy going to the bar in the village."

"No climbing then."

"OK, I promise. I just want to be out and about for a bit. And I think it will be better for you and Oliver if I'm out of the way. I'll be back late. You can talk."

"I hope so. I think I hope so. But don't be surprised if one or the other of us turns up in the bar and joins you."

I leave Caroline and go in to have a wash and change my t-shirt. When I come out again and I'm ready to go off to the village she comes over and hands me an envelope.

"It's your pay for the work," she says. "Thank you for everything you've done. And thank you for being here. I might not see you tonight or tomorrow morning either as I'm going off to work early. So this is good-bye. Take care won't you?"

"You too."

I turn and walk off towards the village. A little way along the road I stop and open the envelope. Inside I find more money than I had anticipated. That's good. And there's a note with Caroline's address at the top.

*Dear Daniel*

*Don't forget to write to me. And do write sometimes to your parents. I'm sure they worry about you. Look after Oliver.*

*Love, Caroline.*

I fold the note carefully and put it in my wallet, in a separate compartment from the money. I go to the village. Get pissed. Try to talk to people. Sing at the top of my voice all the way back. I don't climb anything.

# THIRTEEN

When I get up in the morning Caroline has already driven off to work in her posh car. Oliver is waiting for me impatiently. I have some breakfast and we walk to the village, Oliver carrying his cheap little suitcase, me with my rucksack. We have to wait some time for a bus to the town and we are both uncomfortable and impatient. But then we are on board with the world going past the window. It feels good to be moving on.

Travelling with someone or working alongside them you get a special sort of interaction. Silence is perfectly acceptable. You can say trivial things or talk without embarrassment about something serious. You can drift away into your own thoughts again without seeming rude. I can't help but think about Caroline and of her being alone when she gets back from work. And I wonder what happened between her and Oliver last night when I was out. I don't imagine for a moment that they maintained that awkward polite silence. Beside me this morning Oliver is *serene*. That's not a word I would have used before to describe him but that's how he is today.

"Home tomorrow evening," I say.

"Yes. Home. I think it will be quite late – after dark. And I'll go upstairs and look at Otis and Daisy asleep in their beds. And I will be very happy."

And then we drift off into our own thoughts again. But something comes to the surface and I find myself speaking.

"It must be difficult to love someone and they don't feel the same any more."

"What?"

"Like Caroline. She's still very fond of you. You don't feel the same."

"Lizzie and the kids are my life."

"I know."

"But that doesn't stop me from caring about someone else very, very much."

Oliver didn't tell me this before. I think I misunderstood. Now I wonder. I thought love was pretty much exclusive. One person. Or at least one person at a time. It doesn't feel right to ask him anything more so I just turn it over in my mind. Then we pass by the spot where Caroline stopped the car and told me she wanted to have children. More stuff to think about. But Oliver interrupts my thoughts.

"I heard you singing when you came in last night," he says. "Crap tune. What were the words again?"

"*I'd go the whole wide world just to find her* – was it that one?"

"That sounds like it. I wondered if that was what your travels are all about. Looking for the girl of your dreams."

"Maybe. I don't know. I do yearn for all that stuff but I don't think that's why I'm travelling. I'm just seeing a bit of the world and trying to find out where I want to be and what I want to do."

"And who you are?"

"Yeah, OK. Perhaps that too."

"Daniel, I think you're on a personal Odyssey."

"I like the sound of that. What does it mean?"

"An Odyssey is a story of a man trying to get home," he says.

"But that's not me – that's you. I'm travelling away from home."

"It's all the same."

"I don't think so." Surely Oliver is getting things mixed up in some way. I don't understand him.

"Can I ask you a question, Daniel?" he says.

"Yes."

"What will you be doing when you're my age?"

"I've no idea. It could be anything." I think for a bit. "I suppose I might have settled down with someone and had children."

"OK, so tell me what you're travelling towards."

"I'm.... well, in the short term.... but then again, in the longer view I suppose...." My words peter out.

"What do you suppose?" he says, smiling, coaxing me along so that I give him the answer that he wants.

"I suppose I'm on a personal Odyssey," I say. "Whatever that means."

I look out of the window at the world going past. Little farms with goats, hens pecking at the dust, vegetable gardens, fields of crops. Houses with vines and figs against their walls. Big chestnut trees.

"Oliver," I say.

"Yes."

"Maybe you're right. We are going in the same direction."

Oliver and I catch another bus in town and travel along a bit faster on bigger roads in flatter countryside. Then we change again and are soon on something like a motorway and going even faster. It gets samey at this speed. It seems like the faster you go, the less you see. And the logic of that suggests that you see most of all by staying in one place. That sounds wrong and it contradicts what I'm trying to do by going on this trip. But it's a little bit true I suppose – the places I've stayed still (the Jesus freaks' place, Caroline's) have been the most special, memorable ones. And things happened there. Oliver said something about bringing up kids being a journey too. I'm not so sure about that.

Later in the day we get out of the fast bus in the middle of a hot dirty city. I like cities but not this one, not with the heat, the pollution and no open spaces. The people are rushing around. They have hard faces. Some of them look furiously miserable. Oliver knows his way round the city as he used to come here in what he now calls, giving me a stern look as he says it, *that part of my career that we don't talk about.* We are between the bus station and the train station and walking fast along a street busy with thousands of mopeds as well as cars and pedestrians. Traffic fumes are trapped in between the tall buildings. It's very hot and my rucksack sticks to my back with sweat. We wait to cross at a junction controlled by traffic lights and stand in a row of people facing another row across the street. In all this crowded anonymity one man opposite us stares and stares at Oliver as if in unhappy recognition.

"Shit," Oliver says. But when I look at him he's smiling that smile I've seen once or twice before in the last few weeks – the expression I think of as the mask.

"We'll go this way," he says and we hurry off down the street we were going to cross. The man follows on his side of the road, glancing across at us as he walks. Oliver stares straight ahead and I decide to follow his example and anyway it's hard to keep up with him now, especially with the rucksack on my back. A short way ahead a taxi stops to let out a passenger and Oliver runs a few paces and slips into the back seat. I follow and we're away. I like this. It's like being in one of those old films. We only drive a short distance to the station. We get out, pay the driver, and make for the destination board.

"I don't even know who he is," Oliver says. "That's the strange thing. There are people here who might still think of me as a rival or even an enemy – I don't know. But this guy?"

The train Oliver wants us to get doesn't go for two hours. We go to a platform café and sit by the window (but facing inwards) and drink coffee. I know it's the wrong time to ask anything so we don't talk. But two hours is a long time for me and after the third cup of coffee I wander out onto the platform. *Shit*, as Oliver so eloquently puts it; the man who was following us is walking this way, recognises me easily (of course – I'm so foreign looking here) and comes up to me with a pained expression on his face. He's a little guy, older than Oliver, miserable rather than sinister looking, neatly dressed. He speaks but stops when he realises that I don't understand. He takes a folded piece of paper from his pocket, passes it to me and walks off. I unfold the paper and of course the writing on it is in a foreign language and I can't under-stand it. I go back into the café and hand Oliver the note. Haven't I done something like this once before?

We're on the train and Oliver has been looking concerned and puzzled for a while. The people opposite us got off at the last station and there's no-one close enough to overhear. Oliver decides to talk.

"I don't think it's as serious as it might be," he says. "He doesn't seem like a dangerous man. At least not physically dangerous; that's my guess. I've never met him before and I don't completely understand. But this man has been writing me threatening letters for some time – like blackmail but without demands for money. He says he has evidence against me that could put me in big trouble. And that's possible. Unlikely but possible. Now he wants us to talk. I have to go to this place and meet him and hope for the best. It's over the border and it's on the coast. The good news is that it's on the way home, more or less. But the whole thing's a worry."

"And you don't recognise him?"

"No. But the note makes it clear that he's the guy who's been sending the letters."

"I guess we'll find out more when we meet him."

"When *we* meet him. No, I don't think so. I'd better do this on my own."

I think for a bit.

"I made a sort of promise," I say. "To Caroline. A promise that I would travel home with you and let her know that you're alright. It doesn't make sense, I know, but she thinks I should look after you. That's what she asked of me."

"No."

"But this guy is no real harm. Or is he? Maybe I could be useful in some way."

Oliver turns this over in his mind.

"I'd rather you kept out of this, Dan."

"I made a promise. I'm connected with your stuff now. With you and with Caroline. Neither of you are strangers anymore. And walking away would be wrong."

"I don't know. I suppose if your heart is set on this then you could come along. But I am not *your* responsibility. You can walk away at any time. And don't do anything rash. That needs to be another promise. OK?"

"OK. It's a deal."


And there are more complications. Oliver has got to get over the border without a passport. But he says it's easy and I have to believe him. We get off the train at a town near the border and make preparations. We buy a detailed map of the area and Oliver identifies what looks like a track that connects two villages, one either side of the border. It's an obvious place where people would cross the border informally, just going about their daily business.

"I know this sort of set up well," he says. "The border isn't even marked on the ground in places like this. Just occasionally there will be police around in the villages checking up on anybody who looks suspicious."

"Won't it look funny, walking down this country lane with our luggage?"

"I've thought about that and I want to ask you a favour. Will you put my belongings in your rucksack and cross the border normally? I'll walk the other way carrying nothing, as if I'm just out for a stroll, and I'll meet you later a little further on."

I agree to this. I put some of Oliver's stuff in my bag. He walks away carrying the almost empty suitcase. I suppose he'll throw it away later.

The next day I arrive at the prearranged meeting place and look for Oliver. I'm in a little square in the middle of a quiet town and it's lunch time. I have with me the type of meal that Oliver has got me used to: fresh white bread, dark chocolate and fruit-juice – the traditional Oliver's-family-picnic. I sit on a bench, eat and wait. I'm a few miles over the border and the man-made details of my surroundings have changed. Road signs, street lights, dust-bins, shop fronts, parking spaces, pavements, the list goes on – all of them are a little bit different. It's mildly disorientating. And the longer I sit the longer the list gets and I feel uncomfortable. I'm sitting in the shade but it's still too hot. As the afternoon contin-ues the passing cars dwindle to almost none and the people that were on the streets disappear altogether. I'm alone here.

The houses around the square have overhanging roofs, thick walls and small shuttered windows. As I sit in the silent heat I begin to imagine the cool and comfort of the insides of these houses. And these are people's *homes*. Inside there are families resting away from the heat and brightness of the outdoors. I think being alone is OK or not OK according to the context. Here at this time of the day I feel like an outsider (which I am quite liter-ally), excluded from other people's lives, alienated. Mostly it's because I'm here waiting. Two hours beyond the time Oliver said. Three hours. And now there begin to be a few people about, some of them looking at me with *is-he-still-there?* expressions.

Eventually I have to move. I wander about town hoping to bump into Oliver but I don't. I check into a little hotel and ask, as best I can, for the cheapest room. I shower and lie down on the bed, out of sync with the rest of the world who are now milling about in the streets and being sociable. I'll go back and look for Oliver later and tomorrow too if necessary. Right now I'm thinking about the sea. I've had this feeling before on this trip – that I want to get to the clear blue water and hang out on beaches and swim whenever I get hot. I can remember the name of the place where Oliver and I are to meet this man and I know it's by the sea. That's where I'll go if Oliver doesn't turn up tomorrow.

When I've rested enough I go out again. On the corner of the street there are builders on a low roof, moving tiles, sawing timbers, talking and laughing, calling out to people they know on the street below. I want to be up there. I suppose it's something to do with working with Oliver at Caroline's. It's a nice little turning point for me – realising that the world of work is somewhere I might want to be.

In the town square there's still no Oliver. I sit on a different bench and watch people. The most gorgeous slender dark-haired young woman walks past and I have a wicked thought. And along with the wickedness comes a great romantic yearning. I watch as she walks on. I like the way her clothes cling to her body and I like the way her hair falls onto her shoulders. I think I have a bit of a thing about women's shoulders. I let out a big ludicrous sigh. I think it must be strange to be older like Oliver and be married and everything – not getting these feelings any more. I'm not sure if I would like that. But there's so much to yearn for today. Beautiful women of course. And friends and workplaces and the sea. And all these wonderful things are out there all the time waiting for me. I don't feel so bad.

I eat later. Then I sit again waiting for Oliver and waiting for something to happen. The whole town comes out after sunset and everybody walks round the square and the streets close by. All ages are here, being sociable in the cool evening air. Not one of them will speak to me but it's OK. I felt uncomfortable this afternoon but now I feel fine. I feel a quiet warmth towards my fellow human beings. A warmth and a little sadness and a little buzz of how rich and full life is. And a feeling of anticipation. I wonder what tomorrow will bring.

Now another twenty-four Oliver-free hours have passed and I've moved on. I wonder if he has deliberately given me the slip. I don't think so. Of course I can forget about him now and go my own way if I want to. But it's like I said to him a couple of days ago – I'm connected to him (and to Caroline) now. It's weird but it's true that I feel a bit responsible for him. What happens to Oliver matters to me.

I have hitched and bussed my way up and up into bare hills today because that's the only way to get to this place where Oliver has to meet the blackmailer guy. I'm in the town where the road turns off down to the sea and I've tried hitching but there's almost no traffic. This is a dull place and I'm bored. It's similar to the last town but in a barer and higher landscape – a goat-grazed waterless half-way-to-being-desert scrubby landscape. There's no town square here and the people are doing the walking round at night thing but with a difference; they walk along the wide main street to the edge of town where the outermost houses give way to dirt and scrub, then turn and walk all the way through town to the other end, turn again, and so on. I think most of the local population are walking up and down this one street. A few people sit in bars but I notice they get up and join the walkers after a while and are replaced by others. Well, this is certainly different from home. But I'm restless and I've been sitting outside this bar drinking steadily for a while and haven't even bothered to book myself a room. This isn't really me – pissed and motionless don't go together in my world. I can't sit here any longer.

I ask (by gesticulating) if I can leave my bag by the bar and I do the walking thing with the locals. At the edge of town where they all turn back I carry on in the darkness. There's tarmac under my feet and stars above and the noise of insects – that's all; one thing to feel, one thing to see and one thing to hear. I turn back soon, go to a different bar and try a yellow drink that tastes of glue. I drink a small bottle of this alone and then set off back to the first bar. It's later now and there are fewer people. I'm drunker, restlesser, going to do something crazy. I know I am but I don't know what. I think of Caroline. Nice thoughts. Also the *look after Oliver* thing. Yeah, I should really be with him now, I know that. And it all comes together when I see, leaning at the side of a house, something very useful. I get my rucksack from the first bar and come back; look around to see there's no-one watching; quietly wheel the bicycle away. A little way along the road I get on and pedal out of town.

I ride to the junction and take the road that's signposted for the seaside place – blackmailerville, as I now think of it. The road goes gently up hill and it's hard work with a rucksack on my back. I stop and try to fix it to the rack behind the saddle. I'm far enough away from the street lights now for it to be very, very dark. I use my belt and a pair of shoelaces and I take my time. I like the challenge and I like being very drunk, very altered-state-of-consciousness, and very focused at the same time. I'm feeling my bag into position and the belt and shoelaces around it. I begin to see what my hands are telling me. Wow, this is great. It's like my hands are giving my brain sight messages. It's so real it's amazing. My hands can now see further than the things they touch – I can *see* the bike saddle and the handle bars and every-thing. The glue-tasting stuff I had at the last bar must be very special. I can *see* the road, the bushes and the dirt either side. But no. No, it's just my eyes working better and I understand that they're working better because it's getting lighter. I look all around. There behind me a three-quarter moon is slowly rising above the hills. I lay the bike on the ground and watch the moon rise some more. If I can see it rising that means I'm seeing the world turning. I sway backwards and forwards and I know it's not just because I'm pissed. I can actually feel the world moving gently under my feet.

I mount the bicycle and pedal slowly up the long slope. My legs feel good – full of energy. I push the pedals round and the wheels go round and I go forward across the surface of the slowly turning world. All the time it gets lighter and I can see more of the bare hills. The shapes are clear and hard-edged against the sky but the distances are unknowable. It's a long time before the road reaches a high point between two hills and begins to dip towards the sea.

At first the slope is gentle and the road winds along the course of a valley, crossing a dry river bed from time to time on concrete bridges. The bike picks up speed gradually and the air is cool against my skin. The bends are the best bit. I'm determined not to use the brakes and each bend is dodgier, more hairy, more *will I make it?* Then there's a long straight and I can go no hands. Then a steepening of the slope and a rush of increased speed. It's light enough to see the next bend and the bridge that follows it. Will I slow down? Not if I can help it.

There's a sports commentator voice in my head: *Daniel Brownlow is certainly one of the best young riders in this season's downhill. He's making very good time on the first section. He's really moving along and I wonder how he'll get round this next bend. He's fast. He's very brave. Maximum speed towards the beginning of the curve. The crowd are holding their breath as he approaches the famous Big Bridge Bend. He has perfect style here – the style we've got used to seeing from this promising young rider. The bend comes up very fast indeed and he might just slow a little. He leans his machine over and into the bend, touches the brakes perhaps. The crowd are on their feet – willing him on. But I think it's getting away from him. He's going to lose it. Yes, he's down, man and bike sliding across the road and into the bushes. There's a roar of disappointment from the crowd. What a dramatic exit from one of this year's most important international races.*

I switch the voice off as it's getting irritating. I'm lying on my back on the gravel at the edge of the road, halfway under a fragrant-smelling bush. It's comfortable here. The world still turns underneath me. The sky above is starry but with star-absences marking the shapes of clouds. I can't see the moon as it's on the other side of the bush but I can see its light on the land around. I can hear the sound of running water so the river here isn't completely dried up. And some small animal is scratching its way across the ground. I could lie here all night in the near-dark and near-silence.

The scratchy animal is getting nearer and I raise myself up onto my elbows to look at it. It's closer than I thought – not far from my feet a smoothly shaped stone moves across the ground. I bend forward to look more closely and the thing stops. It's a tiny tortoise, its legs withdrawn now and its head just peeking out from under the shell. I lie back so that it can go on its way. In a while I can hear it moving and when I look again it's gone. I'm restless now and I get up and check that my arms and legs are working. I search around for my little friend without success. Then I pull the bike out of a neighbouring bush, check that my bag is still firmly fixed onto the rack and set off again.

I'm more careful now and I use the brakes. The front brake is very good and I realise that's what made me come off – locking the front wheel so that the bike skidded away from underneath me. The road winds on down the hill and there are lots of hairpin bends and recrossings of the river. I don't do the sports commentator thing but I have other nonsense in my head. It's like I'm a superhero whose special powers include riding a bike. And I'm chasing after a superhero baddy. The wind is in my hair and I roar down the road, clever, fearless and strong. Pissed again. Whoopee.

Now the valley has a twist in it and a big view opens out. I pull on the brakes and bring myself to a stop on a high concrete bridge. The valley has narrowed and steepened and I can hear water falling on rocks far below – the river is flowing down there. And ahead of me is the great mass of the sea, thousands of tiny movements, waves I suppose, catching the moonlight. I spend some time looking at it, thinking vague thoughts of superheroes and the moon and the turning earth. I like this planet.

The water noise below has a predictable effect on me and straight away I know that this is going to be one of my all time best totally-pissed pisses. I let the bike down onto the road and jump up onto the parapet of the bridge. It's quite wide and safe, of course, but I do notice that the world is still turning enough to make me sway back and forth a little. I unzip myself, aim out and up at the stars, and let go. A beautiful moonlit stream of piss arches out towards the sea and into the valley. I listen for the sound of it hitting the rocks below. It's a long time before I believe I can hear my own water noises mingling with the sound of the stream. High or what? This is the best ever. When I've finished I zip up, get back on the bike and carry on down. I swoop around bends. Sing at the top of my voice. I run off into the bushes once when I'm looking too much at the view of moonlight on water. It takes a good while before the sea comes near, the road levels out, and I ride into town.

Or something like a town. Certainly there are man-made structures: huge walls of improbable castles, things like cranes, towers of girders, big empty flat areas the size of football pitches. And I'm relieved to find houses too – a couple of big posh-looking detached buildings and some terraced rows of smaller dwellings. I get off my bike, lean it against a wall and wander about. There are no lights on at all. Some of the houses are boarded up and others have broken windows. I go up to one of the bigger houses and find the front door swinging off its hinges. This place is completely deserted. Everything dark. No human sounds and not even the sound of a dog barking.

The town, if it can be called that, isn't quite on the shore. The closest I can get to the water is to look down from a concrete plat-form to moonlit waves breaking on rocks perhaps fifty feet below. I've been wanting to get to this sea but now I'm here it's not how I imagined it. In the brochures there are gorgeous women in bikinis lying on sandy beaches under the sun and the sea is still, clear and impossibly blue. But here the water is rough and foams white against black rocks. It's harsh, cold, and uninviting. And I'm shivering after my long descent through the cool night air. I need to sleep now but I don't fancy staying in the spooky houses. I find a place between two high concrete walls, away from the noise of the sea and shaded from the moonlight. This will do for tonight. I get the bike, take my sleeping bag out of my rucksack and settle down. Maybe it will all look better in the morning.

# FOURTEEN

I wake up to a still grey morning. There's a thin drizzle falling but I'm close to one of the concrete walls and it barely touches me. I feel as I always do after a serious drink and some craziness, physically rough but mentally renewed – like a carpet that has been given a good beating. I lie still for a while and let my thoughts drift around. In amongst all the vagueness two major concerns take shape: Oliver and breakfast. I get up, take a water bottle from my rucksack and drink. That's better but my head still hurts. Never mind. I set off to explore this strange place.

I walk over and among industrial-seeming structures of unguessable purpose. Mostly there is concrete: walls, platforms, beams, staircases. And there are rusty iron girders making strong towers and a bridge. And there's also wood: a building several storeys high made out of huge timbers that maybe once had some sort of cladding on them but which are now a bare lattice-work against the sky. I go to look down at the sea again. Foaming milky blue breakers crash onto concrete and rock. In amongst the waves are more pieces of iron and concrete wreckage. It's unswimmable here and I look up and down the shore line (though I can't see far through the drizzle) for something better. But there are only huge breaking waves meeting huge broken rocks with maybe the dark shape of cliffs further away.

I turn my back on the sea and look around the buildings some more. It's all something to do with mining or quarrying I think; some big-time ugly activity that fucked-up the place and then went away. Some structures are ruined but some look half-built and suddenly abandoned. It's a landscape of chaotic dereliction – impressive and dramatic but also spooky because all the activities that formed the place have now ceased. It's a ghost town.

I walk away from the industrial structures to the rows of houses. The lower terrace is badly damaged and ruinous but the houses higher up look tidier. I'm very surprised when I see that a semi-detached pair of houses have been subtly restored. From a distance they looked the same as the others but close up I can see new pointing in the stone-work, a new roof, carefully shuttered windows. Then I see more tastefully restored houses, inconspicuous among the ruins, newly habitable but uninhabited. It only makes a little sense for me if I imagine that they are holiday homes, empty because the season hasn't started yet. It's a weird place for a holiday but perhaps there are good beaches close by. So there are two lots of activity not happening here, a double absence. It's a ghost town twice over.

And as soon as I think this I see a ghost, a pale face looking at me from behind a window and then withdrawing into the dark. I have an urge to hurry away but I don't. Maybe it's good to not be entirely alone here, I might need help. I certainly need breakfast. I feel a little uneasy, which isn't like me at all. All the same I go up to the door and knock. Silence for a moment. Then the noises of locks turning and bolts being pulled. The door opens and Oliver emerges, grinning, laughing under his breath, reluctantly pleased to see me.

"I thought I'd got rid of you," he says. "But you'd better come in. Welcome to the place where my past catches up with me. You're lucky you don't have a past. Do you want some breakfast?"

It's a two storey house, attached on one side to a larger building like a workshop. Inside everything is immaculate, freshly painted, modern. It has a state-of-the-art fitted kitchen and expensive new furniture in the living room. It's all very stylish but cold and unhomely. Oliver makes me coffee and unfreezes some croissants. I eat with my usual enthusiasm and when I look up Oliver is grinning. When I've finished we just sit on opposite sides of the kitchen table and smile. I like being English at times like this. Not having to say much, not getting physical. Only that nice understated mutual warmth thing that you get between two guys who have shared a few times together and looked out for each other.

"How did you get here?" Oliver asks.

"I sort of borrowed a bicycle."

"Sounds like you might mean *stole* a bicycle."

"I was pissed. I couldn't help it."

"Yeah, I know." He laughs and pours me more coffee. "Well Dan, the thing here is this: the note gave instructions to come to this place and wait. Key hidden under a stone, food in the fridge and so on. There's a telephone but it doesn't ring. And I'm waiting. Nothing happened all day yesterday."

"And you gave me the slip on purpose?"

"Pretty much. I thought you'd understand. But you're here now and that's OK too. It's good to have some company."

"So the man owns this place?"

"I should think so. Maybe he's quite rich and owns more, I don't know. It would be a nice place to come in different circumstances. I think they are trying to subvert the tourist brochure thing here. It's an interesting spot."

"And what do we do? Just wait?"

"Just wait. And one other thing. Yesterday I discovered that a bus comes down at midday. No-one on it, of course. But I think it's a good idea to be by the bus-stop and be seen so that someone knows we're here. Raise a hand in greeting to the driver. That's it. I have a feeling that I may be required to hang around for a few days."

"I'll wait with you," I say.

"Be my guest."

I look around the little house. Two bedrooms, toilets and showers *en suite*. Better than last night's lodgings. Oliver looks like he's going to sit at the kitchen table and drum his fingers all morning and it's raining outside so I select the unslept-in bedroom and have a lie down. I dream of sandwiches. I guess food has been on my mind this morning. But it's more than that – it's something to do with Oliver getting me food, watching me eat, smiling. I just fell asleep for a moment, dreamt sandwiches and woke up feeling disturbed. What was that all about? Rain hisses on the roof outside. Gutters drip. I fall asleep again.

This time it's a dream that is also a memory. I'm at home and I've suddenly decided that I'm going travelling. It's morning, I've had breakfast, and my bag is packed and waiting by the door. My father crashes around in the kitchen and he's shouting *wait a minute*. I'm ready to go but he's holding me back by calling out my name, *Daniel, are you still there?* And he comes out into the hall with some sandwiches he's made for me wrapped in a plastic bag. Cheese and pickle – my favourite. And then I'm on the train later in the day and I can see myself in the dream, like I'm watching it happen, getting up, picking up my bag but leaving the sandwiches on the seat. I have such a forlorn vivid picture in my mind of myself turning my back on the sandwiches and walking away from them.

I wake suddenly. My stomach turns over wildly and I feel like I'm going to be sick. I stumble into the shower room and kneel down with my head bent waiting for it to happen. My stomach settles and I go back and lie down on the bed. I feel very, very bad and it's not just my stomach. The dream was hurtful like a little nightmare. I daren't go back to sleep again and I try to think of other things. I try to do my usual escapist day-dream of thinking about warm blue sea and sun-kissed beaches. It can't work for me now, here, with that contradictory sea a hundred yards away. And then it comes to me with such relief, the realisation that I did eat the sandwiches. I didn't leave them behind on the train, I know that. They got badly squashed in my bag for twenty-four hours and then on the night ferry I ate them, washed down with a can of beer. I get up off the bed feeling better. Again I think *what was that all about?*

I go downstairs and find Oliver still at the table.

"Where's the bike?" he asks.

"It's by a concrete wall. I can get it if you want it."

"Someone wants it."

"Yeah, I know but there's not much I can do about that. I don't think I can get it back up that hill. It would take days."

"You look very shaky," Oliver says. "Are you hung-over?"

"Yes."

"You'd better have some more coffee."

At midday Oliver, me, and the bike are leaning against the wall waiting for the bus. It's still drizzling but the sky looks lighter; there is a sun up there somewhere. The bus comes winding down the hill, empty except for the driver. Oliver steps on board and starts a complicated explanation in a foreign language. Eventually the driver agrees, Oliver pays some money, I lift the bike on board and carry it to the back of the bus. I get off and the bus goes back up the hill.

"Easy," Oliver says. "Now we can sleep at night. Well, maybe not but you know what I mean. Something done."

I feel restless and I don't know what to do. Oliver reads my mind.

"Go and find the beach," he says. "I think the sun's going to come out. And I don't think the guy will come today. I think he'll make me suffer for a bit longer."

I leave Oliver and walk across a large concrete area like a carpark. On the other side I climb a bank and find a path that looks like it will run along the coast. I pass a short row of single storey houses that look older than the rest of the place, pre-industrial perhaps. They have the same range of characteristics as the other buildings here: uninhabited, re-inhabited, ruinous, restored, half-restored, abandoned. And they are all empty, of course. I go on out and away from the town. The path leads around a steep bluff and then on to more level ground. It runs through scrubby evergreen bushes, glistening wet, and keeps back a little from the sea. The waves here are breaking onto rounded weathered rocks, a more natural meeting of land and sea than the town's shoreline. I can't see far so I notice the flowers, hundreds of them scattered in the gaps between the scrub, blue spikes like the ones in Caroline's garden but much smaller. I carry on for a while. The waves make a continuous pounding noise that, to me, should be accompanied by the sound of seagulls. But there's no sign of animal or bird life – just me, the sea and the rain.

At last the path drops down to a beach. The waves have brought in hundreds of plastic bottles in an array of cheerful colours. And there are washed up single flip-flops and trainers, a deflated beachball, driftwood. Further along the beach the sea has deposited a layer of pulpy seaweed several feet thick. It's squelchy and pungent smelling and makes a ragged cliff at the sea's edge. Would I swim here if the sun came out? I'm not sure. The waves look dangerously powerful. The beach is a sandy rubbish heap.

I turn back, think of lunch, think of sandwiches, think of that dream. Oliver says dreams tell you what you need to hear. Stuff that you know deep down but don't want to consciously acknowledge. When I get closer to the town the hard industrial shapes loom out of the drizzle. A ghost town, yes, abandonment and dereliction big-time. A double ghost town because of all the unhomely little holiday dwellings, empty outside of the season. I know a dream of sandwiches shouldn't be disturbing but as I get closer to the buildings the atmosphere of it comes back strongly and I feel haunted, like it's the place that's doing this to me. There's no need to feel as uncomfortable as I do but I can't help it. Oliver spoke of his past catching up with him. *But not you, Daniel,* he said. *You don't have a past.*

Back in the house Oliver is pleased to see me. He's concerned too.

"You still look rough, Dan," he says. You must have got really wasted last night."

"I drank some of the stuff that tastes like glue," I say.

But that's not really it. This place or my dreams or something is upsetting me. I'm not used to feeling like this. I tell Oliver about the dream. He thinks about it, looks puzzled, smiles.

"I'll tell you about making food for the family," he says. "I cook for Lizzie and the kids all the time at home. I like to do it. The things you do for your family aren't chores, they're acts of love. Really, that's true. Or most of the time it's true. So a man making sandwiches for his son when he's about to walk out of the door and he doesn't know when he'll see him again.... Yeah, I can imagine doing that. What I can't possibly imagine is having teenage children but I guess it's going to happen some time. I hope they eat their sandwiches."

Acts of love. I've never thought about it like that but I suppose he's right. And maybe I knew this at some level otherwise why did I have that dream? But I did eat the sandwiches for God's sake. Why do I feel so guilty?

We are both quiet but I can guess what sort of thoughts are going on in Oliver's mind – I know him well enough by now. He's doing the hunched-up inward looking thing. The shrinking man. Then the phone rings, loud in the silence, making us jump.

"Good," Oliver says. "Something at last." He walks across the room and picks it up. Just silence and he puts it down again.

"Hung up," he says.

He stands by the phone and sure enough it rings again.

Someone speaks, Oliver answers and the guy says some more and then silence again and Oliver puts the phone down. He comes back to the table.

"Well?" I say.

"Not much. He only asked how it felt to be away from my family."

"What did you say?"

"I said it felt bad and he hung up."

Oliver paces up and down the kitchen. He picks up the phone, dials, bangs it down again.

"Shit, shit, shit," he says. He kicks a chair across the room. He walks over and sets it upright again.

"Sorry, Dan. I thought I'd try to phone Lizzie but the phone's set to incoming calls only. The guy is making his point. He's getting to me."

There's another long silence and the room gets darker – perhaps the weather outside is closing in again. I can hear the rain getting heavier. This is not nice.

It goes on. Days pass and very little happens. We meet the bus each day and wave to the driver. The phone rings once a day and the guy says *how does it feel to miss your family?* or something similar. The sky lightens and then gets darker again and it rains some more. The wind blows and the sea stays rough and inhospitable. Thunder and lightning in the evenings.

Oliver isn't sure if he wants me to go or stay but I don't have a choice – I feel implicated. Each day I take walks but I don't feel I should be gone for too long. I stand in the rain and look at the wooden beams of one big old building or the metal girders of the towers or the bridge and work out how I would climb them if I was in a climbing state of mind. But I'm not.

Things that mess with my mind:
1) The place itself. The buildings and structures are massive statements of activity that has now ceased. The houses are empty shells that were once homes. It all says the same thing: absence.
2) The waiting. It's scary and we're tense. The phone rings once

a day and we jump. Sometimes we discuss the man's motives, what information he might have against Oliver, what makes him want to do this to us, what will happen if and when he turns up. 3) The boredom. Nothing happening and only the constant noise of sea, wind and rain. No other stimulation. It's like prison. 4) The things the guy says, usually *how does it feel to miss your loved ones?* or something like that. It affects Oliver terribly. Is the man making some threat to Oliver's family? Is Oliver, by waiting here, allowing bad things to happen to them at home? Mental torture for Oliver and it gets through to me as he's my friend and I care about him. But it's more than that – it touches something in my mind too.

What my mind is doing:
1) Day-dreams. Weird stuff floats into my head on the noise of the waves or on the back of the wind. Day-dreams indoors accompanied by the sound of Oliver drumming his fingers on the kitchen table (I can't believe he hasn't worn a hole in it by now). Day-dreams when I walk to the dirty beach along the rainy seagull-less coast. Day-dreams among the ruined buildings of this non-town.
2) Memories. Oliver said that I don't have a past. Well, it's true that everywhere we go is loaded with memory for him and he has enough memory, enough past, for the two of us. And I believe in living in the moment – in the here and now. And I don't even have to believe in it because it's just how it is for me. Oliver and I are very different from each other in that way. But.... I guess it's the aforementioned things, the things that mess with my mind – the words the man says, Oliver's concerns, etc. They make me remember things I don't want to remember.

I have earlier childhood memories first and mostly they're OK. My mum when she was happy and her face was young and smiley. My dad doing things. Cricket or football in the garden and me having to sneak into the neighbour's to get the ball. Dad helping me over the fence. The *well done, Daniel* when I got back safely. One particular squally sunshine-and-showers day in autumn – him and me climbing to the top of the big conker tree and swaying back and forth in the wind, leaves coming off and whirling away, the plop of conkers hitting the ground far below us, the view across the roof-tops, both of us laughing and feeling very special so high up and away from everyone else.

3)    Dreams. The same old stuff. The my-father-walking dreams when it couldn't be true anymore. I look out of the window and he's walking up the street towards home, an older man now but still smiling. He's walking around the garden and looking at the flowers. Or I'm in town and there, making his way through the crowds and walking towards me...

And the time when he's absent. But he isn't – it's me making an absence where he should be. My eyes going around the room and skipping past him because I don't want to look. My blind spot. Not saving up things to tell him any more but telling them to no-one, just talking in my head to someone who's not there. The door to his room always open and me acting like it's always closed and there's nothing the other side. This is the bad stuff. The stuff I don't want to think about.

On the way to the beach the sun comes out and the temperature rises. The clouds are steadily moving away and soon one half of the sky is blue. Along the path puddles steam away. Bees and butterflies move among the flowers. But the beach looks worse in the sunlight, tatty with rubbish. A sea breeze plays with a plastic bag. The thick pile of seaweed at the far end of the beach gives off a great stink. The sea itself doesn't know about the change in the weather yet and big waves continue to crash onto the sand. I turn back but I'm getting hot and I walk along the rocks at the edge of the sea looking for somewhere to swim. I walk out onto a headland where the water looks deep and the swell rises and falls against the rocks like a big sea elevator.

I take off all my clothes and clamber along to a ledge above the waves. The water moves up and down below me in a regular rhythm. I know that if it sometimes reaches up to the ledge I can get in and out again. After a number of smaller waves there's a strong one that rises up the sheer rock, floods onto the ledge and over my feet, sinks down again. I'm a good swimmer but I'm still undecided when a bigger wave comes in, up the rock, over the ledge and higher still, almost to my waist. When it drops down it takes me with it. This is good, very salty, very floaty water, not too cold, the big swell lifting me up so that I can see the rocks drifting past. But things shouldn't be drifting past like that – I swim hard against the current and try to get back to the ledge. It's too strong and I can't do it.

I don't feel like panicking. I ride the waves and travel along the shore line, only swimming out a little if I think I'll be thrown onto the rocks. A little sea journey. It's not long before I'm close to the beach. There's a big eddy that tries to take me out but I swim hard, get into the surf, and soon I'm thrown onto the sand. I rest on my hands and knees for a moment and the next wave breaks right over me and drags me out again. I swim hard and ride another wave up onto the beach, get up quickly and rush away from the water. I'm shaken and cold but I laugh out loud.

A little way up the beach I clear a space for myself amid the rubbish and lie down on the sand. I'm chilled and goose-pimpled but the sun begins to warm me. I relax and gradually get my breath back. There's a rank smell coming from the pile of seaweed close to me and there are flies settling on my arms and legs. But I feel better than I have done for a few days, released in some way. I shiver and wave the flies off from time to time. I rest, smile to myself, shut my eyes, think of nothing at all.

I walk back half-naked in the sunshine, pleasantly empty-headed. The scrubby bushes by the path are releasing good herb-like smells into the still air. Big brightly coloured butterflies and small drab birds fly about. Lizards bask on rocks. Grass-hoppers make scratchy noises. The rough weather is gone and only the sea remembers.

The town looks different now. It glistens and steams. It looks smaller between the now clearly visible hills and the vastness of the sea. I make my way to the house and find Oliver sitting on a chair outside. The front door is open and before I can speak I hear the phone ringing. He goes in to answer and I lean against the wall and wait. Then he comes out again with his eyes squeezed up against the glare.

"Tomorrow," he says. "The guy is coming some time tomorrow."

## FIFTEEN

How is it that you can spend all day waiting for someone to arrive and when they do you're surprised? It happens. Of course we have tried to prepare ourselves. I described to Oliver the way the guy looked on the station platform when he gave me that note. He was grim-faced, very miserable looking but not scary. Oliver says the man himself will be frightened. We can't know what his motives are or what he intends to do but he will probably be nervous and we mustn't make it worse: nothing around that looks like a weapon; no sudden movements; hands out in the open where he can see them; look relaxed; keep calm. It is late afternoon when we hear a car pulling up in the street outside. There's a knock on the door. I don't feel relaxed at all but I must keep to Oliver's instructions: just observe, don't do anything rash.

Oliver opens the door wide and the man looks in. He's surprised to see me there but Oliver persuades him that it's alright, invites him in, turns his back on him and goes into the kitchen to make coffee for all of us. The man goes into the living room and I follow on behind, careful to keep away from him and look non-threatening. I sit on a sofa and the guy stands in the middle of the room trying to look like he's in control. He's a small man, older than Oliver, grey haired, very smartly dressed. He tries to speak to me but I make it clear that I don't speak the language. Oliver comes in with the coffee and sits down. I think Oliver is a natural psychologist; he puts the man at ease but by playing host he very quietly assumes control. And now he leans back in his chair ready to listen to anything the man has to say. There's a long difficult silence before the man sits and puts his cup down on the table. He perches on the edge of the chair and begins to talk slowly, like he's giving out a carefully prepared speech. He puts his hands on his knees and watches his coffee getting cold rather than look at either of us. I look on and understand nothing. I don't even know what language he's speaking.

The man delivers a monologue for a while. All I can tell is that he is at least slightly nervous, Oliver was right, and deeply unhappy. He talks like we're not there but Oliver listens attentively, nods, says something like *I understand* from time to time. Then the man is interrogating Oliver carefully. It seems to me that he's asking the same few questions over and over again. He gets angry, his words sound abusive now, but Oliver stays relaxed, shrinks and makes himself less visible somehow until the guy calms down. Then there's a pause and both men are looking at their untouched cups of coffee. Oliver starts to speak very slowly and carefully, looking the man in the eye, explaining something simply and sincerely as if under oath. When he has finished the man nods his acceptance of what's been said.

Then Oliver says something else and it's like he's thrown a switch. The man starts to talk again and the words pour out of him in a continuous stream. His voice rises and he waves his hands about. He stands, paces, is angry again, sits down eventually. Oliver says some calm words and the guy is shaking with emotion. I'm surprised to see that Oliver has tears in his eyes. Then both men suddenly rise and embrace in a way very strange and foreign to me. The guy has tears running down his face. Oliver holds onto him tightly for a moment. I'm deeply embarrassed and don't know where to look. Then they part company and the man rushes out to his car and comes back with a large bottle of spirits. He gets glasses from the cupboard, two at first and then a third one for me. We swallow down several shots of a drink that tastes of nothing but has a big alcohol kick. Then Oliver asks me to make more coffee. All the tension of the last few days and the last hour has gone. Now there is just sadness and, for me, incomprehension.

I go outside to get away from it all. I wander across to the edge of a concrete platform and look down at the sea. The waves are much smaller than they have been all week and the water is clearer and a deep blue. It's half-way towards being the picture postcard sea that I expected to find here. I sit down. I'm emotionally shaken even though I understood nothing of what was said back there. It slowly dawns on me that I am not the Daniel

Brownlow that I was a few weeks ago before I met Oliver. I'm not so carefree, independent, self-sufficient. I feel more connected to people. What happens to them is important to me. I don't know if I like this or not.

I watch the sea and feel sad for a while. That alcohol was very strong but the buzz fades gradually. I hear footsteps and turn to see the man walking towards me. I stand and he comes over and shakes my hand briefly but warmly, says something I can't understand, turns and goes. I sit back down and carry on watching the waves.

"OK, it's over," Oliver says. "I can go home. I do not, I really do not believe that anything else will keep me from going home now."

But he doesn't look particularly happy to me, just tired and relieved.

"What was that all about then?" I ask.

"The guy lost his daughter. He's a very rich man, got everything he wants except the most important thing – the happiness of the people he loves the most."

"And what's it got to do with you?"

"Nothing at all. Or almost nothing at all."

"But it's to do with drugs?"

"Yeah, it's drugs. His daughter had money and was wild. Started on dope. Went onto other things that might have been alright but weren't. Have you ever tried acid, Daniel?"

"Yeah. Three times. It was great."

"It isn't great for everyone. But this girl took a load of stuff: hash, acid, cocaine, pills. It didn't all come from me. I tried to keep away from handling the heavier stuff. I never smuggled heroin for instance – it kills people."

"It killed her?"

"No, she's not dead, she's in a mental hospital and it wasn't heroin but acid that did it – that's what they think. It made her schizophrenic. It unleashed something that was in her head anyway. But she's the guy's only child and he's lost her. He had to blame someone. And he wanted to hate someone and he knew about me so he wrote those threatening letters. When he saw me in the street he thought he could do something more."

"What did he intend to do?"

"Just make my life a mess if he could. Make problems. Make me scared that I might lose everything that's important to me."

"So what happened when you talked?"

"They say that if you want to hate someone it's better not to get to know them. He met me, got to know me a little. End of story."

"Try to look a bit happier then," I say.

Oliver's shoulders are hunched like he's got a great weight on them. He looks careworn and tired.

"You don't live in the world without impacting on people all the time," he says. "I didn't know that for a long time and it was great. But all that carrying on as if there are no consequences for people around you – I can't do that anymore. There's Lizzie and the children; Caroline, I'm afraid; the people who work for me at home; a man whose daughter I never met who used drugs some of which I sold. And there's you Daniel. Are you still my friend?"

"Yes, of course I am."

"But that thing with the stolen car – that wasn't good."

I laugh. "It was OK. We got away with it."

"I'm not sure about myself anymore," Oliver says. "This whole trip has been my past catching up with me. And I'm not so sure that I'm a particularly good person. It's not something I used to worry about."

"You're alright, Oliver," I say, meaning much more than that.


It's been a dramatic and an emotional day and now I'm in bed, restlessly asleep, dreaming. The dream starts in the way it usually does: there's a man in a wheelchair by the French doors that lead out into the garden. The curtains are drawn back and I can see that it's dark outside. The man leans forward, turns the handles of both doors and pushes them open. He reaches over and picks up a telescope and tripod that lean against the wall by the door, rests them on his shoulder and wheels himself slowly and carefully out, onto the ramp and down into the garden. He goes down the winding path through the apple trees to the open area near the bottom hedge. He sets the telescope down and adjusts the tripod. The eye-piece is at a right-angle to the tube and he looks down in order to look up at the sky. I've seen this many times: a man in a wheelchair setting off down the garden with a telescope on his shoulder, going to look at the stars. *You have to make the best of things*, he always says, *do the things you can do.*

I follow on down after a while as I sometimes do. He will tell me with great excitement about what he can see tonight: more moons around Jupiter, a far galaxy looking brighter than before, the different colours in the stars. But this is a dream and as I come out into the open space beyond the trees he gets up out of the wheelchair and walks towards me. *Hello Daniel*, he says, *I thought you'd come down.* He smiles, walks around casually looking up at the sky and then across at me. He goes back to pick up the telescope and I notice that the chair has gone. He's walking towards me and I feel a great rush of happiness. *You alright, Daniel?* he says and carries on up the path to meet me. He's walking, of course he is. It's the dream I've had plenty of times before, the my-father-walking one. He told me once that he has the same dream.

I can't sleep after that so I get up and go outside. There's no wind and the sea is very quiet. The sky is cloudless, clear, very bright with stars here so far from any man-made light. There's no moon and I guess it has gone already, a new moon following the setting sun down behind the hills. Some constellations stand out very bright: Orion, the Pleiades, the Plough, all at slightly different angles from normal because I've come south. I should tell my father about this. I'd like him to be here now. I promised Caroline that I would write to them both and I haven't. I'll do it tomorrow and I'll tell Dad how bright the stars are here – he'll like that.

Oliver and I lie on the beach that he discovered this morning while I was still asleep. He found a path on the other side of town, one that I never noticed. It has taken us along the top of spoil heaps of crumbly rock and then down across dry scrubland to the sea. The beach is of gently sloping sand down to calm water. There's less rubbish than on the other beach and none of that squelchy seaweed. This morning we swam in the clearest most beautiful water I have ever seen. The sunlight shines right to the bottom even where it's quite deep. There's a rock at one end of the beach that you can dive from and I did it over and over again. If I could do this every day I would give up my mad drunken climbs. And I understand now why someone is building holiday homes in such a strange place.

We lie naked in the sunshine. There's no-one about and I really don't feel like being embarrassed in front of Oliver of all people. Another hour here and then we will go and catch the midday bus and this extraordinary place will be just a memory. My eyes are shut and I'm aware only of the hot sand underneath me, the sunshine on my skin, the gentle sound of waves breaking.

"You were hard to wake up this morning," Oliver says.

"I didn't sleep very well," I say. "I had a bad dream."

"Well, it's been difficult here. It was very uncomfortable. I'm not surprised that it got to you in the end. It certainly got to me."

"It wasn't that."

"What was it then?"

He sounds sympathetic and I tell him. I've never told anyone about my dreams and I didn't think I would. But I do – stars, telescope, wheelchair, my father walking, everything.

"How old were you when the accident happened?" Oliver asks.

"Nine."

"It must have been very hard for everyone. Very, very hard for him to come to terms with."

"He's had lots of hobbies since he stopped work. Astronomy's just one thing."

"He would have to, wouldn't he?"

"I suppose so. He gets very enthusiastic about stuff. The stars and moon. Music – he's got a keyboard synthesiser. He reads a lot."

"I think your father is a very brave man – to stay sane and happy under the circumstances. And your mum too."

Brave. I hadn't thought of it in that way. I thought it was just coping, it's what people do. But I like Oliver saying that. I'm getting very hot so I get up and go to swim again. I float around on my back for a while. Then I turn over and duck-dive to the bottom, opening my eyes on the hazy blue. When I've had enough and I've cooled down I go back and lie on the sand again.

"What was it like for you, Dan, at nine years old?"

"I don't remember. It was a long time ago."

"I would expect you to remember that more than anything."

"No."

"I don't believe you."

Now there's a long, long silence and all the things that have been drifting around in my head come floating to the surface again. The things I've dreamt and the day-dreams I've tried not to have and the memories I've tried to suppress. I get up off the sand and put my shorts and trainers on.

"We'll miss the bus," I say. "We'd better go."

I don't wait for Oliver to follow but I set off hurriedly on my own. I'm walking across the top of the spoil heaps, the ugly town comes into view, and I think of the man who lost his daughter. Then it all comes clear and I understand what I did. I was nine years old, ten, eleven, maybe it was for longer. I couldn't bear to see my father like that, crippled, unable to do the things he used to do. I blanked him out for years, pretended that he wasn't there. I stand looking down on the town and I don't feel I can go on for a moment. I hear Oliver coming up behind and then he's standing by my side.

"Tell me about it if you want," he says.

"I didn't like it when he couldn't walk anymore," I say. "I couldn't cope with it for a while. For some years. It was a terrible thing to do but I was only a child. Now I understand that it must have been awful for him."

"What did you do?" Oliver asks.

"I pretended he wasn't there. I ignored him. That's all."

I'm not a child anymore and before the year's out I won't even be a teenager. I'm not foreign either, I'm English and I'm reserved and I don't do all that over-emotional stuff. I really don't.

"I pretended that he wasn't there," I say again. But I can't keep it all in and Oliver knows it. He gives me one of his big Oliver-style hugs and I start crying like a child. I don't feel embarrassed or anything. I just cry for a while and then I stop.

We miss the bus and Oliver is going to be away from his family for another day. He must be fairly pissed off but he doesn't say a word. There's still some food in the house and the man left behind the bottle of high octane spirit. So we swim again in the afternoon, survive the evening pretty well and stay another night.

The next day we catch the bus at noon and drive off up the hill and away. Sitting next to Oliver I remember what he said about not thinking of himself as a good man. It's not true. I can't find the words to tell him now but I will some time.

"Home soon, Oliver," I say.

"That's right. I'll be home by tomorrow evening if all goes well. I didn't think it would take this long."

## SIXTEEN

These are some of the conversations I have with Oliver on the last leg of his journey home:

1) Sitting side by side on a bus, chugging slowly up a long slope into bare hills.

"It's been difficult for you at home sometimes," Oliver says. "I'm talking about the things you told me yesterday – you know, your dad and how you wouldn't speak to him for years."

"Yes."

"Excuse me saying this but it seems that you've been feeling guilty about it. I don't think you should feel that but that's what it seems like you're saying – that you feel bad about the way you behaved towards him."

"Yeah, I guess that's right."

"So I just wondered if that's why you're travelling like this. Travelling to get away from all those buried bad feelings. Is it like that?"

I have to think for a while. The bus is even slower now, the road zig-zags up towards a gap in the ridge. The higher we go the sparser the vegetation becomes and there are layers of bare rock showing.

"No," I say, finally. "It sounds right but it's not like that. Things have been more OK at home in recent years. I think it's a natural thing for me to want to get away from ordinariness and go out into a more interesting world. I don't think I'm running away from anything. Towards something maybe."

"I believe you. I just wanted to ask," Oliver says. "And I understand because I was pretty much the same when I was your age. That's how I ended up living abroad permanently. I gradually got attached to particular places where I made friends."

"Or girlfriends?" I say.

"Yeah OK, girlfriends. Lovers. One woman in particular. And the other thing is that I'm good at languages so that there were more possibilities than there might have been. But I travelled in the same way that you are now – randomly, allowing things to happen. The good news is that things do happen. Good things mostly."

2) Late at night in a bar in an ugly characterless city, waiting for tomorrow's bus, slightly drunk. Everybody except me is watching English football on the television. I try to remember something Oliver once said and it comes to me eventually.

"The child is father of the man," I say.

"That's right," Oliver says. "But what brought that up?"

"All this parent stuff. You and your kids. Me and my disabled father. The blackmailer guy. It's all knocking around in my head. I'm meant to be having fun and being wild but all this deep serious stuff is getting to me. Hey, there's even something Caroline said. She said she was thirty-five and she wanted a child before it was too late. She told me when we were…"

But I can see Oliver looking seriously shaken by my words and I stop. He takes a big drink of his beer and his face is hidden from me for a moment. Then he's all smiles.

"The child is father of the man," he says.

"Yes. You said it to me and it got stuck in my head. What does it mean?"

"No idea. It's from a poem about seeing a rainbow – I had to learn it at school and that was a very long time ago. I'll think about it. If I work out what it means I'll let you know."

3) The next morning, in a cheap hotel, after breakfast. Oliver has just tried to phone home but couldn't get through. He's restless and his expression goes back and forth from mad smiles to worried to smiles again.

"Would it be easier for you if I don't come all the way back to your place with you but see you later in a few days time?" I say.

"Yes," Oliver says. "Yeah, it would be better. Thanks Dan. I want you to come and see my place and stay for a time too if you want. But it would be easier if you left a day at least for me and Lizzie to sort ourselves out. I've got a lot of explaining to do. I can show you on the map how to get to some very good places nearby.

There's a beach you can sleep on and there's a café nearby where you can get all your food. I think you should stay there. And it's only about twenty miles away from where I live. Give me a couple of days and I'll be very pleased to see you."

4) On a bus again, travelling across a great plain between far distant hills. We are eating up the miles on a straight fast road and Oliver is glowing with happiness. He always wants me to sit by the window as it's all new to me but actually there's not a lot to see here. We are silent for a long time but then Oliver has a question.

"What about your mum?" he says. "Do you get on with her alright? What's she like?"

"My mum. Well, I don't feel very close to her. She's a sort of angel really – the way she looks after my dad and always has done. But I don't think about it, I just take it for granted that that's how it is. But it's true she's a saint or an angel or something. My sister doesn't get on with her though."

"Why's that?"

I don't know if I want to get into this. But I've talked about things with Oliver that I wouldn't discuss with anyone else so I guess it's possible.

"She is wonderful, my mum. She's a very warm-hearted caring person. She has these big brown eyes. And I've got used to some funny stuff now – I just accept it. I accept it but my sister is screwed up about it."

"About what?"

"My mum has a what you might call a boyfriend. She's nearly fifty so I don't know if they do anything but he is a boyfriend of sorts. But the thing is never spoken about and I don't know if my dad knows or not. I think it's best not to bring the subject up. I'm alright with it because she is wonderful but she's also a human being and has to have fun too. And also it's not my business. But my sister has seen them together once or twice and gets upset. I think it's just how it is. My mum is great but she's human too."

5) Later on in the same bus and on the same road but it's the middle of the day now and it's so hot that the draft through the

open window is like a fan-heater – hot air off sun-baked tarmac. It makes my throat dry. Everyone else on the bus has the windows shut and maybe that's better. I'm thinking about infidelity. I've never been in a serious relationship (not yet) but I can't imagine why you would want to sleep with another person when you've already got someone. And I'm thinking about Oliver and Caroline and what might have happened but didn't happen at her place.

"Can I ask you something," I ask Oliver.

"Go ahead."

"Why did Caroline split up from you that time years ago?"

"That is a really big question."

"You don't have to answer. I just don't understand, that's all."

"It was me," Oliver says. "It was before I had kids so you have to imagine a completely different person – not the man sitting next to you now. I've changed a lot in the last few years. I'm more mellow and more responsible too. But back then... It seems such a long time ago now. I was into cheap kicks. Sex and drugs and rock 'n' roll but without the rock 'n' roll. Sometimes dodgy stuff. And I was very dishonest. Caroline was beautiful, sexy, strong but vulnerable too. All the things that would make you love her. She was, and is, the sort of woman who gets passionate can-I-see-you-again letters from old lovers who haven't got her out of their system. I loved Caroline very much. She felt the same for me. But she had to finish it and was brave and did. I was on a gentle downward spiral of getting further away from anything good. It was getting less and less likely that I would ever turn out to be a good person. Then she split up from me and I got worse for a time. I met Lizzie when I was on the way up again, trying to find a way out. She was the right person at the right time. And she got pregnant and everything changed. Suddenly I had lots of purpose and meaning in my life. It really, really changed me. You can't imagine. I know there's still a bad boy inside but honestly the Oliver sitting here beside you is a great improvement. That's it. Life story. I've been very lucky."

Oliver gets his wallet out and looks at the pictures of his children. Then he pulls out a folded piece of paper.

"Do you know what this is?" he asks.

"It could be the note that Lizzie gave me to give to you," I say.

"It is," Oliver says. "Do you want to read it? You might as well. It will give you a clue as to how sensible and strong she is."

"No, it's OK."

He looks surprised but puts it away again.

"Oliver, I have a small confession to make."

He raises his eyebrows. "Go on."

"After Lizzie drove off and left me at the bottom of that hill waiting for you, I was bored."

"And?"

"I read the note."

Oliver looks so surprised. It makes me smile and after a moment he laughs out loud.

"Of course you did, Daniel," he says. "I would have done the same."

Then, and it seems to happen quite suddenly, there are no conversations with Oliver for the time being. He has gone home and I will see him in maybe a week. Now I'm here alone in a very quiet heaven. It's like this: there's a bar/café and a number of cheap rentable rooms around a square; a big flaky-barked pointy-leaved tree in the middle; rough hand-made outdoor furniture spread about on the dusty grass. All the buildings are painted white and behind them are dark pines against the bluest sky I've ever seen. Blue every day. Leading out of the 'village' there's a pot-holed road to town and a rough track to the beach. The track goes across level ground through planted pines with huge ant hills underneath, then through olive groves, then winds down a steep scrub covered slope to the sea. I've hardly ever been outside of England and have only dreamt of, and didn't believe in, a place like this. The sea is very clear, an unnameable stunning blue, warm (though George, the guy who runs everything here, says it's too early in the year and too cold to even think of swimming), out of this world. The beach is.... but I can't describe it, it sounds like a stupid cliché but it really is heaven to me or, I guess, to anyone from England who hasn't been to places like this before. I didn't know the world could be so beautiful. I'm very happy.

And I'm alone. Every morning George cooks me breakfast in the café and tells me there will soon be more people as the season is about to begin. He talks in broken English about the beautiful girls who will arrive in droves maybe today, maybe tomorrow. He's nice, relaxed, smiling all the time, just with a slight leering expression when he talks about young women and expects me to do some manly dirty-talk thing that isn't my style.

Every day after breakfast I walk to the beach carrying just a bottle of water, a few biscuits and a discarded novel I found in my room. The aloneness is very good. I'm me, Daniel, more completely and happily myself than ever before. And I can see, smell, hear and feel the world so much better with no-one else around. I love the smell of the pines on the first part of the walk. I stop from time to time to look at patches of that blue sky framed between the dark branches. If there's a lizard, or a scorpion or something else interesting on the path I stop and look for as long as I want. And I listen to the breeze coming up from the shore. Then the path goes through olive groves. There are some handsome healthy young trees in their youth, my contemporaries I like to think. Others are seriously ancient rugged things with contorted trunks and branches. Sometimes I pick a particular olive tree, walk around it for a while, then climb into the branches and make myself comfortable, listen to the insect noises.

Then there's the steep slope to the beach and, I suppose it's because it's uncultivatable here, there's scrub. At the top of the slope I have to spend some time looking at the sunlight on the water below. In the morning the sun is reflected as tiny momentary sparks of light coming up off the waves. If you half-close your eyes it's a firework display. The flashes are so bright that you begin to see black spots, absences, where each of the flecks of light has just been. If you look for long enough the sea ceases to exist, there's just a haze and a constantly changing pattern of lights and darknesses. When I've looked enough I go on down carefully, sliding on the loose dry dirt, grabbing hold of bushes and learning all their different smells and, of course, which ones to avoid because of thorns. Then the beach; the water, the sun, the hot sand against my skin.

I do this for days, this great simplicity, stillness of mind, getting to know the place intimately. In the morning a big greasy break-fast, tea in the afternoon with bread and honey, in the evening a big greasy supper and lots of cheap beer. George playing old Beatles songs on the jukebox to his only customer. In all this quiet I expect to be turning over in my mind all the events of the last few weeks. I don't. My mind is wonderfully empty (the books I read on the beach leave no impression at all) and I just enjoy the contrast between all the recent movement and the present stillness.

Then it changes. One night I've drunk more beer than usual, the room swirls around, the bed is floating up and down and I fall asleep quickly. I forget to masturbate for what must be the first time ever. Then I dream. It's not a dirty sexy dream, it's more loving and tender. It's simply and very vividly a dream of a kiss. It's great. But I wake up feeling bereft. And there's something else: the person I was kissing, who kissed me back so tenderly... well, I'm surprised. It's like it really happened. It was Caroline.

In the morning I wake up mildly hung-over. I lie in bed for a very long time thinking how nice it would be if there was someone else lying beside me. I know it will happen one day. Eventually I get up and go outside. The sun is warm and the sky is blue and everything is the same. But different. I have breakfast and I walk to the beach but I'm still halfway in my dream and not particularly aware of my surroundings. I sunbathe and swim but I'm preoccu-pied and lonely. I have such a romantic longing that it makes my stomach hurt. The day stretches on for too long. Back at the café in the afternoon I borrow some paper from George and write a letter to Caroline to let her know that I've more or less seen Oliver home now. The letter turns out longer than I intended. Well, she is a sort of friend. But I don't know for sure that Oliver has arrived safely. I rip the letter up and decide that tomorrow I will move on.

In the morning I pay George the money I owe him and he fetches my passport out of his safe. He insists on making me a cheese and tomato sandwich to take with me on the journey. I try to pay for it but he refuses. When I give in he smiles so sweetly. I set off down the pot-holed road to the nearest town thinking about sandwiches and making a mental note to myself: don't refuse kindness – it's rude and it doesn't make anybody happy.

# SEVENTEEN

I walk for some distance as there's no traffic and no possibility of hitching. But it's OK – it's not too hot at this time of day and my rucksack doesn't do that sticking to my back with sweat thing. The road leads through rough agricultural land with olive trees, thin dark conifers, cactus trees with just-turning-orange prickly fruits. I pass a shack-like house covered with vines and creepers with gaudy purple flowers. A little way further on I realise I'm being followed by a puppy. I try to make it go back by waving at it, clapping my hands, growling, stamping my feet. It thinks I want to play. I walk faster and try ignoring it but that doesn't work either. I pick up the skinny little thing and take it back home. It licks my hands and wags its tail. Back at the creeper-covered house I give the puppy to an old woman dressed in black. She smiles very nicely at me, tosses the dog roughly into a pen and I go on.

A little later the first vehicle of the day comes along and it's going my way – maybe it's from the creeper puppy house. The vehicle is a motor scooter ridden by a young man about my age. I turn and stick out my thumb, joking really. But the guy stops and takes me all the way to the town. I'm wearing a rucksack and we're fairly unstable steering round the potholes. Also the scooter has a sick engine and is so underpowered that I have to get off and walk the uphill bits while the rider goes on ahead (only a little faster) and waits for me at the top. People here are poor but generous hearted. I'm beginning to think that sometimes less means more. And I think that my trip is a personal whatever-Oliver-called-it.

I walk through the small town and start to hitch on the other side. A few vehicles pass and then a sports car pulls up. The driver is a middle-aged man, a foreigner here like me, speaks some English. He tells me that he has lived out here for some time. He's friendly and willing to talk but my mind has gone ahead of me to Oliver's place. I'm looking forward to seeing him again and seeing him for the first time at home with his family. The road goes on across flat agricultural land, through some bare hills, and back to the coast. I should be making conversation but now I can't do anything other than look at the scenery. It's very dramatic here. Big hills roll up to the edge of the sea and end in spectacular cliffs or rugged steep slopes. Sometimes the road goes inland to avoid the most difficult stretches of coast but mostly it's near the sea though often high above it. The driver goes slowly round the bends and I look out across the sparkling water.

Now there's a straighter faster stretch of road followed by a tight narrow bend. We slow down alright but somebody else didn't. As the road straightens out we see that the end of the crash barrier is torn off and the roadside bushes are flattened. We stop a little further on and walk back to take a look. There's a gentle slope down from the road towards the sea and a crashed vehicle is there somewhere, hidden among the olive trees. Closer up we can see the skid marks on the road and the path a big vehicle has forced through the vegetation. We walk down a little way until we can see a yellow bus resting on its side. I don't know how I can tell but it's clear to me that this hasn't happened today. There's a stillness about the place, a past-tense feeling. We both want to look closer and carry on down. When we get pretty close the guy sits down on a rock and looks thoughtful.

"I've been away for two weeks," he says. "I didn't hear about this. I hope no-one was killed."

He's concerned and I realise that as he's a sort of local it's possible that someone he knows was on the bus. I'm not a local and I don't feel the same things and it's interesting. I go right up to the bus and look closely. It's on its side but the roof is badly dented so maybe it turned right over. Every one of the windows is smashed to nothing. There's a noise I don't recognise at first and I think it might come from the engine. Then I understand that it's the buzzing of hundreds of flies. I go into the bus through the back window which, sideways on, is like a doorway. Of course there's no-one inside and no luggage or any other sign of the people who were on board when it crashed. It's uncomfortably hot in the bus and there's a bad smell. I go in a little way, walking along one side of the bus and stepping into the holes where the windows were. I disturb a great swarm of flies and I realise that there is something left from the people who were here. On the seats and on the side of the bus are great dark patches of dried blood. I get out quickly and walk all the way back up to the road. The man follows shortly.

"What was in there?" he asks.

"Nothing. Some blood that's all."

"I think it happened a few days ago," he says. "No doubt some people were killed. And others would have survived."

We get back in his car and drive on. A few miles down the road he stops where a track leads off towards the sea.

"This is where I live," he says. "So I must leave you now. Are you OK? You can come and have some coffee if you want."

"It's alright. Thanks very much."

I don't know what to say about what we've seen. I understand that it's disturbing for him but it's very different for me. I'm a long way from home and nobody I know could have been in the accident. I get my bag out of the car and he drives away slowly.

I walk now. The road continues to wind its way along the side of the hills above the sea. I'm shocked by seeing all that blood but it feels like part of the adventure of travelling. I'm still having a good time on the road. I'm uncomfortably hot but that's OK too because the road is dropping gradually towards the sea and I will be able to swim soon. I walk for an hour and arrive at a village on the coast, a nice place, fishing boats in the harbour, small hotels, a few tourists. I find a spot where I can swim from the rocks and cool myself off. Then I make for a cheap café and get something to eat. I don't think it can be far to Oliver's place now. There's no hurry and I like it here. I have a beer. Wander round the harbour and look at the boats. Find a small beach and swim again. Sunbathe and fall asleep for a while. When I wake up a couple of not-so-brilliant thoughts drift into my head. Number one: the *nobody I know could have been on that bus* thought. Number two: the *I can't be far from Oliver's place now* thought. The second thought seriously contradicts the first.

And so now I'm not relaxed any more. Of course it's a slender chance – there are probably several buses a day and there's no reason that Oliver should have been on that particular one. But it's a worry. I walk up from the beach to where the main road passes the town. I'm in a hurry now so it's good that one of the yellow buses comes along. I wave for it to stop, climb on board, fairly successfully pronounce the name of Oliver's place, pay the right fare. The bus is full of mainly locals plus a few tourists, some of them speaking English. The driver pulls away, hooting his horn and waving at people he knows. Suddenly everyone seems more carefree than I am. And now that I'm on the bus my memory plays a nasty little trick on me. I can hear flies buzzing. I smell dried blood.

The bus takes me along a further stretch of the coast road that I was on this morning. It's spectacularly beautiful but it doesn't feel the same. I look out of the window at views of the sea from varying altitudes and perspectives. The colours and the light change all the time. Inside the bus there's the sound of lively conversation in a number of different languages. What I concentrate on is the quickly approaching (I hope) meeting with a happy healthy Oliver and his family at home. After we've gone a few miles I get up and walk to the front of the bus. I say the name of Oliver's place to the driver with a question mark in my voice. He says something that I believe means *sit down and relax and I'll tell you where to get off.* I sit down but I don't relax. I'm trying to remember the names of Oliver's children and recreating the sound of his voice in my head in case that works when the bus stops and the driver speaks to me. He points the way down a road that leads to the sea. I pick up my rucksack and get off. The names Otis and Daisy come to mind. Yes. Otis and Daisy, here I come. And Oliver.... I'm going to be so pleased to see him.

I set off down the well maintained track. I pass through a young plantation of eucalyptus trees and then there's a bend and I can see what I imagine is Oliver's place. The land is flatter here than much of this coast but it slopes a little and I can see the sea. On the water's edge or perhaps a little way out is a big rocky outcrop with some white painted buildings on top. A flag flies from the highest one. I still have perhaps a mile to walk. I don't think I've ever before been in one of these it might be OK but it might be really terrible situations. It's not comfortable so my mind goes blank. I look down at my feet treading the dusty road and only occasionally look up to see the rocks and buildings getting closer. I begin to feel better as I get near. It's such a beautiful spot that really everything must be OK. Oliver's place is like a small rocky island but connected to the land by a narrow causeway that has rocks down one side and a thin beach down the other. The sea here is different again, more green than any other colour, green like a precious stone, impossibly clear.

I walk this last stretch of road. It's like the end of a journey, or at least I'm very aware that it's the end place of Oliver's journey, his happy destination. I'm more conscious of what the place means to him than I am of what it means to me. At the foot of the rock outcrop the road ends and a few very posh cars are parked under the shade of structures covered in vines. A flight of wide steps leads up to the group of buildings that make up the hotel. At the top of the steps, between two palm trees, a woman stands and watches me. When I get closer I recognise her as Oliver's wife, Lizzie. She doesn't recognise me but looks down with an expression that's half manufactured welcoming smile and half curiosity. I suppose I don't look at all like the sort of people that usually come here. I bet none of them come on foot carrying a rucksack. I pause at the top of the steps and she politely waits for me to get my breath back. I can't help but think of the bus crash and I'm not sure what to say.

"Is Oliver here?" I ask.

"No, he isn't," Lizzie says firmly. "I haven't seen him for some time. Are you a friend of his?"

I panic. "No," I say. "Or at least, yes, but it was a long time ago."

Lizzie still doesn't recognise me and I guess there's little reason that she should. She looks at me suspiciously and says nothing.

"It doesn't matter," I say. "I just thought he might be here."

"He isn't."

"OK."

She turns her back on me and walks into the hotel. I stand for a while. I really don't know what to do. A little girl with blonde hair comes to the door and watches me. I wave to her but she doesn't wave back. *Daisy*, I think to myself but I can't say anything. My rucksack feels very heavy and it's sticking to my back with sweat. I can't stay here all day. I turn around and make my way back down the steps.

# EIGHTEEN

What to do? It feels wrong to knock on someone's door and say *I think your husband has been killed in a road accident but I'm not sure.* And it's true that I'm not at all sure – perhaps there's some other explanation for Oliver's non-appearance. I very much hope so. So I can't go back to the hotel and speak to Lizzie yet. I have to at least try to find where Oliver is and what has happened to him.

When I get to the road I stand and hitch. An hour passes and plenty of cars go past without stopping. It occurs to me that I'm not so pick-upable as I was. I'm tired, hot, very worried and probably frowning or scowling or in some way looking unapproachable. I try a sweet smile for the next car but the driver looks away anxiously – I guess it came out as a grimace. I think it would be good to swim in the sea. It will cool me off and maybe make me feel calmer. I walk back down the track towards Oliver's (Lizzie's, I suppose I should call it), hiding my bag in the eucalyptus trees on the way. When I get near to the sea I cut across country and find a place where I can swim from the rocks. I'm in sight of the hotel, I feel I could be watched and I find myself acting almost furtively. But the water is fantastic, implausibly clear, a colour beyond imagination. I duck-dive a few times and swim along the bottom with my eyes open. I can't see much but it's an escape into something other-worldly and it helps. I spend a long time in the sea and I'm shivering when I get out. I put my shorts on and walk back to the road, drying off as I go, gradually getting warm again.

I feel better and must look better because the second car stops. The driver is an amiable man who speaks no English. He's going to the town I hitched from this morning and I decide I should go all the way with him – maybe somebody there will be able to help. We drive past the fishing village, past the scene of the accident, and all along the beautiful coastline. It looks sinister to me now. The light is too bright and everything is foreign. I want to be home. That's a new thought.

Back at the town I find the police station and go in. The man behind the counter doesn't speak English. No-one in the building can speak English. I'm stuck. I walk around the town, too hot again, hungry but not wanting to eat. I find the tiny tourist information office and discover that it opens only for an hour in the evening. But the person who runs it will be certain to speak English so I'll come back later. I find a café and sit in the shade with a cold drink. At the next table two old men argue but only for the fun of it, like they do here. A radio plays weird music. People wander past slowly. The proprietor stays inside and plays pool on his own. I have another drink. My patch of shade moves and I have to move too. There are different types of waiting and different ways of doing nothing. This the worst sort. But I can't think of what else to do.

Eventually it's time for the tourist information office to open. The man turns up late, of course, but he does speak good English.

"I've got a bit of a problem," I say.

He smiles. "No, I don't believe you. Here everything is OK. No problems. Relax. Please take a seat."

I don't sit down. I really can't do it.

"I need to know about the road accident," I say. "You know, where the bus crashed." I point in the direction of the road out of town.

"A terrible thing. Very terrible. Why do you want to know about this?"

He's a nice gentle type of guy, laid back, unshaven, kind brown eyes. I want to tell him all about it but I try to be focused. As I speak I can hear the quavery sound in my voice and I realise exactly how upset I am. He looks at me sympathetically.

"I think a friend of mine might have been on the bus," I say. "I need to find out if he's dead or in hospital or whatever."

The man gets a newspaper from behind the counter and turns over the pages slowly.

"Maybe don't worry so much," he says. He picks up the phone and makes a very short call. He looks at me again. "Please wait a few minutes."

I pace around the tiny office. I look at the posters of gorgeous women in bikinis lying on sun-drenched beaches but I can't get interested – that's how bad things are. Then a little boy comes in with a pile of newspapers. The man smiles broadly, takes the papers, picks the boy up, kisses him on both cheeks, gives him a small coin and sends him on his way. He looks through the papers carefully.

"OK," he says. "A week ago it was. The bus went off the road to miss a car. Some people were OK. Five are very bad in hospital. Two are dead."

"Does it give people's names or descriptions or something?"

He reads again. He looks carefully through another paper. Then another one.

"It says the names of the local people but not the others. It says the dead were two men, foreigners. That's all. I don't think I can help you more. You must try the police."

"They don't speak English."

The guy spreads his arms in a gesture of hopelessness. He smiles an *I-would-help-you-if-I-could* smile. I don't know what to do. I pick my bag up but don't walk towards the door. I just stand there.

"I will phone the police for you," the guy says. He dials and waits a long time but no-one answers. "I am sorry but they have gone home to their wives and childrens," he says. "No crime tonight. There is little crime here."

He starts to turn the pages of the newspapers again and I put my bag down and wait to see if he comes up with more information.

"OK," he says, eventually. "I will write it for you. This is the name of the hospital where some of the people were taken. And look on the map here, this town is where the hospital is. You can go there tomorrow. For now don't worry."

I spend the next day on buses and in bus stations, waiting hours for missed connections. In the afternoon I manage to get on a bus going in the wrong direction. But I have a serious mission and I'm patient in a grim sort of way. In the evening I arrive in the town. It's bigger than I expected, a city really. It's a long way inland, in a valley between the hills, has a river running through it (or at least a space where a river ought to be), is surrounded by quarries and cement works. Huge lorries trundle around and fill the air with obnoxious fumes.

It takes me a long time to find the hospital and when I get there it's nearly dark outside. I can't go in tonight but at least I know where it is. I look for somewhere to stay and end up at a cheap hotel by the side of a busy road. I'm out of place among the small-time business people and travelling salesmen but it will be OK for one night. Tomorrow will be different.

The next morning I shower and try to make myself look tidy. I check out of the hotel but they agree that I can leave my ruck-sack there for a while. I walk to the hospital and go straight to the reception desk.

"Excuse me," I say. "Do you speak English?"

The woman behind the counter shrugs and indicates that she doesn't understand.

"Is there anybody here who speaks English?" I ask.

She looks at me without interest, turns and speaks to a colleague, turns back to me and says something incomprehensible. Other people, patients and visitors, are coming in and she deals with them. Soon I'm invisible to her so I sit down on a plastic chair in the corner. When a whole crowd of people come in I slip past into the main part of the hospital. I wander down a corridor and look through the glass-topped doors into the nearest ward. I can see only two beds and both of them are occupied by women. I decide to go down every corridor looking into wards in this way. There's a chance I will find Oliver.

When I've done the ground floor I go upstairs and carry on doing the same. I get a couple of dirty looks from nurses but I don't hang around and nobody stops me. I do the same thing on the second floor and then start on the third. Here it goes wrong. Some sort of senior nurse with a very stern manner asks me a whole load of questions that I can't possibly understand.

"I'm terribly sorry," I say. "Do you speak English?"

She stops the questions and starts telling me off. I think I'm being asked to leave. But as I make for the stairs the nurse stops a porter and directs him towards me.

"Can I help you?" he says, in English, and with a kind manner. Phew.

I can at last explain to someone that I'm looking for my friend who might have been in a bus accident. At this point I realise that my enquiry is very vague; I can't describe exactly when or where the accident happened. At least this guy understands what I'm saying. But now the nurse seems to be telling him off too.

"Wait downstairs," he says to me. "I will come and help you when I can. Not now but later. Please?"

I return to the foyer again and after a half-hour wait the man turns up. He's not wearing the green uniform that he had on upstairs so I suppose he's finished his shift. But he has recognised my complete helplessness and is willing to try to do something for me. I explain the situation all over again and he listens carefully.

"I will ask," he says, and goes off again. Another half an hour passes and I imagine that he must have walked out of a different door and gone home. But he comes back and sits down next to me.

"It is very strange," he says. "It is like this: there was a man here from the bus accident – a foreigner with a beard like you said. He was here for only one day because he wasn't badly hurt. But he had lost his memory and he had no papers. The police came but they were not interested. And no-one came to find him. What to do? He could not stay here because we need the beds. So he was sent to a hospital for the mind. He might still be there now – I don't know. And he might be the man you are looking for. I can get you a taxi there. OK?"

Yes, I think it might be OK. If the man is Oliver then it explains a few things. I agree to the nice porter guy getting me a taxi though it sounds expensive and I've never in my life used one before. I'm driven three or four miles to a leafy suburb on the edge of town. We pull up at the gates of what looks like a school, a single storey building, brand new it looks to me, surrounded by a small area of grass and trees and enclosed by a chain link fence. The taxi driver speaks to the man at the gate who goes into a tiny wooden office and phones for someone to come. A smartly dressed professional-looking woman (a doctor I guess, though she doesn't wear a white coat) steps out of the main building and comes over to talk to me.

"I understand you are looking for someone," she says, and smiles.

I explain.

"What is his name, this man?"

"Oliver McBride."

"He is not here. I'm sorry."

I can't say anything else for the moment. I feel pretty bad. The woman looks at me sympathetically and there's a funny silence. I think she will walk away and leave me here feeling helpless again.

"But you have an Englishman here?" I blurt out, as if any Englishman will do.

"We have a man who was in an accident. He is probably English. He remembers very little except for his name and we don't know what to do with him. He is not nice, not helpful. I don't think he can be your friend."

"What is he called?"

"He only remembers his first name, Otis. We call him Mr Otis."

"Can I see him?"

The woman thinks, seems reluctant but nods and motions for me to follow her. We go to the main building and walk along a corridor past some wards and into a large recreation room. A group of mildly deranged looking middle-aged men stand around a pool table. Other men sit reading newspapers or staring into space. I follow the doctor to the corner of the room where a man sits at a table with his back to us.

"Mr Otis, please," the doctor says.

He turns and looks round at us.

"Oliver," I say. "I thought you were dead."

"Who the hell are you?" he says, but he doesn't wait for a reply before turning his back on me.

## NINETEEN

The doctor and I are in her office and I explain as simply as I can some of the events of the last few weeks. She listens, nods encouragingly, is thoughtful when I finish. She unlocks a drawer in her desk and brings out a wallet. She takes from it a folded piece of paper and two photographs.

"This was in his pocket," she says. "The note you speak about and these photographs."

"Oliver's children, Otis and Daisy."

"Otis," she says, and smiles. "But he says this belongs to somebody else. And he has been very unhelpful. He has lost his memory – this is not unusual after such an accident. Sometimes it will be just the bad thing, the accident, that the mind doesn't want to know. It protects itself. Sometimes more is forgotten. But it comes back in time. It is not a problem. Just the trauma may stay hidden for a long time and it is best to leave it that way. He may have seen someone dying – been unable to help and so forth. We will leave it for his mind to discover. Now with this man, Oliver – his memory is coming back perhaps. But he won't talk to us. And we want him to go. He swears at other patients and frightens them. It is bad for their health to have him here. He is, I don't know the word – he controls people with his moods, he creates fear. How do you say it in English?"

"Manipulative?" I say.

"Yes, perhaps it is that. I say this thing to you: the man we have here is your Oliver – it must be so. But the description you give of him... that is not the same man. The man here is not a good man."

"Maybe I can help."

"Yes, you can help. That would be good. But I suggest that you are careful. Wait here for one minute please."

The doctor leaves me in her room and goes off to make some arrangements. I can't imagine that things will be too difficult.

Perhaps some time today we can phone Lizzie and get her to come and pick Oliver up. Surely seeing his family will sort him out. I feel good now, relieved that my friend is still alive, pleased to see him, intrigued by all the loss of memory stuff. The doctor comes back into the room.

"Mr Otis, or Mr Oliver, is waiting to see you. I suggest a short talk in which you tell him what you have told me. Any problems and you can walk out – you will see that he is behind the table and you will sit nearest to the door. But there will be no-one else in the room. He asked for that. Are you ready?"

I follow her to a small room containing only two chairs and a table. Oliver looks up as I come in. The doctor goes off, leaving the door ajar. I sit down on the chair opposite Oliver and smile at him. I don't say anything for a moment because he looks so different. He has shaved off his beard leaving only a heavy moustache. And he looks older, the boyishness in his face has gone and he has hardened. I'm not comfortable about the way he looks at me.

"Relax," he says, but in a tone of voice that makes me do the opposite. Then he gets up quite quickly and moves around me to shut the door. He stands behind me for a moment and I can't see what he is doing. Then he sits down again and stares at me intently.

"Relax," he says again, unnecessarily loudly, as if to intimidate me. Then, having achieved what he wanted to, he leans back in his chair and smiles.

"Tell me what you want," he says.

"I'm here to help you get home."

"Home. And where's that?"

I tell him the most important things I know about him – that he has a home and a wife called Lizzie and two children called Otis and Daisy. Surely he must be able to see from my manner that I don't mean him any harm. He softens a little and shrinks into himself. His eyes wander around the room aimlessly and then they settle on me and he looks at me carefully, weighing me up.

"You *seem* alright," he says. "It's just that I don't believe you. It's true that I've lost my memory. But it's coming back a little more all the time and I don't need your help. I'll be clear of here in a few days." His mind drifts off now and he says a few words under his breath, not meaning to let them out, "I've just got to get back."

"Back where?" I ask.

"Wouldn't you like to know?" He gets up quickly and opens the door. "Nurse," he calls out. "Interview over, thank you very much."

He walks off down the corridor. He doesn't say good-bye and he doesn't look back. I carry on sitting at the table in the little room. I'm shocked, saddened, unable to think clearly. After what seems like a long time the doctor comes in and joins me.

"What do you think?" she asks.

"I don't know. Except that you're right about one thing – he isn't the same man. I mean he is, he's Oliver. But then again, he isn't."

"I think there is nothing you can do," she says. "You should forget about him. He is not detained here and he has a little money. I think he will go soon. And if he doesn't we will have to ask him to leave."

"OK" I say. I get up to go. But it's clearly not OK. I can't walk away from this.

"Can I come back to speak to him again tomorrow?" I ask.

"Yes, you can. In the morning. I will expect you."

I spend the rest of the day looking for cheaper pleasanter accommodation but I don't succeed. In the evening I'm in the same soul-less cheap hotel. I don't understand about Oliver. All I can think of is something like Dr Jekyll and Mr Hyde, a split personality, one part of him suppressed or destroyed and the other part, the nasty bit I saw today, taking over. Perhaps the doctor is right and I should forget about him. But I'm not ready to do that yet.

I sleep badly and wake in the middle of the night after a bad dream. I lie on the too soft bed in the hot little room looking at the pattern the street lights make on the ceiling. Every now and then a big lorry rumbles past and shakes the building. Gradually the dream comes back to me. I was dreaming of Oliver as he is now but even worse, hard-faced and angry too. He wasn't angry with me but with someone else, someone not able to stand up to him: Caroline.

I think of Caroline and I wish I could speak to her now. I get up, turn the light on, find the note that she gave me with her address on it. If there was a phone number then maybe I would phone. I could write but it would take too long, would achieve nothing and it would make her worry. No, I can't involve her. I remember that not so long ago I did write a letter to her with the news that Oliver had arrived home safely. It wasn't true but I thought that it was. And I wrote a lot of other stuff too and never posted it. In a way I wish I had.

It's morning, sunny and hot outside, comfortably cool here in the mental hospital. But I'm not that comfortable. I walk into the little room that Oliver and I were in yesterday. He sits at the table waiting for me.

"Hello Oliver."

"Hi. I didn't expect to see you again."

He looks different today, shifty and suspicious but also haggard.

"Did you get a good night's sleep?" I ask.

He looks at me but doesn't answer.

"I didn't," I say. "I had bad dreams."

"Me too."

Then there's a long silence. I've already thought of what I will tell him if he's willing to listen but I wait. Perhaps he has something to say to me. Maybe that's better.

"You're Daniel, aren't you?"

"Yes."

"You were in my fucking dreams."

"I'm sorry. I can't help that. Was I a friend or an enemy?"

"Daniel," he says, as if practising saying my name. "Yeah, you were a friend. So I'm here and you can talk."

"All I know about you is what I've learnt in the last few weeks. Maybe not everything you said was true. You did get me to steal a car at one point."

He laughs. "Yeah, that figures."

"But if I tell you about it, the things we went through together, the things you told me about yourself – well, maybe you'll remember more."

"I don't get it. Why are you trying to help me?"

I look at the hard-faced man sitting opposite me. I put a few words together in my head and I know they're not true, not at this moment, but I must say them anyway.

"I'm your friend."

He stares at me and I recognise something of him from before but not the best part. It's that thing he does when he doesn't want you to see what's on his mind. A particular type of smile which I think of as *the mask*. But he's willing to listen to me and waiting for me to start so I do. I tell him about the red estate car with Lizzie and the kids in it; the car that we stole and how he took it back (he opens his eyes wide at this); how I met up with him at the Jesus freaks' place. Then I mention Caroline.

He gets up out of his seat quickly and starts pacing around the room. He goes round three times and then opens the door and looks out along the corridor. He closes it again and returns to his seat.

"Shut up for a bit," he says. "I'm thinking."

I wait while he runs his hands through his hair a few times, shuts his eyes, opens them again.

"I don't really trust you, Daniel, but I need some help. I've got to get back to Caroline."

"No."

"What do you mean, no? You said you would help me. You said you're my friend. Why won't you help me to get back to her?"

"That's not why I came here. That's not what we've been trying to do. Don't you understand?"

Oliver gets up and walks around the room again. Then he sits back down and looks at me carefully.

"I think you're OK, Daniel. I think you're a good guy and I don't know how you got mixed up with me. You don't look much like a criminal and I can see you're not an addict. So I ask you again – take me to Caroline. I'll make it worth your while."

"No."

"Fucking hell man, I can't believe this. Listen to me, will you? I have to get back to that woman because I'm not a complete shit whatever some people think. I'm not a complete shit and I have to get back to Caroline." He lowers his voice and looks away. "She's carrying my baby."

Oliver said the last words quietly but his fists are clenched and he looks full of suppressed anger. At this point I appreciate what the doctor did in putting my chair closer to the door. I get up and walk out quickly. I take a few steps down the corridor and then I wait. The door opens and Oliver comes out looking apologetic.

"I didn't mean to frighten you," he says.

"I'll come back tomorrow," I say. "I'll come and speak to you again. Perhaps you'll have remembered more by then."

The doctor has come out of her office and is watching us.

"Can I come back tomorrow?" I ask her.

She nods her head. I walk out of the building into the bright sunlight.

The next day, hot outside, cool inside. When I walk into the room he's drumming his fingers on the table.

"Morning Oliver," I say.

"Hello Daniel. Thank you for coming again."

These first words surprise me and I fall silent. I don't know if it's the sound of his voice or my paranoia but something in my head says *be careful.*

"It's OK," I say, and there's more silence. This reminds me of one of those macho card games. It's stupid.

"Yesterday you were telling me a story," Oliver says. "And it got interrupted. I'd be very thankful if you carried on from where you left off."

"Caroline's place?"

"Yes."

So I describe what it was like there: the building of the bridge in the woods, him and Caroline not speaking to each other. Oliver tries to keep a cool detached expression on his face. He tries but he can't do it – he looks puzzled and he frowns as if in some sort of pain. Maybe he's got a bad stomach. When I've finished the Caroline part of the story I stop and wait to hear if he has anything to say.

"I don't understand. You tell me I have someone else now. And children. So what did Caroline think she was doing? What was her game?"

"I think she wanted you back," I say. "She made that a possibility by having you there. But it was up to you. Something like that."

"What's the name of the place again?" Oliver asks, casually. A bit too casually, I think.

"I can't remember."

Oliver gets up and goes to the window. He speaks with his back to me, "They want me to go. I'm not mentally ill and I shouldn't be here. I have to go in a day or two." He rests his head against the glass for a long time. Then he comes and sits down again.

"I want to explain something," he says. "I'm not as bad as I seem."

"OK."

"How I treated you a couple of days ago when you first came in.... I'm sorry about that. I apologise. But I have to do that until I can be sure I can trust someone. In my line of work I have to be like that. I need an edge. But that's not the real me."

"What is your line of work?"

"If you don't know I can't tell you."

Now I know that Oliver is a businessman, a hotel owner. Before that he was a landscape gardener and a drug dealer. *In my line of work* he said and it didn't sound like he was talking about managing a hotel. It didn't sound like he was talking about landscape gardening either. And he was talking about what's happening now – *his* now.

"Oliver, you know it's 1978, don't you?"

"Very funny."

"I can prove it."

I get up and go to the doctor's office. The door is ajar so I knock and go in. She smiles at me.

"How are things going?" she says.

"He's stuck in the past somewhere."

"That's not so strange. It happens in cases like this."

"But the *now* Oliver is a better man. He's not that nasty manipulative guy you see here."

"I already know that. He is more complicated – as people are. If I thought the unpleasant Mr Otis of a few days ago was all there was I would have discharged him. In fact he has to go very soon."

"Have you got a newspaper?" I ask.

"Wait please," she says and leaves the room. She comes back with an English language magazine that has the date written very clearly on the front page.

I take it and show it to Oliver. He sees the date, turns over the pages for a while.

"I understand," he says.

He gets up and paces round the room again. He runs his hands through his hair. Then he's standing to one side and a little behind me so that I can't easily look at him as he speaks.

"Where did you say Caroline lives again?" he says.

I don't want to answer this question. "I think I should go now," I say. "Will you still be here tomorrow?"

"I have nowhere else to go. I'll be here if they haven't thrown me out."

I get up to leave but I think of something and sit down again.

"You do have somewhere to go," I say. "It's a rocky place with some white buildings on the top and it's surrounded by clear green sea. There's a big flight of stone steps to walk up and there are two palm trees. There's a flag flying from a pole on the highest building. A little girl with blonde hair stands in a doorway. When she sees you she comes running over. She calls you Dad maybe, Daddy, I don't know."

Oliver listens but my words have no effect. I guess it was worth a try.

"OK, I'll be back tomorrow," I say.

"Yeah. If I'm here I'll be expecting you."

I wander into town, eat a too expensive crap lunch in a cheap café, buy a bottle of beer, go to a park and get told off for sitting on the grass, walk to the river and lean on the railings of the bridge wondering where all the water's gone, wish it wasn't so hot, long for the sea, feel more and more deeply pissed off. I can't face my hotel room so I find a bench to sit on in a square that has less traffic than other parts of town. *I don't have to do this* I think. *I'm free to not be here.* I remember how at the beginning of this trip I found it easy to make friends and easy to part from them if things didn't work out. And when Oliver got me into trouble for stealing a car I walked away and was happy to never see him again. *I don't have to do this* I think. *I'm free.* But it doesn't feel like that at all. I really don't want Oliver to go to Caroline's – I want him to go home. And for the time being I'm caught up in his stuff. I have a connection with him and I have to sort him out. It feels like his journey is my journey.

Day four in this crap town. Slept badly. Angry about everything this morning. I walk to the mental hospital. The doctor comes to the door and meets me.

"Come to my office for a moment please," she says.

I do as she asks but I'm impatient to see Oliver. I quite fancy having an argument with him today.

"He has gone," the doctor says. "He went early this morning."

"Did he say where he was going?"

"No, he would say nothing. He was very upset but decided."

"Shit."

"But you have done everything you can. Go on with your holiday. Forget this man."

"Maybe you're right. Yes, that's what I want to do. But what about his wife – surely I have to go and tell her what I know. Or do I have to? I don't know."

I look to the doctor for help. She has kind brown eyes, well, everyone here has brown eyes so maybe that's not the point. But she's intelligent, clear thinking, a psychologist or something.

"What shall I do?" I ask.

"I cannot tell you. You know him better than I do. I think he is still stuck in the past but he will have some present things on his mind too. He will be very mixed up for a time and then his memory will come back and everything will be OK."

"I don't think it will be OK," I say.

"But it will be. Why not?"

I think about how Oliver should be with his family – that's what he wanted so much all the time I was with him. But now he's stuck in the past and he wants to go back and see Caroline. Then his memory will return and he'll want to be with Lizzie and the children. Lizzie won't have him back because he stayed with another woman. I can't explain all this to the doctor.

There's nothing more to be said or done here. I thank the doctor for her time and I leave. I go to the hotel and check out. On the way to the bus station I think about what I should do next. I ought to go to Lizzie and tell her everything I know. But for some reason I want to go and see Caroline. I want to see her very much and I don't know why. But if Oliver is there when I arrive.... No, I can't face that. I don't think I could cope with that at all.

# TWENTY

The bus station is like every other one I've been in. I guess they're like this the whole world over. Lots of concrete, oil-stained tarmac and diesel fumes. A huge dirty roof blocking out the sky. People hanging around in a between-places limbo; sitting on their luggage; standing uncomfortably; smoking desperately as if the air isn't polluted enough for them already. I think the man sitting in the corner is a tramp; he looks defeated, purposeless. The other people look pissed off but expectant; this grotty underworld is only temporary for them. But this man looks like a permanent fixture, marooned, trapped, lost, exiled, I don't know, something like that. Perhaps he simply has nowhere to go. I only glance at him for a moment and all this stuff comes into my head. I guess it's my feelings projected out onto my surroundings – I'm always doing that. My eyes come to rest on the man again and he looks up, stares at me, allows himself a weary smile. How strange that I didn't recognise him at first, but then he's never looked quite as low as this. I go over to speak to him.

"Oliver," I say.

"Daniel. Will you help me? I don't know where to go."

I sit down next to him and think for a moment. I get out my map.

"I think anywhere is better than here," I say.

Oliver and I are sitting side by side on a bus. We are going to George's place and we will stay there tonight. I don't know what we will do tomorrow. Meanwhile the same dusty goat-grazed land speeds past us and I've lost interest – I don't even bother to look out of the window. Oliver sits with his hands on his knees, patient like a well behaved school-child. I don't know but it looks like all the manipulative stuff has gone for the time being. I suppose he spent quite a few hours in that bus station and now he's helpless and subdued. I don't expect it will last. Eventually he speaks.

"Daniel, I've been thinking," he says.

"Yes."

"You've been my friend, you say?"

"That's right."

"I've got this note in my wallet, you know about that?"

"Yes, I've told you. That's how I got mixed up with you – Lizzie gave me the note to give to you."

"Mixed up with me, that sounds bad. Do you regret being mixed up with me? I suppose you must do."

"I don't know. The jury is still out on that one."

"I've been thinking."

"You said."

"You've been to see me the last few days in the hospital, right?"

"Yes."

"And you also spent some time with me when we travelled together but I can't remember that. The thing is – what was I like then? Was I different from now? You see I've sunk very low sometimes, done bad things, lost the plot. I know I'm not a good person and I could be better. What I want to know now is..." but his words peter out.

I don't exactly know what his question is but I give him an answer anyway.

"The man I travelled with over the last few weeks was, is maybe, a better man than the guy in the mental hospital. Is that what you want to know?"

"Thank you." Oliver smiles.

"And younger too. Not so hard. Maybe it's to do with having kids or something."

"I have to get my memory back. Bits come to me. Last night I remembered you and I building a bridge – is that true or did I make it up?"

"It's true."

"At Caroline's?"

"Yes, I've told you about it."

"So it's coming back. I hope it doesn't take too long. Did I sleep with Caroline?"

"No, I don't think so. You would hardly speak to her. And you asked me along as a sort of chaperone."

Oliver shakes his head in disbelief. He looks out of the window. I'm waiting for more questions but he goes very quiet and inward looking again. That's OK by me.

We travel all day and Oliver stays shrunken and withdrawn so I have to take responsibility for everything. There's no bus from the nearest town to George's place and we have to walk the last bit in the dark. Before we arrive I know things have changed there – I can hear it. We walk into the square that has George's bar on one side and the white-painted bedroom buildings on the other three and the place is heaving. Lots of people of my age have turned up since I was last here. There's loud music: not the old Beatles songs that George was always playing before but exuberant punk rock – it sounds like the Stranglers. I feel at home. And as I glance around I do the usual thing, I can't help it, I notice the sexiest looking girls and wonder if they've got boyfriends.

But I'm lumbered with Oliver and I wish I wasn't. I turn to him to see what he makes of all this; he looks well out of place with that silly moustache he got left with after shaving off his beard and he looks very confused. It occurs to me that these people with their punky clothes and the music too.... it must be like time travel for him. People are looking us over the way English people always do but they're smiling. My eyes try not to rest on a girl with spiky hair, too much make-up, and too few clothes. Did I say *too few clothes?* I don't think so. I'm smiling at her but I'm aware that I've got this strange man at my side. And here comes George, always ready to greet new customers.

"Daniel," he says. I like it that he has remembered my name. "And Oliver," he says too. "It's been a long time no see. How are you?"

Of course, we're not far from Oliver's home here and he's bound to be known. I look at him to see his reaction and I see him looking confused and helpless. He stares and stares at George like he's seeing a ghost. Eventually George starts speaking to him in the local language. I can't understand a word but it sounds gentle and kind. Oliver answers his questions in the same language and he seems to be speaking very openly – he's not the suspicious shifty man of the last few days. After a bit George takes him off inside and I feel a huge buzz of relief. I'm free.

I walk over to the nearest table and plonk myself down on a chair. Someone pushes a bottle of wine towards me and grins. I see that some people are getting up to dance. I will do the same later when I'm pissed. It's good here. I'm in the right place for a change.

I wake up in the morning on the beach. There are a few of us who came down last night with sleeping bags and blankets, went for a swim under the stars, fell asleep together on the sand. I raise my head and look at the others. The guy nearest me is half-covered by a blanket, has tattoos and a squashed mohican, is snoring softly. There are a couple of blonde-haired girls cocooned in sleeping bags. The rest are a mess, a pile of sleeping bodies of indefinite gender. We all lie in the shade of the cliffs and not far from the sea. The little waves make a good sound, the light is clear on the water, the air soft and warm. For a long time I'm motionless and happy. I've got a delicate head and stomach, it's true, but my mind has been purged and renewed by last night's alcoholic craziness. I let images of that craziness drift around in my head. We danced, pogoing mainly, to the Clash and the Sex Pistols. When George couldn't cope anymore he put on weird local music and we played hide-and-seek like big kids. I hid with and kissed the spiky-haired girl whose name I can now almost remember but not quite. I think we cuddled a bit too but that was it. On the way to the sea everyone got into the olive trees and we made up names for them and talked nonsense. I think there was some sliding and tumbling down the slope to the beach. We got into the water and floated around naked on our backs, looking up at the milky way. Yes, it was a good night out.

I get restless after a while and I get up and go for a swim. Now I'm really thirsty and I scramble up the slope and go back to George's. Tea and toast. Yoghurt and honey. A shower. It gradually dawns on me that I asked for a bed last night but they were all taken and George said sleep on the beach and eat here. I sit in the square and nod and sometimes grin at people as they emerge from their rooms or come up the path from the beach. More tea. Bread and jam. I start to talk to people who remember more about last night than I do. I get told about some of the things that I did. Never mind.

Later on I go to the beach again and say hi to the people who are just waking up. Swim again. Back to George's. Beer at lunch time and a siesta under the trees. When the sun sets I'm eating omelette and tomato salad and talking to one of the blonde-haired girls. I keep asking her about herself and she's flattered and smiles a lot. When she asks me questions I divert the conversation back to her and her friends and in the back of my mind I know why I'm doing it. Finally she asks me about the man I was with when I arrived – *who is he? Why was I with him?* I've tried, without really trying, to forget about Oliver all day but I can't get away with it any longer. I wonder where he's got to. I go into the bar and ask George. I want him to say everything is alright, Oliver's gone home. Instead he leads me through the back of the bar into his kitchen and out into a little private garden that I didn't know existed. Oliver sits in a comfortable chair in the shade of grape-vines, a pile of old newspapers by his side. He's staring into space but smiles when he sees me. And it's a new smile because he's shaved off his moustache.

"Daniel. I thought you'd forgotten about me."

"I tried to."

Oliver waves his hand over the newspapers, "I'm catching up. It's interesting – like travelling into the future but of course I know it's only the present."

"Are you getting your memory back?"

"Bits. Yeah, it's happening."

We look each other over for a while. I try to get used to how different he looks clean shaven. He guesses what's on my mind.

"I usually shave off my beard in the summer," he says. "I've been doing it for years."

"You remember that?"

"No. But George told me, so I did it."

"Are you remembering Lizzie and the kids at all now?"

"A bit."

"And what about Caroline? You wanted to go back to her – have you changed your mind?"

"I think so. I think I have to. You know George keeps telling me what a great guy I am. How good I am with my kids and so on. He tells me that stuff and then he goes off and a little bit more comes back. I remember Otis and Daisy more and more and I want to be with them. And I want to be that person George describes. Someone worthwhile. A good man called Oliver."

"What are we going to do now?" I ask, and I'm surprised that I used the word *we* but I can't take it back.

"I've talked to George and he has an idea but he can't do much himself...."

"What do you want me to do?"

"Will you go to Lizzie and tell her everything? Prepare the way for me. Be completely honest I think. Yeah, just be honest, tell her about us staying at Caroline's. See how it goes. Explain about my loss of memory. See if she will have me back. Can you do that for me Dan?"

"Tomorrow. I'll do it tomorrow."

I'm walking down the track to Lizzie and Oliver's again. Last time I did this I didn't know whether Oliver was alive or dead so this time is better. I pass through the eucalyptus plantation and some olive groves and then I'm at the beginning of the causeway that leads out to the rock with the white hotel buildings on it. The sea is clear and green, like it was before but darker because the sky is overcast. Even on a dull day this is a beautiful place and it seems right for the ending of an epic journey, an epic story. That's how it feels to me now. But it's not the ending because that only happens when Oliver comes this way. It might not happen. Both Oliver and George made it clear that Oliver can only go home if that's what Lizzie wants. George is in touch with local gossip and he's not so sure. It seems that all these weeks of Oliver wanting to be home and travelling towards home aren't enough. Home isn't just a place on the map, it's a state of mind. More than that it's two people's states of mind – Oliver *and* Lizzie in this case.

I walk across the causeway, past the parked cars (one of them the red estate car – that's good), up the flight of steps, between the big palm trees, and in through the open front door of the hotel. A young man greets me and I tell him that I want to speak to Lizzie. He goes off to fetch her and my mind goes blank. A minute or two passes and she comes in and gives me a cool smile.

"How can I help you?" she says.

"It's about Oliver."

"He's not here. I told you before. I'm sorry but I don't know where he is."

"I do."

Lizzie looks at me carefully, trying to work out what sort of person I am. I guess she sees someone who looks awkward and nervous – that's how I feel.

"You'd better come through," she says, and opens a door into an office.

"You are...?"

"Daniel. I've been travelling with Oliver for the past few weeks."

"Daniel, please take a seat."

She takes a deep breath and sits down opposite me. Her professional smile has gone and she looks worn out. I guess she's been pretty busy running this place on her own. She fidgets in her seat, takes another deep breath and I realise she's worn out in another way, *a where is Oliver? what's going to happen to all of us?* way.

"So where is he?" she asks.

"Do you know a man called George, a little way down the coast from here?"

"Of course. Everyone knows George."

"Oliver is at his place."

"Why?"

And I have quite a story to tell. It starts with a bus crash and loss of memory and then goes back to the beginning and Lizzie giving me the note to give to Oliver.

"I thought I recognised you," she says. "But I couldn't think how or where."

Then there's more story and I know that I have to explain the

Caroline bit but I leave it to last. I remember the word Caroline used to describe me.

"I was a sort of chaperone," I say. "I can't exactly explain but that's why I was there. That's what Caroline called me – *the chaperone.*"

Lizzie stands up suddenly.

"Tea or coffee, Daniel?" she asks. "Which would you like?"

"Coffee please, that would be nice."

Lizzie is out of the door before I finish answering and I have to guess that it's because she's pretty upset. It takes a while for her to come back and she brings tea by mistake. She doesn't have a cup for herself and she sits down awkwardly, trying to look calm but not completely succeeding.

"Oliver would hardly speak to Caroline," I say. "One time she said something nice about him being there and he said *I'm only here because I want to be somewhere else.* All the time he was just trying to get back here."

"That's what he told you to say, I suppose."

"He can't remember much. He told me to tell you the truth."

I try sipping the tea but there's no milk in it and it's very hot. Lizzie looks pissed off and angry. Then she looks like she might start crying.

"Thank God he wasn't killed in that bus," she says.

Now I don't know what else to say and there's a long silence before she speaks again.

"I'm sorry you had to get mixed up in all of this."

"It's OK."

More silence.

"Thank you for coming here, Daniel. And thank you for looking after Oliver. I can't think straight at the moment. Can you tell him that I'll let him know? Would you go back to George's and say I'll be in touch? I'm sorry to have to ask this of you."

"It's OK," I say, but it's not OK – I want this to be sorted. I put my tea down.

"I'd better be going."

"Yes, thank you."

Lizzie turns her head away from me and looks out of the window.

I walk back across the causeway and along the track towards the main road. I'm having *his journey is my journey* thoughts, vague thoughts that I don't quite understand. Then I have some *home is not a place, it's a state of mind* thoughts and I don't completely understand that stuff either. I want to get back to my new friends at George's place but I know that I won't get right into the holiday mood until Oliver is sorted. I think about Lizzie but no way can I guess how it is for her, what's going on in her mind, what she's going to do. But I feel that Oliver won't be completely reunited with his family again. He'll be in some sort of limbo, living nearby and seeing the kids occasionally – I know that sort of set up sometimes happens. Or perhaps this part of his life is over. He'll start again somewhere else. Maybe with someone else.

It feels now like I've spent a long time helping this man get back to something that doesn't exist anymore. I remember the time Oliver and I were in the car driving down a valley towards a rainbow that moved away from us all the time. The faster I drove, the faster the thing raced off ahead. It was unobtainable but I guess it was fun trying. Has this whole trip been like that? A deep unsettling thought drifts into my mind – is this how my life is going to be, chasing things that I can't catch up with? Fun trying but nothing more than that. Perhaps it doesn't matter, I don't know. But I feel the ground under my feet isn't as solid as it might be. I'm not that happy right now.

I'm walking very slowly but I've nearly reached the main road. I'll have to try to smile if I want to get a lift and it's going to be quite an effort. I can hear a car coming down the track behind me but I don't turn round to look at it. It slows as it gets closer and then it pulls up beside me. It's the red estate car and Lizzie is in the driving seat. She reaches across and pushes the passenger door open.

"Do you want a lift?" she asks.

"Yes, OK."

I get in and she looks across at me with a kind expression on her face. I guess that I'm more unhappy than I realised and it shows.

"Cheer up," she says. "I think things are going to be alright. I'm going to pick up Oliver and bring him back home."

# TWENTY-ONE

Lizzie and I drive to George's. We don't say much on the way. It's a wonderful road, great views of the sea, sometimes from very high up. I think I would like to come along here on my own one day, stopping the car a million times to look at the view, getting out and walking a little way from time to time. And there are a few people doing that, tourists parked in lay-bys, cameras at the ready. We pass a couple riding touring bikes, pedalling gently along one of the flatter stretches of road high above the sea, going very slowly and taking it all in – yeah, that would be a nice way to do it, maybe one day.

But this isn't just a stretch of road – for me it's marked by memory. I've been along here three times before and each time my journey had a different purpose and emotional charge. The first time I was going to see Oliver at home with his family (that's what I thought). It felt good until I found out about the bus crash. Then I was on my way back but with no idea where I was going – I just had to find out somehow if Oliver was dead or alive. Then back to Lizzie's again this morning with the responsibility of telling Oliver's story and seeing if she still wants anything to do with him. So as we go along the road now I see little landmarks along the way that bring back the feelings that were on my mind before. Oliver was like this when we were travelling together, the landscape full of ghosts for him. But for me it was fresh and new. That's what I want soon – to be in a new place, somewhere that isn't cluttered with emotional memories.

But first I have to see what will happen between Oliver and Lizzie. Oliver has been spending time in the past and he's been emotionally attached to the wrong woman. So how will he behave when he sees Lizzie again? I can't guess. But I don't have time to think any more about this nonsense because Lizzie drives fast and we soon pull up in the square outside George's bar.

We get out and George comes rushing over to speak to Lizzie, his face full of warmth and concern. Then he takes her into the bar and through the door at the back to where, I guess, Oliver is still sitting in the shade reading old newspapers. Then he returns, gets a couple of beers out of the fridge and gives them both to me.

"Free of charge. For you, Daniel," he says. "You are a good man."

Nobody's ever said that to me before.

Later in the day I've drunk both bottles of beer and lie asleep under the pointy-leaved flaky-barked tree in the square. I'm woken up by someone nudging me on the shoulder. It's Oliver and he's smiling a youthful smile that I don't think I've seen before. I have to get up because he wants to give me a hug.

"I can't tell you how much...." he says, and it's true, he can't tell me, he just shrugs and smiles some more. "But we'll see you soon. Come and visit when you're ready. You'll promise to come soon?"

"I promise."

Lizzie comes over and shakes my hand. "Thank you for everything. We'll look forward to seeing you," she says.

I watch as they say good-bye to George, get in the car, and drive off. Then I lie down under the tree and fall asleep again. When I wake up I wonder which of all the strange and wonderful things that come into my head are true.

I sleep on the beach and eat at George's for a week. I get pissed a few times and I try to get off with the girl with spiky hair. She's very sexy but my heart's not in it and I guess it shows and nothing much happens. The people here are a laugh and George is brilliant and very tolerant. I'm half-way popular but part of me is elsewhere and I feel like an outsider. It's always like that for me. Here I am with people who are on the fringe of things, like I am, but I'm further out again – on the fringe of the fringe. All the same I have a good time. I swim and sunbathe everyday and I get very brown except for my shoulders that start peeling spectacularly. My hair goes blonder like it was when I was a kid. It's a good time. Easy. Carefree. The days pass by and I put Oliver out of my mind for a while. Then one night I'm in the bar and telling the story to some people and I feel the story's not over for me until I see it with my own eyes – Oliver at home. I set off the next morning.

I'm half-way across the causeway when I see the red estate car coming towards me. Oliver stops in front of me and gets out, gives me a hug, puts my rucksack in the back. We get in the car and he reverses back across to the rocky almost-island, his home. He carries my rucksack up the flight of steps like I'm an honoured guest. At the top he shouts for Lizzie and she comes out. They stand together in front of me, smiling broadly and looking younger than they did before. I think they want me to see this – they stand there like they're posing for a photograph.

Then there's the sound of a child screaming inside the hotel and Oliver rushes off, still smiling. He comes back out again carrying a tearful little girl. She clings to him with her arms around his neck and he kisses the top of her head. When she has quietened down he introduces us.

"Daisy, this is Daniel, my friend. He helped me to get home. Dan – meet Daisy, the best girl in the world."

Then the boy, Otis, comes up and takes his mother's hand.

"I didn't do anything," he says. "Daisy made me do it."

He doesn't understand why we start laughing and he glares at us. Then Oliver bends at the knees and manages to scoop his son up with his free arm. The children start to poke each other but Oliver carries on smiling. "See what they're like?" he says, pretending to be critical but proud and happy and wanting me to know.

"What about a treat for everyone? Ice-creams all round?"

End of story. Or at least end of Oliver's story. I stay there for a few days – that's all. Oliver and Lizzie are very busy with their posh guests, problematical staff, and, of course, the children. The children are impossible sometimes. They argue when there's nothing to argue about, fight for no reason, burst into tears just because they're tired. But they are fun too. And they're excited about the small things in life, going for a ride in the car, new guests arriving, the postman bringing letters, everything.

I watch Otis sometimes. Oliver has brought him a new brightly-coloured plastic football and he carries it around in the netting bag it arrived in and bounces it against his knees as he walks. He also bounces it on the floor and on walls, swings it around his head, uses it to sit on. He never takes it out of the bag. I haven't seen him kick it and don't think I ever will. But this football is so important to him, special and magical like a fetish. It's part of his identity at the moment. And Daisy is the same with her teddy, fixated on it, projecting funny stuff out of her head onto the toy. Little things seem fantastical to Oliver's kids. Their small world is pure magic.

When Daisy smiles she smiles not just with her eyes but with her whole self, outside and inside too – that's how it seems to me. It's good to be around the kids when they're like that. If it feels good to me then how must it feel to Oliver and Lizzie who love them to bits? I know the answer to that – I can see it in their faces. But I can see that they get pretty fed up sometimes too. There are times when the kids are impossibly impossible. I can't believe how patient Oliver is. The guy was a drug-dealing minor gangster sort a couple of weeks ago and now he's on his hands and knees picking up pieces of jigsaw puzzle or carefully wiping sticky hands and faces. OK so it's a bit cringe-making at times but really it's good and as there are no young children in my family it's something new to me. I liked it when Oliver asked me to read Daisy a story after she'd fallen over and was crying. She sat on my lap and fell sound asleep. I didn't move for ages because I was scared of waking her up.

On Saturday afternoon Oliver and I pack a picnic and take the kids to a beach a little way from the hotel. It's sunny and hot, as every day is now, but there's a breeze off the sea and even one or two white clouds in the sky. The beach is tiny, about twenty yards long, and has smooth rocks rising up into pine woods at each end. We are the only people there. Daisy plays in the sand and Otis climbs the rocks. Both of them are completely absorbed in the place and in the things they're doing. Otis talks to himself as he climbs. I can see that he's on a big adventure.

Oliver and I are the grown-ups. We have inflated the two airbeds we brought with us and set them floating close to the rocks so we can practise running and jumping onto them, trying to land standing up. We work out more tricks: somersaulting off the big rock and landing lying on our backs on the air-beds; simultaneous dives onto air-beds to see who can scoot the furthest across the water; a handstand on the edge of a rock followed by a controlled plunge into the sea (Oliver can't do this one).

When we stop for our picnic Otis looks at me closely.

"Are you a man like my dad or just a very big boy?" he asks.

"I'm a big boy," I say. "And Oliver is too, he just hides it better."

A little later Otis and Daisy have abandoned their egg sandwiches and are sitting on the air-beds pretending something. They are on the beach but they look like they're crossing vast oceans in their heads. Oliver and I sit on the rocks watching them.

"Are you completely yourself now?" I ask him. "Have you got all your memory back?"

"No," he says, but he smiles. "No, not everything but it's coming along. I'm rediscovering myself – who I was, who I can be, what my relationships are. It's a journey of discovery and it's good."

"A journey, eh?"

"Yes. Why not?"

Otis is swaying from side to side on his air-bed boat and making sea noises. I think a storm has blown up. He rides out the waves and looks bravely ahead for sight of land.

"See how he's a hero to himself?" Oliver says. "That's how he feels inside."

"I was like that as a kid," I say.

"You know those old stories of heroic adventures and journeys?" Oliver says.

"Maybe."

"Well I have a theory. I think the story-tellers were just trying to get back those childhood feelings. You know all that mythical stuff about golden ages long past? It's just recapturing childhood. That's all."

This reminds me of something Oliver once said but never explained.

"The child is father of the man," I say. "You were going to tell me what it means, I don't suppose you remember that."

"I do as it happens. I remember quite a lot of our adventures together."

"Well?"

"I think it's something to do with childhood coming first. We start off with all that excitement and imagination. And a sense of wonder about the world. That comes first in us. And we shouldn't ever lose it. You, for instance, Daniel – you're still in touch with your inner child."

At this point in the conversation I've decided to stand on my head. I'm listening to everything Oliver says but I'm also looking at the upside down sea and sky.

"You may be right," I say. "And you're not doing so bad yourself."

Oliver has his hands out in front of him and he tries to do a head-stand too. He tips over onto his back a couple of times but he finally manages it. We stay like that for as long as we can. An upside down boat drifts into view, Oliver recognises the fishermen and tries to wave. He falls sideways onto the sand and then rolls onto his back and laughs. Daisy comes over and sits on his stomach.

"Daddy," she says.

"What is it, sweetheart?"

She sings a little song, like a nursery rhyme but with rather repetitive lyrics.

"Daddy, daddy, daddy, daddy, daddy, daddy, daddy."

"Yes, yes, yes, yes, yes, yes, yes." Oliver says.

## TWENTY-TWO

Oliver got the impression that I was going straight home after I left his place. I didn't deliberately mislead him.

I get off the bus in the village and walk a little way down a country road that runs along a ridge. On one side of me are corn fields, the crop ripening already and changing in colour from pale green to dirty yellow in patches running down the slope. On the other side there are pastures. There were cattle grazing here before but now they've gone and the grass is a stubbly aftermath – I think it's been recently cut for hay. There's a constant buzz and movement of insects in the heat: butterflies mainly, but also bees and grasshoppers and things I don't know the names of. It's uncomfortably hot until I turn down a track that takes me into the shade of the woods. But I'm soon out in the open again with the sun on my head and sweat building up where my rucksack rests against my back.

Caroline's house is at the edge of the next strip of woodland. I thought it was hidden, or at least obscured, by trees but I can see it already from something like a quarter of a mile away. I'm nervous and excited – how strange. But I had to come here, I really did. I promised to let her know that Oliver got home safely and I couldn't explain everything in a letter. As I get closer the dog starts barking. I can see Caroline leaning on the gate waiting for her unexpected visitor. She waves when she recognises me and I wave back. Then there's that awkward bit when you're walking towards someone but you're not close enough to speak yet. And I arrive, drop my bag, make an unnecessarily big fuss of the dog.

"Tea?" Caroline says. She doesn't seem at all surprised to see me.

"Yes, please. That would be nice."

She smiles and waits for me to say more.

"He got home. Oliver got home. I came to tell you. That's why I'm here. There's lots to explain."

She nods and doesn't speak. We just stand and look each other

over appreciatively for a while. I think she looks different. There's
a stillness about her as if she's at peace with herself. And she radi-
ates some sort of sensual contentment. I start to think how
beautiful Caroline is and I wonder if I'm blushing. I'm relieved
when she turns her back on me and goes inside. I sit down on a
wooden bench under the vines at the side of the house and try to
sort out my thoughts. Then Caroline comes out again with a tray
of tea things and sits down opposite me.

"Everything's alright with that man, then?" she says. "He got
home safely?"

"Yes. I've come straight from there to here. We had some problems and he only got back a week ago. He was involved in a road
accident and there was a man sort of blackmailing him and he lost
his memory. But not in that order. It's going to be hard to explain."

"You've been with Oliver all this time? I don't understand."

"Well, it's not been a laugh a minute. I mean, it's been good,
I'm fond of Oliver, he's a great guy and everything. I suppose I've
been a bit responsible for him and that was hard work. Yeah, very
difficult actually."

"So you haven't had a holiday as you intended?"

"A holiday? No. An adventure maybe. A struggle sometimes.
Definitely not a holiday, not as good as that. Except that it was
better than a holiday in a way. Yeah, better."

Caroline looks increasingly puzzled and I have a lot of explaining to do. The only way is to tell her everything from when Oliver
and I left her place right up to the present moment. It takes some
time. Of course I leave out some of the Oliver-Lizzie-and-the-
kids part of the story because I don't want to upset her. But she
seems very calm and asks questions if I don't make sense. When
I've finished she goes indoors and makes more tea.

When she comes back she looks at me very seriously.

"Thank you," she says. "It was very good of you to do so
much for Oliver, for all of us. You're a very special person."

I think I'm going to blush again and that will be twice in one
day. I thought I'd stopped doing it years ago.

"It must have been very hard for you when he lost his
memory. You were good to stay with him."

"I don't know, I suppose so."

Caroline gives me a smile full of warmth and sympathy. I pour out the tea and help myself to biscuits.

"Perhaps I should explain about how it was when you were here," she says. "I'd like you to understand. I'm not such a terrible person as you think."

"I don't think you're terrible at all. I think, well, you know..."

"But you must have thought I was trying to break up Oliver's marriage by trying to keep him here?"

"I don't know."

"Well I was. And I wasn't. I just wanted a chance for us again. If his marriage was no good and he still cared for me then something could happen. I loved Oliver very much, you understand that don't you?"

"Yes."

"So it wasn't me being a bad evil woman like people might think. I just wanted a chance, a possibility. And I helped him get home in the end."

"I think you're wonderful," I say. I don't mean to say it but it just comes out – Caroline is saying bad things about herself and they're not true and I have to say something. And what happens now is that she gives me the most beautiful smile I have ever seen.

"Will you stay?" she says. "Stay tonight and you can have the room you had before. And perhaps in the morning you can help me with some things that are too heavy for me to lift. Do you mind if I ask your help with a few things, Daniel? While you're here?"

"Anything you want," I say. I think it comes out sounding rather serious.

Caroline laughs at me and gets up as if to go indoors again. But she stops beside me for a moment and puts her hand on my shoulder.

"You're very sweet," she says. "No, that sounds patronising. I mean you're..." and now it's her turn to run out of words. She bends, kisses me on the cheek and goes quickly into the house.

In the evening Caroline cooks supper for the two of us. I offer to help but she says I'll be in the way. I sit down in the living room but on a chair that allows me to see her through the open kitchen door. From time to time she calls out the names of various ingredients and asks me if I like them. We had pesto last time I was here but I've never heard of the others. The list goes on and on and I realise that she's teasing me. I can't help being young and English and from an un-posh background. But I don't mind and I'm sure it will taste fantastic. As I watch Caroline moving around the kitchen I think again that she looks different from before. She smiles to herself as if she has some good secret she doesn't want to share. She glows with inner contentment. Her movements are slower and I think she's not so slender and light on her feet as she was. But Caroline can only look beautiful and sexy. That can't change. But my thoughts are going in the wrong direction so I move to another chair and look through some of her expensive art books.

We don't talk much during the meal. Afterwards I wash up and Caroline plays the piano. When I've finished she offers me more wine but won't have any herself. It's a very warm evening but she shuts the windows to keep out mosquitoes. It's very quiet and Caroline slumps back into her chair and loses herself in a pleasant day-dream.

"You seem different," I say.

"What do you mean?" she asks, looking surprised.

"You look different from how you were when I was here before."

"You do," she interrupts me. "You're tanned and your hair is longer and nearly blond from the sun."

Caroline now has a teasing wicked smile on her face. "You must have met some beautiful young women on your travels," she says.

"I've been busy with Oliver."

"Of course." And me saying his name sends her off into her own thoughts for a moment. Then she's doing the wicked smile thing again. "Did you have girlfriends at home?" she asks.

"A couple of times. Nothing serious. I haven't met the right person."

"Does one ever?"

I'm not sure what she means by this so I can't answer.

"Did you go to bed with these girls?" Caroline asks very straight-forwardly. There's no wicked smile now but I don't know if she's just suppressing it. It's a cheeky question but it's OK. Right now it's like Caroline is my older sister.

"I'm not a virgin," I say. "But I've never spent the night with someone and woken up with them in the morning. Sometimes I think that would be good. Something different again."

"Yes."

She begins to look sad and thoughtful and I wonder if she's thinking of Oliver. She withdraws into her thoughts and I can't guess at what's going on in her head. There are some questions I would like to ask her but I don't feel I can. I suppose that it's because she's older than me that it's alright for her to ask me personal questions but not the other way round. Maybe that's OK.

When I look at her again she's nearly asleep.

"I ought to go to bed now," I say. "I'm keeping you up."

She stirs. "You know that tomorrow is Sunday, don't you Daniel? There will be very little public transport. You had better stay tomorrow night too."

"Is that alright?"

She nods and smiles. "I like you being here."

I say good night and go up to my room. I've had plenty of red wine to drink and I feel good. I'm going to sleep well. I wonder if I'll dream of Caroline.

When I wake up in the morning Caroline is already up and about. I look out of the window and I can see her at the edge of her herbaceous border, a big woven basket in one hand and a pair of secateurs in the other. She's cutting flowers to bring indoors, I guess. She doesn't notice me watching as she's completely absorbed in her task in a way that reminds me of a child playing. I think about when I was here before and Caroline was critical of herself for being too business-like and not creative. It's not true – her creativity comes out in her garden and I think she's put a lot of work into it over the years. Or maybe it's something between work and play. Something that involves self expression. I don't want to disturb her so I just pull my shorts on and go downstairs to see if I can find some coffee.

I sort myself out some breakfast and then I go outside to see what she's doing now. The dog bounces up to me when I open the door to the garden. Caroline looks up and I'm amazed to see that she's still cutting flowers.

"Good morning, Daniel. I've been thinking about you."

"Hi."

"I've cut more flowers than I can fit into the basket. Will you hold the rest for me as I go?"

She hands me a few chrysanthemums and carries on carefully selecting and cutting blooms and passing them to me. This goes on for a while. I follow her about the garden and she remains absorbed in her task so we don't talk. My feet are bare, I'm only wearing shorts and as the bunch of flowers gets bigger and they begin to pile up against my chest I feel more aware of being nearly naked. Each time Caroline hands me more flowers I can see a little light in her eyes and hers lips are tightened together as if she's trying not to smile. Eventually she stops what she's doing and starts to laugh.

"You look lovely," she says. "But that must be enough now. I think I was getting carried away. Come on, we'll take them all into the shade before they start to wilt."

Caroline and I take the flowers up to the wooden table under the vines and she sorts them into small bunches and wraps them in damp newspaper.

"I take some bunches to the local hospital once a week," she says. "Quite a few this week. It brightens the place up. Do you want to come with me?"

"Can I stay here?"

She doesn't answer my question so I guess that's a yes. She's so self-contained now, comfortable with talking or not talking. I think she must feel at ease in my company. She's still smiling to herself but I'm not going to know why.

In the afternoon I offer to do some chores for Caroline – she'd said something about moving things that were too heavy for her. She has a large pile of logs stored in an outhouse and asks me to split them with an axe and stack them at the side of the house to season. Winter time and log fires seem so far away that the task feels a bit meaningless but Caroline is my friend and I want to do something for her so it's OK. The things that are too heavy for her to move turn out to be a number of large stones that were set out along the edge of the path to the woods and which, it's true, don't look very good there. I load them into the wheelbarrow and take them off into the woods out of the way. Caroline watches and I'm surprised that she doesn't help. It's like she doesn't want to get her hands dirty. She is my friend but her manner is patronising sometimes and now I feel like I'm playing a servile role for her. And I remember that when I was here before she helped me cutting down some overhanging branches off the trees next to the garden; we worked together and it was fun. So what's different now? I don't understand. I think she reads my mind.

"I'm sorry to make you do all this for me," she says.

"I don't mind. It's OK."

"I would do it myself in normal circumstances but I have to be careful at the moment."

I still don't understand and I want to ask more but Caroline turns quickly, moves away and starts fiddling with some plants. When I've moved the stones I feel I'm not so bothered about Caroline's company right now and I set off down the path through the woods, across the bridge that Oliver and I built, and out to the viewpoint where the ruined building stands. I sit overlooking the valley and think of home because tomorrow that's where I'm going. I'm looking forward to it. Then I think of how Oliver sat here one evening with similar thoughts on his mind. Except that he loved Caroline so his thoughts must have been more complicated.

I turn a few things over in my mind – things to do with travelling, home, family, love. I think that I was very independent when I first started this trip and I saw travel as an end in itself. I liked being free and unconnected to people. That didn't last very long. I've changed now and I think that's OK. I feel positive about the whole experience. I can puzzle it out a bit more when I'm sitting on buses and trains all day tomorrow and the next day too.

I'm far away in my thoughts and I don't hear Caroline until she's quite close by.

"Do you mind terribly if I sit here too?" she asks.

I shake my head.

She sits down on a flat stone quite close to me, faces out across the valley and looks out at the view.

"I think of you as a close friend, Daniel," she says.

This gives me a good feeling. I turn to her and smile.

"Me too," I say. "I mean I think of you... you know what I mean."

"I think I had better tell you something. It seems wrong to keep it from you."

Caroline is very solemn. I can't imagine what this is about.

"I think you didn't like me not helping you this afternoon."

"It's alright."

"No, you weren't happy about it. But I have to be careful at the moment. I have changed as you said. I didn't think anyone would know for some time but if you've noticed I suppose others have. I expect it's all around the village now."

"What is?"

"Daniel, I'm pregnant. I'm going to have a baby."

"Oh."

"You're meant to say *congratulations.*"

"Congratulations. Really it's good. I know it's what you wanted. I'm pleased for you."

"Is there something you want to ask me?"

Caroline looks me in the eyes very frankly and I feel that special connection with her again – a sort of brother-and-sister or best friend connection. Or something more perhaps. There is one obvious question.

"Not Oliver?" I say.

"Yes."

"How did you manage that?"

She hesitates for just a moment before speaking. "You remember that you went off on your own to the village on the last evening you were here. Oliver and I had a chance to have a good talk."

"A bit more than a talk," I say, and realise that I spoke rather bluntly. "I'm sorry."

"No, you're right. It was more than a talk. And it doesn't feel now that what we did was a mistake."

A great mass of weird thoughts and feelings rush through my mind now. I feel hurt for a moment – that surprises me. Then I wonder if Oliver will tell Lizzie. I don't think he will and perhaps that's the right thing.

"Of course, Oliver must never know about the child," Caroline says. "He thinks it was safe. I'm afraid I misled him."

"But he knows."

Caroline shakes her head.

"I didn't tell you everything about the time he lost his memory," I say. "You see he was trapped in the past – in the time when he loved you. He wanted to get back to you. I wouldn't help him. I'm sorry but it seemed like the right thing. And he said you were going to have his child. He said he had to get back to you because you were expecting his baby."

Caroline holds her breath. Her eyes have gone quite round and she doesn't look like herself at all.

"Oh, my God," she says.

She starts crying, silently at first and then sobbing and catching her breath. I move over and put my arms around her. I hold her quite tight as if somehow that will help. It occurs to me that I might have chosen not to say some of the things I've just said.

"I'm sorry," I say. "I really am."

Her sobbing gets louder and I hold her tighter. When she quietens I let go and she wipes her face with the side of her arm. There are still tears in her eyes but she manages a smile too.

"Oh, Daniel," she says.

The rest of the day I feel so close to Caroline and so warm towards her that I can't really speak. She soon recovers and brightens and in the evening she cooks for the two of us again. She puts a lot of time and energy into preparing the food and opens a bottle of red wine. She won't drink, of course, but I have a strong feeling that it won't be difficult to polish off the bottle on my own. When we sit down at the table it's in a mood of celebration. We touch our glasses together.

"Santé," Caroline says.

"Many of 'em."

"What?" She smiles at me across the table.

"Many of 'em. It's what my father always says."

Caroline takes a drink of her mineral water and puts the glass down.

"Did you write to your parents?" she says.

"Yes, I did. A few times. You asked me to so I did. I didn't tell them anything that I thought would worry them. I told them about you though."

"I wonder what you said."

"I said you were very cultured and very beautiful."

"Daniel!"

"I'm sorry."

"Will you stop saying you're sorry?"

I feel it might be safer not to speak for a while. Caroline reaches across and pours me another glass of wine.

"Many of 'em," she says. "Tell me about your father."

I do want to talk about home and about my dad but I decide to hold back until later. Caroline and I eat a wonderful three course meal. I wash up and tidy the kitchen while she takes the dog for a walk. Then the light is fading, it's mosquito time and the windows are shut, and Caroline and I sit opposite each other on her comfortable sofas. It's very quiet in the room. I think about the things from my childhood that I've only confided to one person. That person was Oliver. I decide not to speak of him tonight.

"My father had an accident when I was young," I say. "It left him disabled and it was very difficult for all of us. Difficult to cope with..."

Telling something like this, talking about things you would normally keep quiet about, things that you've been hiding even from yourself, brings you close to the person you're talking to. It doesn't take long to explain how I ignored my father for some years because I couldn't face up to what had happened. Caroline is sympathetic. And it's true that I was only a child. But I find myself using a word that I haven't used before. Maybe it's the wrong word – too big a word to be attached to a child; that's what Caroline says. The word is *betrayal* and alongside it comes the feeling of guilt. OK it's true that I was only a child and I coped the best way I could. But it doesn't stop me feeling bad now. I'm shaken by all this and I don't mind that she comes over and gives me a hug. I let out a big sigh. Caroline, Caroline, Caroline, Caroline. I have my head on her shoulder and her hair touches my face. She smells very good.

She lets go of me but doesn't go back to sit on the other sofa. She's leaning back and I don't see the expression on her face when she speaks.

"Will you sleep with me tonight, Daniel?" she says. "I'm afraid I mean *sleep*. We could sleep together as friends."

I think about this.

"I don't know. I sleep with no clothes on. I'll get an erection, I won't be able to help it."

"Better not then."

I think again.

"No, I want to. It will be alright, I promise to behave myself. You know it will be a first for me?"

"I know."

I wake in the morning to find Caroline nuzzled against my back. She has one arm resting over my waist and I can feel her breath on my shoulder. I don't move for a long while because I think she's still asleep. There's very little light in the room even though the curtains are drawn back. Perhaps it's very early.

"Daniel. Are you awake?"

"Yes."

"Are you happy? I am."

"Yes, I'm very happy."

Caroline moves away from me and I roll onto my back. She kisses me on the cheek. She touches my hair with her fingers.

"You're going home today, aren't you?"

"Yes."

"Will you promise to go?"

"Yes, if you want me to, I'll promise."

"Are you happy?"

"You asked me. Yes, I'm happy. But I'm confused."

"What are you confused about?"

I don't say anything because I don't think I can explain. But it feels as if part of me has left already. So I'm sad. Sad and happy too. It hurts a bit.

"After breakfast I'll drive you down to town and you can catch the train. Is that alright?"

"Yes, it's alright. I'm going home."

Caroline kisses me on the cheek again.

"Promise?"

"Yes, I promise."

She kisses me on the lips and is doing wonderful things with her hand under the covers.

"Daniel, would you mind terribly if I made love to you?"

*Would I mind terribly?*

"No," I say. "I don't mind."

# About the Author

Richard Collins has been a farm labourer, gardener and estate worker. His first novel, *The Land as Viewed from the Sea*, was shortlisted for the Whitbread Book Awards and the Welsh Book of the Year. Richard Collins lives with his family in west Wales and teaches at the Institute of Rural Sciences in Llanbadarn.